HIDDEN SECRETS

Avon Flare Books by
Audrey Barcus

Dangerous Secrets

HIDDEN SECRETS

AUDREY BARCUS

AN AVON CAMELOT BOOK

HIDDEN SECRETS is an original publication of Avon Books. This work has never before appeared in book form.

AVON BOOKS
A division of
The Hearst Corporation
1350 Avenue of the Americas
New York, New York 10019

Copyright © 1996 by Audrey Barcus
Published by arrangement with the author
Library of Congress Catalog Card Number: 95-96210
ISBN: 0-380-78369-X
RL: 5.5

First Avon Camelot Printing: July 1996

CAMELOT TRADEMARK REG. U.S. PAT. OFF. AND IN OTHER COUNTRIES, MARCA REGISTRADA, HECHO EN U.S.A.

Printed in the U.S.A.

OPM 10 9 8 7 6 5 4 3 2 1

One

"MY MOTHER WOULDN'T RUN AWAY, WOULD she?" Allie McKenzie slammed the bedroom door and leaned against it.

Her best friend, Kristi Kennedy, sat cross-legged on Allie's bed. "Is that what the police think?"

"Yes. The cop downstairs said, 'It's possible that Mrs. McKenzie's disappearance is deliberate.' " Allie mimicked the policeman's voice. " 'If that's the case, then she doesn't want to be found.' " She threw herself full length on the bed next to Kristi.

"What did you say to the cop?"

"I told him he was wrong. My dad got mad. But I *know* my mom wouldn't run away."

"Then where is she? She's been missing for five days."

"Something awful must have happened to her, but no one will listen to me." Allie punched the pillow. "The cops think what does she know, a dumb eighth grader. They don't believe me."

"And your dad?"

"He's so upset, he'll believe anything the police tell him."

1

"What did they say?" Kristi grabbed a brush from Allie's dresser and back-combed her curly red hair.

"That they'd covered all the usual bases in a missing person's case here on Staten Island. They sent her picture to every hospital, clinic, airport, bus station, and train station in the entire New York City area." Allie bit her lip. "Even the morgues."

"How gruesome!"

"They didn't turn up one tiny clue. Nothing."

"What about her car?"

"No sign of it anywhere. The cop said if she'd met with foul play, they probably would have found out by now."

"That's good news. They'll find her soon, Allie. Wait and see."

"They never found the hit-and-run driver who killed my brother."

"Maybe your mother was still upset about Jimmy's death."

"That was five months ago. Why wait till now to run away? She went to pieces when he was killed. So did my father. So did I." Allie rolled over on the bed.

"Maybe she's taking a break and will come back."

"She wouldn't just leave for work in the morning and not show up at night. No way. Not my mother."

"Yeah, she'd at least have left a note."

"She'd look me square in the eye and say so. She wouldn't run away. We made a pact after Jimmy died, my mom and me. We promised to be here for each other."

"The police say anything else?" Kristi rummaged in her purse for a stick of gum, unwrapped it, and popped it in her mouth.

2

"You're not going to crack that gum, are you?" Allie sat up, her hands around her knees.

Kristi grinned. "I can't help it. What else did the police say?"

"They found out my mother had been going to a shrink. Can you believe that?"

"A psychiatrist?"

"Yeah. A Doctor Diamond in Manhattan. She went once a week during her lunch hour. And she never even told us. She went to see him the day she disappeared."

"Did your dad know?"

"Uh-uh. She never even told him."

"Wow, that's weird."

"Why didn't she talk to me? I'd have been here for her the way she was for me." Allie grabbed the brush from Kristi and combed out her long hair—sleek and dark just like her mother's. Then she shook the brush at her friend. "If I tell you something, will you promise not to tell anyone else?"

"You know I wouldn't." Kristi leaned on her knees.

"If you dare, I'll . . . I'll tell Freddy Vunder that you like him. He's such a nerd, he'd believe me."

Kristi smiled. "Yeah, he would. What's the secret?"

"I never told you, but ever since Jimmy was killed, I get awful nightmares. I wake up screaming. My mom always came in and stayed until I fell asleep again. Sometimes she'd sing silly songs or rub my back."

"I didn't know you had nightmares. Is that why you won't spend the night at my house?"

Allie nodded. "I still need a light on when I go to sleep. My dad said my mom was treating me like a baby. But she let me leave the light on anyway."

"Your mom would."

"Why would she leave me when cheerleading tryouts are coming up? She wanted me to make the squad. She promised to help me do round off backhand springs this weekend."

"Speaking of tryouts, guess who made the JV basketball team at Curtis High School?"

"Who?" Allie was annoyed that Kristi would talk about such trivia right now.

"Shane Schroeder. My sister told me."

"Big deal." She didn't want to admit to Kristi how much it hurt to talk about Shane.

Kristi bit her lip. "I thought you'd want to know. You did go with Shane last year."

"That was last year. Everything's changed.

"I wish I could wave a magic wand and have your mother reappear." Kristi paused. "I wish I could make you laugh again. I miss the old Allie." Her voice broke.

"I'll never be the same again." Allie swallowed down a sob. "I'm scared, Kristi. Really scared."

"Ouch!" Kristi yelled from the foot of the bed.

"What's the matter?" Allie stared at her.

"Something jabbed my funny bone." Kristi rubbed her elbow. Then she reached under the comforter and drew out a book. "Do you always keep books in your bed?"

"I wondered where that book had disappeared to."

"It's overdue at the library." Kristi read the due date. "You'll have a fine."

"I don't care. I'll never read another mystery as long as I live."

"What? This from the Nancy Drew of Staten Island?" Kristi placed her hand over her heart in mock horror.

"Cut it out. I'm not in the mood."

"I'm surprised you're not helping the police look for clues."

Allie drummed her fingers against her cheek.

"What are you plotting?" Kristi asked. "Whenever you start tapping your face like that, something's up."

"You gave me an idea. If the police can't find my mother, maybe I can."

"How are you going to do that?" Kristi frowned.

"Where's the first place you'd look for clues if someone was missing?"

Kristi screwed up her face in thought. "In the missing person's house, I guess. Probably her bedroom."

"Exactly." Allie jumped up. "Come on. We're going sleuthing."

"In your mother's room?"

"Of course. What do you think? The North Pole?" *Sometimes Kristi could be so dense.*

"No need to be cranky."

"Hurry up." Allie pulled Kristi off the bed.

"What if your father sees us?"

"He's still downstairs with the police."

Allie opened her door a crack and listened. She heard the murmur of voices from the living room.

"The coast is clear," she whispered. "Let's go."

Two

THE DOOR TO HER PARENTS' BEDROOM CREAKED open. Allie slipped inside with Kristi hanging on to her arm.

"Stop cracking that gum in my ear." Allie turned on the light.

"Didn't the police search your mother's room?"

"Yeah, but they don't know my mother like I do."

"What are we looking for?"

"Anything suspicious."

"How do I know what looks suspicious?" Kristi muttered.

Allie searched her mother's dressing table. Just a few weeks ago her mother had taught her how to use eye makeup. "It has to look natural to be good, Allie," she'd said. "You want people to notice your eyes, not the makeup." She remembered the feel of her mother's fingers on her eyelids, the smell of her perfume. She dropped a tube of lipstick.

"Shh. Your father will hear us!" Kristi warned.

"Look in my mother's closet."

"I feel funny going through your mother's things."

"Do it." Allie rifled through the dresser drawers.

"Wow! This is a great dress. It would be perfect for the dance next week." Kristi pirouetted in front of the mirror.

"Knock it off, Kristi!" Allie grabbed the dress and went to hang it back in the closet. "Ouch!"

"What's the matter?"

Allie picked up a big metal flashlight from the closet floor. "I stubbed my toe on this."

"Clumsy."

"This isn't ours." She turned the flashlight over. "A label says, Forest Avenue Playground."

"That's suspicious." Kristi popped her gum behind Allie.

"It is. How did it get in my mother's closet?"

"What are you two doing in here?" her father boomed from the doorway.

Allie spun around. She hid the flashlight behind her leg. Kristi backed against the bed so hard she sat down with a thump.

"What's going on?" Her father looked around at the open drawers and closet.

Kristi jumped up. "I was just leaving. Call you later, Allie." She darted out the door.

"What are you looking for, Allie?" Her father closed a few drawers.

She took a deep breath. "Clues."

"Clues? For what?"

"Where Mom is."

Her father sighed. "We all wish we knew that."

"I don't believe the police. Mom wouldn't run away."

Her father loosened his tie. "Allie, sit down." He pointed to the bed.

She hesitated. Ever since she'd started eighth grade, her dad was on her back about something—talking on the phone too much, staying in the band, wearing makeup, boys. She didn't want another lecture.

"I said, sit down." He sounded angry.

Allie scooted back against the headboard. She slipped the flashlight into the wide sleeve of her sweater while her father pulled up the chair from the dressing table.

"First of all, you need to go back to school tomorrow. You can't stay home waiting for your mother to show up. We can't count on that."

"She's coming back, Dad."

Her father ran his fingers through his brown hair. She had always thought he was handsome, but today he looked like he sagged. This was rough on him too.

"The police could be right, Allie. Your mother may have left because she wanted to."

"How can you say that? You know Mom. She wouldn't do that." She was spitting mad.

"Your mother and I weren't getting along. You heard us arguing. Ever since Jimmy died, nothing's been right in this house. You know that."

"Dad, don't!" Allie ran to the window, her back to her father.

"I don't want to hurt you, honey." She heard the sadness in his voice. "But coping with your brother's death has been the hardest thing any of us have had to do, especially your mother. I'm beginning to agree with the police. I think she left because she couldn't handle it anymore. It may be a long time before she gets in touch with us."

Allie spun around. *"No!"* she screamed at her father. "I don't care what you say. Or what the police say. Mom wouldn't leave me. You probably hope she doesn't come back. All you cared about was Jimmy. You're sorry he's the one who's dead and I'm alive!"

She burst into sobs and ran from the room to her bedroom.

"Allie!" her father called, but she slammed her door.

She sobbed into her pillow until her chest hurt. She'd finally said it. For five months she couldn't look her father in the eye for fear she'd see disappointment that she was the one who was alive, not Jimmy.

Jimmy had been Dad's favorite. They'd gone to Mets and Giants games. They were always throwing footballs and baseballs around outside and talking about fishing trips they were going to take. They hardly ever invited her.

A knock sounded on the door. "Go away!"

"Allie, it's Mrs. Brumbaugh."

Great. Old nosybody herself. "I don't feel good," she called to the old lady who lived next door.

"I've got something for you."

She sat up. Might as well get it over with. "Okay. Come on in."

Mrs. Brumbaugh poked her white head around the door. "Howdy. Your father told me to come on up. I've got a plate of warm brownies for you. Your mother can eat a whole plate of these by herself."

"Thanks. Just put them on my dresser." Mrs. Brumbaugh thought food was the answer to every problem. When Allie had broken her leg in sixth grade, the old lady had come over every day with a plate or bowl of something.

9

"You're looking pale, Allie. Fresh air would do you a world of good." She plunked the brownies down, then straightened out the blue gingham apron that covered her green checked housedress. She always wore an apron. She made them herself and gave them away as gifts, too. Whenever Mrs. Brumbaugh came over for dinner, Mrs. McKenzie made Allie wear one of the ones she'd given her.

Allie pointed to the rain trickling down the window. "It's raining out."

"It's only a drizzle. Nothing like a good walk in the rain to clear the brain, I always said to my children. Your mother's a great one for walks in the rain, you know."

Allie swallowed. "I know. And thank you, Mrs. B."

The old lady shook her head. "The brownies are nothing. I wish I could do more."

"Not for the brownies."

"Oh?" She opened her faded blue eyes wide.

"For not talking about my mother in the past tense. Like she's dead or never coming back—the way everyone else does."

Mrs. Brumbaugh sat down on the edge of the bed. "If I know your mother, she'll move heaven and earth to get back to you. Don't you give up on your mom. I feel it in my old bones that she's alive. Peggy McKenzie's a fighter. And so are you. You're the spitting image of your mother in more ways than one." Whenever the old lady got excited, her false teeth wobbled like crazy.

Allie said nothing, afraid she might cry.

Mrs. Brumbaugh struggled up from the bed. She had something wrong with her feet. It made her hobble like

10

a bowlegged cowboy. "I'd best be going. Eat those brownies. And if you need anything, give me a holler."

The only thing Allie needed or wanted was her mother. But she said, "Thank you."

After the old lady left, the room seemed too quiet. Even the rain drizzled down without a sound. It trickled on the window like tiny teardrops.

Everything reminded her of her mother. Her mother had hung the green paisley wallpaper, bought the matching comforter, hung the ruffly yellow curtains, and refinished the big dresser and matching desk.

Allie unwrapped the brownies. The smell of warm brownies made her want to cry. On rainy days she and her mother baked chocolate chip cookies or brownies, and the smell of them would fill the house, cozy and warm.

Why did Kristi have to mention Shane? She didn't want to think about him either. She rolled over on the bed. Her hip hit something hard. The flashlight. She carried it to the window where the light was better. About a foot long, heavy, black metal, and a strip of adhesive on the handle labeled FOREST AVENUE PLAYGROUND.

How did it get in her mother's closet? It couldn't have been there when the police searched the bedroom. They would have noticed it and asked her father about it.

Allie sat and ran her fingers over the rough surface of the flashlight until it grew dark outside.

Tomorrow, she'd have to go to school. But tomorrow she was also going to look for her mother.

Three

THE NEXT MORNING SHE MET KRISTI AT THE COR-
ner of Harvest Avenue. Allie's backpack felt like a ton
of bricks on her shoulders.

"I wish I could run away right now." Allie kicked
at a rock on the sidewalk. "What if the kids at school
look at me weird?"

"Why? It's not your fault your mother's missing."

"But it's been in the *Staten Island Advance* for days.
And you said everyone was talking about it."

"I'll stick by you all day."

"Thanks, Kristi.

At the front gate of Susan Wagner Junior High, Kristi
nudged Allie. "Don't look now, but guess who's
coming."

Allie sucked in her breath. Shane Schroeder was
headed their way. It was too late to turn around. He'd
already seen them.

"Hi, Kristi." He stuck his hands in his jeans pockets.
"Hi, Allie."

"Hi," Kristi almost sang.

Allie could only stare at him. He had the most gorgeous blue eyes with long dark lashes. And a smile that took her breath away. She couldn't believe how tall he'd gotten.

"What's the matter?" Shane frowned at Allie. "Why are you staring at me?" He smoothed his brown hair.

"You wish," she said, and then instantly regretted it. "What are you doing here? Did they kick you out of high school?" She wanted to bite her tongue off.

"Still a junior high brat, aren't you? For your information, I brought my sister her lunch." Shane pushed past them and out the gate.

Allie groaned. "Why did I act like such a jerk?"

Kristi shook her head. "I don't get it. Why do you treat him like that? And why won't you talk about what happened between you two? He's a hunk. How do I look? I bet my hair looks like crud."

Allie hit the gate with her fist. "Who cares? Let's go to class and get this day over with."

They walked into the band room just before the bell rang. Everyone stared at Allie. Some of them whispered. She wished she were invisible.

"Darn it," Kristi muttered. "He's here."

"Rothenburg's never absent. He lives to torture kids."

She slid into the second seat in the saxophone section. Kristi was first chair flute.

Mr. Rothenburg pounded on the podium with his directing wand. "Time's a-wasting. Settle down, ladies and gentlemen. We need to oil those squeaks and grind those squawks."

Allie rolled her eyes at Kristi. Rottenburger, as the kids called him, said the same thing every day. He'd probably been saying it for twenty years.

13

She couldn't concentrate on the music. She'd never make first chair at this rate. But she didn't care anymore. Being a band nerd was the pits. If it hadn't been for her father, she'd have dropped out long ago.

At lunch she and Kristi sat by themselves on the soccer field away from the in crowd by the basketball courts.

"Thanks for sticking by me, Kristi."

"You're my best friend. I'd rather be with you."

Allie chewed her peanut butter sandwich. "Most of the kids act like I've got lice or something. They walk away or won't look at me."

"They just don't know what to say."

She threw her crumpled up lunch bag against the fence. "Kristi, do you think my mother's coming back?"

Kristi sighed. "I don't know, Allie. Don't keep asking me that."

"This is different from when Jimmy died. We knew he'd never come back. But what do you do when someone's disappeared?" Allie closed her eyes. "How can I go to school every day when I don't know where my mother is!"

She jumped up and ran across the field, sobs choking her. She heard Kristi running after her.

She stopped at the fence and banged her head against it hard. The pain jolted her.

"Allie, don't." Kristi pulled her away.

"If my mother doesn't come back, I won't make it. I'll kill myself. I will." She stood absolutely still, afraid of the words she'd spoken.

Kristi looked white as a ghost. "Don't say that." Her voice broke. "Don't ever say that."

14

"Then tell me how I can go on living as if nothing has changed?"

Kristi put her hands on her hips. "Stop feeling sorry for yourself. Yesterday you said you would search for your mother. Have you changed your mind?"

She wanted to slap Kristi's face. Instead she turned and scanned the playing field.

"Well?" Kristi challenged.

"I've got to get out of here. Can I climb over this fence?" Allie shook the chain-link fence to test its strength.

"You can't do that. You'll get caught!"

"I have to. My mom may be trapped somewhere. Or maybe she has amnesia. Maybe someone kidnapped her. Maybe she witnessed a murder. Maybe some weirdo grabbed her and is holding her prisoner."

"Allie!"

"Don't you listen to the news? Bad things happen to nice people. Look what happened to Jimmy. The hit-and-run driver who killed him never even stopped." Allie kicked the fence. "You're right. I have to find her. No one else cares. Not even my father. So, help me over the fence."

"What will I tell the principal if he asks for you?"

"Tell him I disappeared. It runs in the family."

"Where are you going?"

"To Manhattan to find Doctor Diamond, the shrink. If that doesn't turn up anything, I'll go to the Forest Avenue Playground."

"Did you ask your father about the flashlight we found in your mother's closet?"

"Not yet. Come on, give me a boost over the fence."

Allie stepped into Kristi's linked hands and sprang

for the top of the fence. She stuck the toes of her shoes into the fence and climbed up and over it. She landed on her feet on the sidewalk.

"Run," Kristi urged. "Good luck. I'll call you later."

Allie raced down the street, not even looking back over her shoulder.

Four

SHE RAN ALL THE WAY HOME. WAS THERE RE-
ally a truant officer looking for kids who ditched school?
If there was, Allie crossed her fingers he wasn't in the
West Brighton part of Staten Island today. She had
never ditched one class in her whole life.

Mrs. Brumbaugh was out front raking her lawn when
Allie came racing down Bosworth Street. Great, just
great! Mrs. Nosybody herself.

"Home early today, aren't you?" Mrs. Brumbaugh
leaned across the white picket fence that separated their
yards. Her white hair looked like a wild bird's nest.

"We only had half a day." The lie slipped out easily.

"Have you had lunch?"

"Yeah. I've got a doctor's appointment."

Allie ran up the front steps and inside the house.
From her secret hiding place in her bedroom, she drew
out a ten-dollar bill and some change and shoved them
in her jeans pocket. Then she rushed from the house for
the bus stop.

Usually she avoided North Burgher Avenue where
Jimmy had been hit, but today she was in a hurry, and

this was the shortest route. Jimmy'd always been in a hurry. Whenever they'd been going somewhere and she was still doing her hair, he'd shout up the stairs, "Come on, Allie, get a move on! You look beautiful already." Allie's breath caught in her throat. She remembered how he'd bragged to his friends in the sixth grade that his sister was the prettiest girl in junior high.

At the corner of North Burgher and Forest Avenue, she caught the bus for Saint George and the Ferry. She scrunched down in her seat hoping no one would notice a girl who should be in school.

She made the two o'clock ferry, racing through the turnstiles just in time. At the snack bar, she bought a fat pretzel and a Coke. She didn't dare look at the Statue of Liberty. Whenever she and her mom had ridden the ferry they'd told the same dumb joke about Miss Liberty getting her feet wet. Her mom would laugh and laugh.

As soon as the ferry bumped into the pier, Allie raced off the gangplank, out of the ferry terminal, and across the network of streets to South Street. Then she slowed down. She didn't want the bums who hung out around the docks and parks to notice her. If you watched, you could even see creeps buying drugs.

She'd never been here alone before. When a dirty vagrant looked like he wanted to stop her, Allie ran, her heart hammering, all the way to Wall Street.

Her mother worked at 120 Wall Street near the East River. Every summer vacation she and Jimmy would take turns going to work with their mother for a day. They'd lunch in one of the restaurants in the narrow streets near Wall Street and go to the South Street Seaport Museum.

At the eighteenth floor, Allie shot out of the elevator.

She crossed her fingers that Irene Iaconne wasn't home sick or ditching work.

She breathed a sigh of relief when she saw her mother's friend at the receptionist's desk of the sugar company where her mother worked. Her dark head was bent over some papers, her owl glasses on her nose.

Irene looked up from her work. "Allie! What are you doing here? Has your mom come back?"

Allie shook her head, afraid she might cry. It felt so good to see someone who cared about her mother.

Irene came around the desk, putting an arm around Allie's shoulder. "It's my break. Let's go to the lounge to talk."

Allie followed her down the corridor to the lounge. They sat on a couch by the window. Irene lit a cigarette and blew smoke to the ceiling.

"I thought you quit smoking, Irene."

"I did. But I started again five days ago." She made a face.

"I know what you mean," Allie said. "I've done some things the last few days I never thought I'd do either."

"It's awful, isn't it?" Irene had tears in her eyes.

Allie nodded. Then she squared her shoulders. "But I'm mad, too! Because everyone believes my mother ran away, and I know she didn't."

Irene nodded. "That's what I find hardest to understand. She was crazy about you, kid. You meant the world to her, especially after . . . I mean . . ."

"You mean since Jimmy died."

Irene nodded.

"You know, Irene, I'm sick of hearing and saying

19

that. It's like B.C. and A.D. at our house—before Jimmy and after Jimmy." Allie's voice broke.

"I know. Life doesn't stop just because someone dies," Irene said.

"You don't know the half of it! Jimmy's room is locked up like a shrine. Nothing's been touched since the day he left it. My dad acts like he's in a daze. Mostly he's never even home. When he was, he and mom were arguing and yelling."

Irene handed her a tissue. "Your mom was very unhappy, especially with your dad. You kept her sane. She loves you so much."

Irene stubbed out her cigarette. "I don't know if I should tell you this, Allie, but maybe it will help. Your mother was thinking of divorcing your father."

"What?" Allie felt like the floor was caving in under her. "You're making that up."

Irene shook her head. "She didn't see any other way out. Your father was so torn up by Jimmy's death, he started taking it out on your mom."

"What do you mean?" Allie whispered.

"A couple of times he came close to hitting her."

"No! He wouldn't do that."

"Your mother was afraid he might, someday."

"Are you saying she ran away because of that?"

Irene touched Allie's knee. "It's possible. When she didn't come in to work and the police came asking questions, that's what I thought happened."

"But you said she loved *me!*"

"She does. But sometimes a woman can only take so much. Maybe she just needs time away. I think she'll come back when she sorts things out in her mind."

Allie shook her head.

"I wish I could tell you what you wanted to hear."

Allie lifted her chin. "There is something you can tell me. Did you know that my mom went to see Doctor Diamond, a shrink?"

"Yes. She went every Thursday during her lunch hour. He helped her through the rough times."

"Where's his office?"

"On William Street. Why?"

"I want to talk to him."

"For yourself? Or about your mother?"

Allie hesitated. "Both. Can you give me his address?"

"It's in the Rolodex on your mom's desk."

As they walked down the corridor, Allie asked if her mother acted differently the day she disappeared.

"I've racked my brain to remember, Allie, but, honestly, I didn't notice anything different about her. I was shocked when they said she was missing. I figured she'd have told me if was leaving your father."

"Me too." Allie smiled. "The police said she saw Doctor Diamond last Thursday."

"Yes. She left here at noon, but she didn't come back here afterward."

"She called, right?"

"At twelve forty-five. She talked to Betty, the woman who fills in for me at lunch. According to her, your mother said she was taking the afternoon off and to charge it to her vacation. Your mother had never done that. I was afraid she was sick or something. I called your house a couple of times, but no one answered."

Irene wrote down the address and handed it to Allie.

"Thanks, Irene. Thanks for everything."

Irene hugged her. "If you need to talk, give me a call. Your mother will come back, Allie. Just give her time."

Allie walked away to the elevator. Irene was wrong. Her mother didn't have time. She had to find her before it was too late. Her stomach churned on the ride down to the first floor. What Irene said about her father couldn't be true. He would never hit her mother. Would he?

"*No!*" Allie shouted at Wall Street. People turned to stare. She ran as fast as she could. Dr. Diamond had to help her. He had to have some answers!

Five

ALLIE FOUND DR. DIAMOND'S OFFICE ON WILliam Street.

"Do you have an appointment?" the receptionist asked Allie.

"No, but I need to talk to Doctor Diamond about my mother. It's very important."

"Doctor Diamond doesn't see anyone without an appointment."

Allie swallowed her anger. "This is an emergency. My mother, Peggy McKenzie, is his patient, and something awful has happened to her." Allie tottered and grabbed the edge of the desk.

"You all right, kid?"

Allie closed her eyes. "I hope so."

"I tell you what. Sit down, and when the doctor's finished with his patient, I'll see what I can do."

"Thank you." Allie sat on a plastic chair and leaned her head against the wall. She tried counting the ceiling tiles to pass the time. Finally, the doctor's door opened. A tall woman came out and fussed about making another appointment.

Allie coughed.

The receptionist tapped on the doctor's door with long red fingernails before she entered. In a minute she came back. "He said he'd see you, but make it quick. The doctor's a busy man."

The doctor, bald with a chubby face, sat behind a big desk. He removed his glasses and pointed to a chair where Allie could sit.

"Hello, Allie. You look like your mother—the same dark hair and pretty brown eyes." He smiled, kind of like a chipmunk but nice. "How can I help you?"

"The police told you my mother's disappeared?"

"Yes, they did."

"Everyone thinks she's run away. I don't. Do you?"

He raised his eyebrows. "She didn't reveal any such intention to me, if that's what you're asking."

"Do you think she would have run away?"

Dr. Diamond put on his glasses. "I was your mother's doctor, her counselor. I consider the confidentiality between a patient and her doctor sacred. I could never break that trust and reveal anything she told me. Do you understand?"

"Do you understand what it's like to have everyone tell me my mother ran away when I know she didn't?"

"You were very important to your mother."

"I know that! What I need to know is where she is."

"Have the police uncovered anything?"

"No. They think she's a runaway mother." Allie leaned her arms on the desk. "You were the last person to see her before she disappeared into thin air. She called her office at twelve forty-five. When was her appointment over?"

"Her appointment was from twelve fifteen to twelve forty-five."

"I bet she used your secretary's phone. Did she?"

Dr. Diamond sighed but reached for the intercom button. "Gina, come in here, please."

She walked in, carrying a pen and pad.

"Gina, did Mrs. McKenzie use your phone last Thursday after her appointment?"

Gina tapped the pencil on her chin. "Yeah, she did, come to think of it. Said she needed to call her office. Mrs. Wunderlich came in for her appointment then, so I didn't hear what she said."

"Thanks, Gina." The doctor nodded, indicating that she could leave.

Allie waited until the door closed. "Something made my mother change her mind about going back to work. She never did that. So I figured it had to be something important. I also figured it had to be something she talked to you about."

The doctor waited, his hands steepled under his chin.

"My brother died five months ago and now my mother's gone." Allie's voice shook. "I couldn't stand it if she didn't come back. Please help me. You don't have to give away anything secret. Just tell me what she talked about that day. Maybe it will give me a clue about where she is. Please?"

He stroked his jaw. "I'll tell you as much as I feel I can. No more. Okay?"

Allie exhaled, nodding.

"Your mother was dealing with your brother's death, getting stronger every week. Last Thursday, she decided it was time to clean out his room."

Allie sucked in her breath. "She did?"

"She hoped it would be a healing process, so she could go on from there."

"She kept his room locked," Allie whispered.

He nodded.

"Why didn't she tell me? We could have done it together."

"Some things we need to face alone."

Allie hit her fist into her hand. "I bet that's what she did instead of going back to work. She's like that. She acts on the spur of the moment. My dad says she's impulsive."

"How is your father doing?"

"Was my mother afraid of my father?" she asked.

The doctor checked his watch. "No more, Allie. Besides, I have to leave."

Allie jumped up. "Thanks, Doctor. You've helped a lot. My mother was right in coming to you for help."

He shook her hand. "I hope you find your mother."

Allie ran all the way to the ferry. She caught the five o'clock boat. Commuters streamed down the aisles. Most of the seats were taken. She was too tense to sit anyway. She stood outside, staring into the dirty water.

The wind blew cold and raw for April. Her insides felt as choppy as the water. She wondered how her mother had felt when she rushed home to clean out Jimmy's room.

Allie was scared. Maybe her mother felt strong enough to see Jimmy's things, but Allie didn't know if she could handle it. She couldn't even deal with what had happened with Shane. Dr. Diamond said some things needed to be faced alone. And Allie had never felt so alone.

Six

IT WAS DARK BY THE TIME SHE RETURNED HOME. For once she would have welcomed Mrs. Brumbaugh in the front yard. The dark house seemed spooky. She turned on every light, even though her father would be upset that she was wasting electricity.

He would be home soon. She raced up the stairs. In front of Jimmy's room, she stopped. "I can't," she whispered in the empty hallway.

She had to. Her hand turned the doorknob. Someone had unlocked it. Her mother *had* been here. She pushed the door open. She snaked her hand around and found the light switch on the wall.

She walked into the room like someone stepping into ice-cold water. On the floor by Jimmy's bed lay his pajamas, just as if he'd stepped out of them. His baseball glove, bat, and cleats were jammed into the corner where he always threw them.

The pretzel and Coke she'd eaten earlier surged into her throat. She wanted to run. *Jimmy. Oh, Jimmy, I miss you. You were the best brother a girl could have. Everyone loved you. You were true blue, Jimmy. Why did you have to die?*

27

She wiped her face on her sleeve. *Stop it.* She couldn't fall apart. She had to think of her mother.

Her mother had piled some of Jimmy's clothes on the dresser. On the floor by the closet boxes lay strewn about. One of the boxes was packed with games from his closet shelf. Allie smiled. Jimmy'd loved to play Risk.

She sank to the floor by the boxes. Her mother had been in the middle of cleaning out Jimmy's closet. A pair of tennis shoes still stood on the floor, and shirts still hung from the rod. Why had she stopped? It wasn't like her mother to leave things messy.

It looked like she just up and left in the middle of everything. Maybe she couldn't handle going through Jimmy's things. Maybe she had run out.

Allie walked around the room, stopping at Jimmy's desk. His diary lay open, facedown. Jimmy wouldn't have left his diary like that. He always kept it hidden in the Monopoly game. She had found it once when she and Kristi had wanted to play Monopoly. She knew all Jimmy's hiding places.

But she'd never read his diary. That would be like peeking into someone's private thoughts. She knew she wouldn't want anyone looking inside her head.

Her mother must have found the diary in the games. Allie picked up the brown leather diary and turned it over. It lay open in her hand. A page had been torn out. She checked the date. Tuesday, the day before Jimmy had been killed! That was the page that was missing.

Jimmy wouldn't have done that. He was a real freak about books. Even when he was little, he never scribbled in them.

It had to be her mother. But why? What had Jimmy

written that made her tear the page out like that? The edges were all ragged like she'd torn it in a hurry.

Allie sat on the edge of Jimmy's bed. She flipped through the pages of the diary. On Monday he'd written:

Should you beef on a friend? Suppose it was something bad? I'll ask him tomorrow about R. M.

Jimmy never beefed on anyone. He hadn't tattled about the times she'd stopped at the candy store with her friends and was late coming home from school. Allie swallowed hard. If only he had told on her, he'd . . .

Stop it. Concentrate on Mom.

Whatever Jimmy had written must have been real important for her mother to have torn it out. Maybe he wrote the name of a friend he wanted to tell on or what the "something bad" was. Who or what was R. M.? Whatever it was must have made her mother bolt from the room in one heck of a hurry.

Allie tapped the diary against her lips. Could Jimmy have left any other clues? She skimmed through the diary but found nothing else important. She searched through his desk, but all she found were his mementos and toys and junk.

Allie snapped her fingers. His secret hiding place. Once she made Jimmy tell her where he kept his money, in exchange for half her Halloween candy. Jimmy was a candy freak.

She ran to the corner where Jimmy had tossed his baseball stuff. She pulled them away from the wall. Then she dropped to her knees and ran her hand along the wood floor until she found the uneven edge of the board.

With her fingers, she pried the board up. In the cavity underneath lay Jimmy's old tin chest. Her hands shook as she lifted it out. Cradling it like a baby, she carried it to the bed.

Inside, stacks of baseball cards lay bound with rubber bands. She pulled them out. On the bottom lay a small plastic bag half full of tiny green leaves.

Allie dropped it like a hot potato. She knew enough about drugs to know marijuana when she saw it.

She shook her head. Jimmy would never have done drugs. He had only been in the sixth grade when he died. If Jimmy had been into drugs, she'd have known. Besides, Jimmy was as straight as they come. Straight as an arrow, her mother always said.

Plus, they'd made a pact that if either of them tried drugs they would tell the other and not keep it secret.

Could this marijuana be the "something bad" he'd written about in his diary?

It would kill her father if she showed him the drug. The police were out, too. They would see the drug as another reason why her mother had run away.

She'd have to find the friend who Jimmy was going to beef on. She'd start with his friends from the neighborhood. One of them would know about the drugs. At least she hoped so.

6:45—Her father would be home any minute. Allie shoved the plastic bag in her pocket and ran to her room. She grabbed her jacket and raced down the stairs. In the kitchen she wrote a note to her father:

Kristi's mom invited me for dinner. I did all my homework. I'll be home by 9:00. Mrs. Kennedy will drive me home. School was okay today.

Allie

As she ripped the paper from the pad, headlights lit up the driveway. Her father. She propped the note on the kitchen table, and tiptoed to the back door.

She waited while her father rang the front doorbell twice. When she heard the jingling of his keys in the lock, she slid open the back door.

"Allie! I'm home!" he called. She slipped out the door and into the night.

Seven

ALLIE CROUCHED BEHIND THE OLD ELM TREE until her heart stopped hammering. In the lighted kitchen she saw her father pulling food from the refrigerator. She should at least have made him dinner.

Too late now. She dashed for the picket fence, climbed over it and into Mrs. Brumbaugh's backyard and out to the sidewalk. Then she raced down the street to Bement Avenue.

Once she was around the corner, Allie stopped. She sat on the curb between two parked cars, deciding which of Jimmy's friends to question. They'd probably think she was crazy, knocking on their doors to talk about her dead brother. Let them. She had to find her mother.

She decided to start with Eric Jenson, Jimmy's best friend. Eric lived on Harvest Avenue in a gray two-story house. Mrs. Jenson opened the door.

"Allie. Come in. Is everything okay?" Mrs. Jenson held a dish towel in her hand.

"Yes, fine. Could I talk to Eric?"

"Eric?" She frowned, like she wasn't sure she liked a junior high girl talking to her sixth grader.

"I wondered if he wanted my brother's baseball cards," Allie blurted out in a panic.

"Oh. I'll get him. Sit down, dear."

She perched on the edge of the living room couch while Mrs. Jenson yelled up the stairs for Eric and then disappeared into the kitchen.

When Eric came down the stairs, Allie was surprised how tall he'd grown since November. Would Jimmy have been this tall?

"Hey, Allie." Eric lifted a thumb in greeting. "What's up?"

"Do you still collect baseball cards?" she asked.

"Yeah, why?"

"I was wondering if you'd want some of Jimmy's."

Eric looked at the floor. "Gee, you don't need to . . ."

"Jimmy would have liked it."

"Thanks," Eric mumbled, clearly uncomfortable.

"You and Jimmy were best friends, right?"

Eric nodded.

"If something was bothering him, he would have told you, right?"

"Probably."

"Did Jimmy ever do drugs?"

Eric's head jerked up. "Jimmy do drugs? No way!"

"One of his friends was doing drugs. Do you know who?"

Eric stared at her. "Did Jimmy say that?"

"No. But I read his diary today, and he wrote about telling on a friend who was into something bad."

Eric wrinkled up his forehead. "You know, Jimmy was talking about that, just before . . . just before . . ."

"He died." Allie knew how he felt.

"I remember now. We were at school and he asked

33

if it was okay for a friend to tell on a friend, if the friend would get hurt by what he was doing. When I pumped him about it, he just clammed up.''

"Who did you think he meant?''

"No idea. But I remember he said he was going to talk to some guy after school. Something about checking out if it was true or not before he told anyone.''

"Do you know what day that was?''

"Jeez. That was a long time ago. And then Jimmy, you know, died, and it didn't seem important.''

"Was it the day he died?'' She held her breath.

"Maybe. Why? What does it matter?''

"Just wondering.'' Allie jumped up. "If you want the baseball cards, come by after school some afternoon.''

"Yeah, maybe. Thanks.''

Eric didn't walk her to the door. He stood in the middle of the living room, as if he was thinking about Jimmy. She could tell it hurt a lot.

Outside, she shivered even in her jacket. She scratched Eric's name off the list in her head. His surprise at her drug question seemed real.

She ran the three blocks to Darrel Kaskey's house. No one was home. A dog barked inside, sounding lonely. Allie fingered the smooth plastic of the bag in her pocket.

Steve Ingino lived across from the Staten Island Zoo. His mother blocked the doorway like a football player.

"Steven has homework to do. What do you want?''

"My brother borrowed some money from Steve, and I'm returning it. Could I give it to him?''

"Well . . . I guess so.'' The woman left Allie standing on the front porch and went to yell for Steve.

Steve looked surprised to see her. He scratched his head till his hair stood on end.

She pulled the plastic bag from her pocket. "I found this in my brother's stuff. He said it was yours."

He wrinkled up his face. "What is it? I never had anything like that."

"It's marijuana. Jimmy said you used it."

He jerked back like she'd socked him. "What? He's crazy. I don't smoke pot!"

Allie believed him. He didn't look guilty, just scared to death his mother would hear her.

"Sorry. Wrong Steve, I guess. Thanks anyway." She ran down the front steps, shoving the plastic bag in her jacket pocket.

This was getting her nowhere. But she was probably already in trouble with her dad, so she might as well finish the list.

Jason Densmore lived a few blocks from the zoo. Rain started coming down in a fine mist. She'd probably get a sore throat if she got wet. She always did. And her mom wasn't here to take care of her.

She sighed and rang Jason's front doorbell. Jason answered the door. He frowned when he saw Allie.

"Hey, you're Jimmy McKenzie's sister. What do you want?" The way he said that, and the way he quickly shut the door behind him and came out to the porch, made Allie's pulse beat faster. She was real good at reading people.

"I came to return something of yours my brother had."

Jason flipped back his long blond bangs that fell down his forehead. "Yeah? What?"

She drew the plastic bag from her pocket. "This."

Jason looked back at his house and shoved his hands into his pockets. "How do you know it's mine?"

"Jimmy told me."

"Big mouth jerk," he muttered.

"Excuse me?" Allie raised her voice.

"Forget it. What else did he say?" He sounded worried.

"He was going to tell on you, wasn't he?" she said on a hunch.

Jason narrowed his eyes. "You're just guessing."

"No. He wrote it in his diary. He knew you were doing drugs, didn't he?"

"Get lost." He turned to go in the house.

"Fine. Then I'll talk to your parents."

He let out an angry breath. "What do you want? A confession? Yes, I smoke pot once in a while? Is that what you want me to say?"

"Who was my brother going to talk to the day he was killed?"

Jason sucked in his breath. Then he tried to act cool. "I don't know what you're talking about."

"Yes, you do. Who is R. M.?"

Jason backed away. He was no longer the cool kid trying to act tough. Now he looked like a scared little sixth grader.

Allie moved closer. "Who is R. M.? Did he run my brother over?"

She didn't know who was more scared after she'd said that, Jason or her. He stood there panting like he'd been running the mile in a minute.

Jason broke the spell. He whirled and grabbed the doorknob. "You're crazy! Get out of here before I call the police."

The screech of tires and the squeal of brakes in the driveway made them both turn. A guy jumped out of the car and ran up the steps to where they stood.

"Hey, Jason. What's happening?" The guy stared at Allie. "Who's the cute chick?"

Out of the corner of her eye, she saw Jason shake his head ever so slightly at her. If he thought she would protect him, he was nuts.

"She's just leaving," Jason said.

"My brother has no manners. I'm Tim Callahan, Jason's brother." He smiled in a way that made her uncomfortable.

"Stepbrother," Jason corrected.

"What's your name, kid?" Tim was tall, blond, and wore lots of gold chains around his neck.

"Allie."

"Be kind to my brother, Allie. He's a jerk with girls." He laughed and reached around Jason to open the front door.

Jason flipped him off as Tim went in the house. Then he shook his fist at Allie. "Get out of here before I punch your lights out." He slammed inside the house.

Allie started to cry. She sank to the bottom step and buried her face in her arms. She cried for Jimmy. For her mother. For her father who waited at home, hurting and alone. She had to talk to him. Maybe Jason was right. Maybe she was crazy.

She raced down the sidewalk. At the corner, she barreled head-on into someone coming in the opposite direction.

A strong hand grabbed and steadied her. "Whoa! Watch where you're going!"

She looked up at a handsome guy with wavy brown hair. "Shane," she whispered.

"What are you doing here? It's late—and it's raining."

"I'm going home," she mumbled.

"You shouldn't be hanging out by the zoo at this time of night. I'll walk you home."

"I don't need your help." Allie started walking away.

Shane blocked her way. "Why do you act like I'm dirt? Come on, Allie, talk to me. We used to be friends."

"Yeah, but you're in ninth grade now, in high school. Why would you waste your time on a junior high brat?"

"Sometimes you act like a brat."

"Thank you."

"I'm sorry, but you dumped me—without even telling me why. You never even gave me a chance to say sorry about your brother. You never answered my phone calls. When I waited for you after school, you ran away from me."

A sob threatened to break loose from her throat.

"Did I do something to hurt you? Did I say something wrong?"

Allie shook her head. She brushed past Shane. "I have to go home."

Shane grabbed her arm. She wrenched free. Something fell from her pocket. Shane picked it up. He stared at the plastic bag, then at her.

"Marijuana? I never figured you'd do drugs, Allie."

"I don't!"

"Then what are you doing with this?" Shane waved the bag under her nose.

"It's not mine. You don't understand." Her voice broke. "Please, let me go home!"

"Okay. But I'm walking with you. I want an explanation. You owe me one." They crossed Broadway and headed up Harvest Avenue. Shane kept talking. "I liked you a lot, Allie. Don't you remember? I asked you to go steady. You said you wanted to. What happened?"

"Please, stop, Shane. I can't talk now."

"All right. I won't push you. But I'm not taking no for an answer. Will you meet me tomorrow after school? At Foster's Freeze?"

"No. It's over, Shane. Can't you accept that?"

"Not without a reason. If you don't say yes, I'll tell your father about the marijuana."

Allie jerked to a stop and looked up at him. He meant it. He stared her down. Her heart skipped. She looked away so he couldn't see how she felt about him.

"That's blackmail."

"Promise you'll show up?"

"I don't have a choice, do I?"

She wouldn't let him walk her all the way to her house. Her father would blow a fuse if he thought she was out late with a guy.

Allie ran in the house. Her father waited in the living room. He looked ready to commit murder.

"Where have you been?" He folded his arms. "You lied to me. I called Kristi's house, and Mrs. Kennedy said you hadn't been there all evening. Get in here and tell me the truth!"

Eight

THE GRANDFATHER CLOCK CHIMED NINE-THIRTY. Allie stood in front of her father like a doomed prisoner waiting for the axe to fall. He sat in his black leather chair, his arms folded. She remembered what Irene had said about her mother being afraid.

"Why did you lie to me?" Her father watched her with the saddest expression she'd ever seen. He looked old. The skin around his chin hung loose. She'd never noticed the gray hair at his temples.

She started to shake her head, but something about the way he waited for an answer made her change her mind. "Because, I didn't think you'd let me go."

"Go where?"

"I needed to talk to some of . . . of Jimmy's friends."

Her father's lips tightened. "Why?"

"I had to ask them something about Jimmy."

"What?"

She hesitated. Then she blurted out about her mother cleaning out Jimmy's room and the diary. He looked so sad and so lost she said nothing about the marijuana.

"Peggy tore a page out of Jimmy's diary?" he said as if to himself.

Allie nodded.

Her father ran a hand over his hair. "Why did this make you want to talk to Jimmy's friends?"

"I thought what Jimmy wrote might have made Mom disappear."

"Allie . . ." Her father shook his head. "Is that why you went to see Doctor Diamond?"

"How'd you know that?"

"He called. He was concerned about you."

Sometimes you just couldn't trust adults.

"Your principal called too. He said you ditched school today."

Again Allie could only nod.

"I should punish you for what you did." He paused.

She didn't know what he wanted her to say. So she said nothing.

"But under the circumstances . . . I mean because of . . . What I'm trying to say is that I understand." He loosened his tie as if it were choking him. "I've done some things lately too that I can't explain. I know how you feel. It's like the old rules don't apply anymore. You do things you never thought you'd do."

She stared at the rug while he pulled out his handkerchief and blew his nose like a foghorn. This was crazy. He wasn't talking like her father.

When he spoke again even his voice sounded funny. "I know how much you miss your mother, Allie. You were so close, sometimes I was jealous. I never could talk to you the way she could." He cleared his throat.

"Dad . . ." She wanted to run to her room. He'd never talked like this before.

"Let me finish. I miss your mother as much as you do."

"You do?" The words slipped out before she could catch them back.

"Of course I do. Why would you even ask that?"

"Because . . ." She'd gone too far now. She'd have to finish. "Because you were always fighting. And because Irene said Mom wanted a divorce," she ended in a rush.

With a sigh, her father reached out a hand to Allie. She shook her head and held her hands behind her back.

"Just because two people argue, doesn't mean they've stopped loving each other. Your mother and I had stopped talking, stopped sharing. Jimmy's death tore us apart. It was my fault. Your mother locked Jimmy's door. I locked up my feelings. I was never there for her."

He stood up. "You're too young to understand, Allie. And it's late."

She headed for the stairs.

"Wait. I'm not going to punish you. But no more ditching school. No more running off to find your mother. Promise me."

Allie nodded.

"One more thing. I'll be coming home earlier from now on. But after school, you're to go to Mrs. Brumbaugh's house and stay there until I come home."

"What?" she exploded.

"You heard me. Mrs. Brumbaugh's agreed to watch you until I get home from work."

"Dad, I'm thirteen years old. I don't need a babysitter!"

"It's not good for you to be alone."

"I can take care of myself."

"Mrs. Brumbaugh's a kindly woman."

"She's a nosy old witch!"

"Allison! There'll be no arguing. That's the way it will be. Now go to bed."

Allie charged up the stairs to her room, slamming the door so hard the whole house shook.

She lay awake long after she heard her father climb the stairs to bed. The clouds disappeared from the sky and stars twinkled like diamonds. They made her angry. How could they shine when her life was so miserable?

She couldn't search for her mother with Mrs. Brumbaugh on her case. And she had to meet Shane at Foster's Freeze after school tomorrow. If she didn't show, he'd tell her father about the marijuana. She'd just have to think up a way to get around old Mrs. Brumbaugh.

She was drifting off to sleep before she remembered she hadn't even turned on the night light. She'd been too busy thinking of how to find her mother to be afraid of the dark. She already knew what she'd do tomorrow. Tomorrow she would follow a suspect.

Nine

"WHERE WERE YOU LAST NIGHT?" KRISTI ASKED at school the next day. "I called a million times."

She looked like her eyes would bug out of her head when Allie told her about going to Wall Street, seeing Dr. Diamond, finding the diary and the marijuana, and talking to Jason Densmore.

"I can't believe you did all that. My mother would kill me if I snuck out."

Allie shoved her backpack into her locker. "I can't believe my father didn't ground me for life."

"Yeah, that's weird."

"But how can I meet Shane when Mrs. Brumbaugh's waiting to baby-sit me?" Allie slammed the locker shut.

Kristi snapped her fingers. "How about I call Mrs. Brumbaugh and tell her you had to stay after school to make up the work you missed."

"Great! She'll fall for that. I knew you'd come up with something."

"Years of practice. I've got two older sisters." Kristi shoved the gym door open. "Aren't you excited about meeting Shane?"

"No. I can't let him complicate things when I need to find my mother."

"He's such a hunk. If you don't want him, I'll take him." Kristi examined her hair in the wall mirror.

"He's all yours." Allie pulled her P.E. shirt over her head.

"I want to know every gory detail of your meeting." Kristi shook her tennis shoe. "I mean everything."

After school, Allie's courage deserted her as she neared Foster's Freeze. All the high school kids hung out there. The guys were so tall, and the girls seemed so sure of themselves.

Shane sat on one of the outside tables, his feet on the bench. When he saw Allie, he jumped up. He must be close to six feet tall. He looked so handsome in a navy blue sweater, blue jeans, and Nike high-tops.

"You want a soda?" he asked.

"Sure." Allie tried to sound like she met guys here all the time.

"Want to sit inside?"

"Fine with me."

They ordered root beer floats at the counter and carried them to a table back in the corner.

Allie sipped the soda too fast. Her throat stung from the coldness of it. She tried to keep from staring at Shane's eyes. She'd forgotten how blue they were.

"I read about your mother in *The Advance*, Allie. It must be awful not to know where she is. Is there anything new?"

"No. She's still missing."

"I'm sorry."

She didn't say anything.

45

"I guess it's not my business, but you scared me last night. What were you doing with marijuana?"

Allie watched the way his hands slid the straw up and down through the lid on the float. How much should she tell him? She searched his face. He seemed concerned. He wasn't stuck on himself or out to use people like some of the other jocks. They'd been good friends last year. They used to hold hands at school. Everyone said they made a cute couple. But that was last year. Could she trust him now?

"You okay?" He touched her arm.

Tears filled her eyes. What a jerk he must think she was.

"Maybe I shouldn't have mentioned your mother." He looked uncomfortable.

Allie got a grip on yourself. "No. It's okay. I was just trying to decide how much I could tell you."

"About what?" He removed the lid and spooned up some ice cream.

"My mother, my brother, and the marijuana."

Shane frowned. "There's a connection?"

"I think so." She drummed her fingers on her cheek. "If I tell you everything, would you do me a favor?"

He narrowed his eyes. "It's not something illegal, is it?"

"No. I just need your help."

He bit his lip. "After what you did to me, I ought to say no. But something tells me you're in some kind of trouble. What is it?"

"Promise you won't laugh or tell me I'm crazy?"

Shane raised his hand. "I promise."

She relaxed against the chair. "Okay, here goes." She began with her mother's disappearance and everything she'd found out yesterday. Shane listened without flinching or interrupting.

He whistled low when she was finished. "Wow, this blows my mind. No wonder you looked like you'd seen a ghost when I ran into you last night." He shook his head. "What's the favor?"

"I want to follow Jason Densmore."

"Follow him?"

"Yeah. Jason was lying through his teeth. I'm sure the marijuana was his. And he knows who my brother was going to blow the whistle on. My guess is it wasn't Jason. It could be someone who was selling drugs to Jason. He was scared out of his skull. Not because he smoked pot, but because he'd be in trouble from someone else. Maybe he can lead me to that person."

Allie sagged on her elbows. She felt drained.

"What do you want me to do?"

"I can't go out after dark. My dad cracked down on me after last night. You live near Jason, don't you?"

"Across the street."

"Do you know him?"

"Some. He's just a kid. His brother's a senior at my school."

"Do you know him?"

"Not really. They haven't lived there very long. Tim drives. He's got a brand-new limited-edition Mustang GT. It's great—black with gray interior, tinted windows. The frame is lowered a little. Boy, would I like that car. Got a five point eng—"

"Shane," Allie interrupted. She wasn't interested in Tim Callahan's car. "Could you tail Jason? See where he goes, who he hangs out with—if he connects with anybody suspicious?"

47

Shane scratched his chin. "I don't know. Sounds corny to me. I'd feel pretty stupid, sneaking around like a little kid."

"Like me?" She wanted to throw her root beer float in his smug face.

"I didn't mean you were a little kid."

"Just a junior high brat?"

He grinned. "Okay. I'm sorry about that statement. Let's call a truce, okay?" He reached out his hand.

Allie hesitated, then shook his hand. It felt warm and strong. She dropped it quickly.

"Will you follow Jason?"

"I suppose I could."

"Great." Allie checked her watch. What if Mrs. Brumbaugh called her dad? She stood to leave.

"Wait." Shane held her arm.

"I've got to go."

Shane shook his head. "Don't you realize if what you told me is true, then your brother may have been killed on purpose?"

Ten

SHANE'S FACE BLURRED. ALLIE HELD ON TO THE table.

"Are you okay? I didn't mean to scare you." He sounded scared himself.

She shook off his hand. "Let's get out of here."

Shane followed. They walked along Forest Avenue.

"I could be wrong, Allie. It probably was just a hit-and-run."

She shook her head. "Jimmy was murdered." The words shocked her. But for the first time in five months she knew she was right.

"Murder's a strong word." Shane held her hand as they darted across the street. She dropped it as soon as they reached the curb.

"It's the truth, though. My brother was dangerous to someone. I think he found out who was selling drugs to his friends. And knowing my brother, I bet he went straight to that person to find out the truth."

"How old was your brother?"

"Eleven."

"Was he a tough kid?"

Allie smiled. "Tough when it came to being right."

"Like you." Shane grinned.

She ignored that. "My mother read something in Jimmy's diary. I bet he wrote down his suspicions. Maybe he even wrote the guy's name. His friend Eric said he was going to talk to someone the day he was killed."

"Maybe that's why your mother is missing." Shane stopped dead in his tracks in the middle of the sidewalk.

Allie shivered in fear.

"You have to tell your father—or the police. You can't go poking around to find this guy. He might kill *you!*" Shane reached out to her.

She ducked under his arms and raced down North Burgher Avenue. Shane pounded the sidewalk after her. "Allie, wait!" he yelled.

She didn't stop until she reached the place that lived in her mind like a nightmare. Then she sank to the curb and sat with her hands between her knees.

Shane sat next to her. "What did you run for?"

"This is where Jimmy was hit. The police came to my house and said he'd been hit by a car on North Burgher Avenue." Allie choked on a sob. "I ran like crazy to find him. The ambulance was there—paramedics—people all crowding around. Then a paramedic who'd been bending over Jimmy stood up and told the cop there was nothing he could do. The cop held me back, but I started yelling that he wasn't dead—he was only sleeping. I still remember the smell of the cop's uniform as he lifted me back to the sidewalk."

"How did it happen?"

"Jimmy was riding home on his bicycle. It was almost dark. The cops said the guy driving the car probably didn't see him. And then he panicked and just drove off.''

''Did anyone see the car?''

''No.''

''Where had Jimmy been?''

''The playground. The one we passed on Forest Avenue. He used to hang out there with his friends—shoot baskets, play Ping-Pong. His friends said he'd left a lot earlier than the time he was hit. He must have gone somewhere else. We never knew where. It didn't seem important then.''

''That was the day I asked you to go steady with me, wasn't it?'' Shane picked up a pebble from the street.

''Yeah.''

''Why wouldn't you talk to me afterward?''

Allie started to get up, but Shane grabbed her arm. ''Don't run away again. Answer my question.''

''Ouch! You're hurting me.''

Tell me why you dropped me like a hot potato.''

''I can't.''

''Too chicken?'' He threw the pebble into the street.

What was it Dr. Diamond had said? Sometimes you had to face something head-on. She lifted her chin.

''I wanted to go steady with you, Shane. I liked you a lot. But I wasn't supposed to stop at the store after school. I was supposed to go right home and watch my brother.'' Allie's voice shook.

Shane put his arm around her shoulder.

''Jimmy usually came home at two-thirty. I got home at three o'clock. He was supposed to wait until I got there before he went out to play.'' Tears trickled down her cheeks.

''Jimmy never told on me. He never tattled that I'd

stop by the store with my friends and not get home until three-thirty.'' Her lips shook so badly she could hardly talk. Shane bent closer to hear.

"He always waited for me. He never left until I got there. Except for the day he died. That day, he was gone when I got home. He'd been there. His backpack was by the door. An empty milk glass was in the sink.''

"Did he leave a message or anything?'' Shane asked.

"No. Nothing. At first I was mad at him. I thought I'd be in trouble. But when it started to get dark and he wasn't back, I got worried. And then the cop came.''

"I don't get it. What did that have to do with me?''

"Don't you see?'' Allie cried. "Because I went to the store to be with you, Jimmy was killed. If I had come straight home, he might have told me what was going on. I could have stopped him. It's my fault Jimmy died!''

Eleven

ALLIE CRIED INTO SHANE'S SHOULDER UNTIL HIS
sweater was damp. It felt so good to be held close by
him.

She broke away first. "I have to go home."

"I'll walk you." He held her hand.

Mrs. Brumbaugh was sweeping her front porch, and
she looked worried. She waved when she saw Allie.

"Howdy, Allie. Your friend Kristi called. I'm glad
you let me know you'd be late. I made a fresh batch
of peanut butter cookies. I bet you're hungry." Mrs.
Brumbaugh spoke to Allie but her eyes in their wrinkled folds of flesh assessed Shane. Allie introduced
him.

"Come on in. There's enough cookies for an army."
She hobbled into the house. Allie questioned Shane with
a look. He shrugged and ducked through the door behind her.

"How was school?" The old lady motioned for them
to sit at the kitchen table. She poured milk into sparkling
crystal glasses.

"It was okay." Allie gobbled up a warm cookie.

"Your mother told me how smart you are and how you got all A's on your report card."

"Not all A's." Allie didn't want Shane to think she was a brain.

"She told me you want to be a cheerleader."

"Are you trying out, Allie?" Shane looked skeptical.

"Don't you think I'd make it?"

"Maybe you would. Maybe you wouldn't. How would I know?" He shrugged.

"Your mother would be disappointed if you didn't give it a good shot." Mrs. Brumbaugh shook her head.

"How do you know so much about my mother, Mrs. Brumbaugh?"

"Your mother visited me often. When my hip gave me trouble she went to the store for me. In the winter she'd look in if she hadn't seen me for a day or two." The old lady smoothed the tablecloth before she finished. "She's a genuinely good person."

"Would she run away?" Allie waited.

The old lady's faded blue eyes widened. "Run away? From you? Never. And don't you let anybody tell you she did."

Allie pressed her lips together to keep from crying. Mrs. Brumbaugh passed the cookies to Shane.

"What do you think happened to Mrs. McKenzie, Mrs. Brum . . . Brumbach . . . Can I just call you Mrs. B.?" Shane grinned like a charmer.

"Sure. That's what Allie's brother, Jimmy, used to call me. He was another good one." She stopped and wiped her eyes.

"You didn't answer Shane's question." Allie grabbed another cookie. "Where do you think my mother is?"

The old lady raised her hands and let them fall into her lap. "I wish I knew. All I know is she rushed out of your house, putting her jacket on as she ran down the steps. Then she backed the car out of the garage and drove off. That's what I told the police too."

"Did she seem upset?" Allie asked.

"I couldn't tell from my kitchen window. But she did seem in a hurry. Just like your brother did, the day he was hit by the car."

"You saw my brother leave the house?" Allie leaned closer.

"Yes. I was getting the newspaper from behind the hedge. I looked up and saw Jimmy running down the street like a house afire. 'Hey, Mrs. B.,' he called like he always did. Then he raced into your house. I had barely climbed my front stoop when out he came again. He took off real fast down the driveway on his bicycle."

"Are you saying he was only in the house for a couple of minutes?" Shane leaned on his arms.

"Yes. I called to him that he would get in trouble for not waiting for you, Allie, but he didn't hear me."

Allie pressed her hands to her face. "It wasn't my fault then," she whispered. "Jimmy left before I could possibly have come home."

"So that's what it was." Mrs. Brumbaugh sighed.

"What?" Allie asked.

"Your mother knew something was worrying you."

"She did?"

"If only you'd told her, you could have spared yourself a lot of grief." Mrs. Brumbaugh reached for the milk and refilled both their glasses.

"Mrs. B., could I walk Shane partway home?"

Mrs. Brumbaugh puffed out her lips. "I don't see

why not. Just be home when the streetlights come on. That's what I used to tell my children, a long time ago.''

Allie jumped up from the table. "Thanks, Mrs. B." She and Shane hurried from the house.

"You don't have to walk me home," Shane said, outside.

"I'm not. I want to find Jason Densmore."

"Why?"

"I want to keep an eye on him—maybe ask him some more questions."

"What if he's not home?"

"You could find out, and if he's not, ask where he is."

"What would I want with a sixth grader?"

"Make up something. Say you want to sell your bike."

"I don't want to sell my bike."

"Just pretend!" Allie wanted to pound his arm. "We just want to find out where he is, for crying out loud."

"Okay, okay. Don't get excited. And quit pushing me around."

When they reached Jason's house Allie waited by the curb, while Shane marched up to Jason's door and rang the bell. A younger girl answered. They talked for a minute before he ran back down the walk.

"He's not home," Shane reported. "His sister said he went to the playground."

"Good. That's where I'm headed then." She turned to walk away, then stopped. "Thanks, Shane."

"I'll go with you. Jason could be trouble."

"I can take care of myself." Allie shrugged his hand off her arm, then slapped her forehead. "Wow! I didn't make the connection, but this is weird—the Forest Avenue Playground.''

''What are you talking about?''

She told him about the flashlight she'd found in her mother's closet. ''Jimmy was at the playground just before he was killed. And now we find out that Jason hangs out there.''

''Could be more than a coincidence. How did the flashlight get in your mother's closet?''

Allie shivered. ''I'm not sure I want to know.''

''Maybe your mother found it in Jimmy's room?''

''Uh-uh. The police would have noticed it when they searched my mother's room. The flashlight got there *after* the police search.''

''Who could have dropped it then?''

''That's what scares me.''

''Let me go with you, Allie. Please?''

''If you really want to.''

''I do.''

Shane's smile made her heart jump like crazy. How could she go weak in the knees over a pair of blue eyes when her mother was missing?

Neither of them said much on the way to the playground. Allie kept thinking about the flashlight. They ran down the steps to the playground, past the swings and the pool.

She stuck her head in the door of the big brick recreation building. She checked out who was playing Ping-Pong and pool. No Jason Densmore. The director looked her way, but she ducked out again.

''He's not in there,'' she said to Shane.

The basketball courts were behind the rec building and down another set of stairs. Allie paused at the top.

57

She nudged Shane. "Look over there on the far court in the red shirt."

"That's Jason, all right. He's playing with a bunch of older kids. I know them from school."

"He thinks he's so hot." Allie made a face.

"Want to play a little one-on-one?" Shane challenged. "There's a free court next to Jason's."

"Okay. But I'm warning you, I stink."

"Let's get a ball and see."

In the rec room, Shane gave his watch as security.

"I haven't seen you two around before." The director handed Shane a basketball. The guy must pump a lot of iron. His muscles were huge. He was maybe twenty or so. His black curly mop of hair hung to his shoulders. Something about him was scary.

"We haven't been here in a while," Shane explained.

"You live around here?" He was asking a lot of questions, Allie thought.

"Yeah." She tapped her cheeks. "Maybe you knew my brother, Jimmy McKenzie."

His eyebrows rose. "Yeah, I knew Jimmy. Nice kid. I liked him. I went to the funeral."

Allie and Shane ran down to the courts.

"I'm not sure I like that guy," Allie said.

"The director? He seemed okay to me."

On the court, Allie dribbled the basketball like a clumsy nerd. She missed most of her shots. Shane made all of his. He let her make a few easy layups. She hated it when guys went easy just because you were a girl.

Out of the corner of her eye she watched Jason. She knew he saw her, because he frowned and turned his face away. The guys he played with looked tougher than the group Jimmy used to hang out with.

Jason made crude remarks about girls. He laughed real loud when she missed a shot.

"You want to leave?" Shane asked her.

"No way!"

Allie was winded. The ball slipped from her hands and rolled to Jason's court. She ran after it. Jason charged for the ball and deliberately rammed into her. She fell flat on her back.

The other guys laughed. Jason bounced the ball right next to her face.

"Watch it, Jason." Shane elbowed him back and stretched a hand to Allie. She ignored it and scrambled up on her own.

"You all right, kid?" The director stood behind Jason, frowning at Allie.

She nodded.

"Jason, it's time you went home." The director squeezed Jason's shoulder so he winced.

"What if I don't want to?" Jason bounced the ball.

The director squeezed harder. "Beat it, twerp."

Jason threw an angry glance at Allie, slammed the ball to the ground, and stalked off in a huff.

"Hey, Mad Dog, shoot some hoops with us," one of Jason's friends called.

"Mad Dog?" Shane and Allie said in unison.

The director grinned. "The name's Rick Madison. Between my name and my hair the kids call me Mad Dog. I don't mind. Keeps you guys intimidated. But if you like basketball I'll give you a few pointers sometime." He saluted Shane and Allie and loped over to the other court.

They watched as he hooked shot after shot. He moved like a graceful cat around the court.

"We'd better go." Allie shivered. "It's getting dark."

In the rec room, Shane exchanged the basketball for his watch. A tall guy with huge hands and thinning hair handed them each a flyer. "Come to the basketball clinic tomorrow night," he said.

Allie looked at the flyer. The guy's picture was on it. He had once played for the New York Knicks.

The guy smiled. He had big teeth. "That's me, Bob Meer."

"You came to our school and spoke at an assembly about drugs last year." Shane shook his hand.

"I'm a recovered drug addict. Now I like to help kids not get hooked." Someone called Meer's name. "See you at the clinic." He walked away.

Allie exhaled. Drugs again. She knew kids who smoked pot or did drugs. She was too smart to get hooked on something so stupid and so dangerous. Maybe she'd been too smug, thinking drugs could never hurt her family. Maybe drugs were behind Jimmy's death and her mother's disappearance.

They hurried up the playground steps. Allie pulled Shane backward.

"What are you doing?" He grabbed the fence to keep from falling.

"Look." She pointed across the street. Mad Dog held on to Jason Densmore's bike like he wouldn't let him go.

"I thought Jason went home," Shane said.

"They're arguing. What's going on?"

Finally Mad Dog backed off, and Jason sped like a streak down the sidewalk. Mad Dog watched until Jason was out of sight.

"What was that all about?" Allie asked.

Shane shrugged and they continued homeward.

"Will you stake out Jason tonight?" Allie stopped at the corner of Bosworth Street.

Shane folded his arms. "Tonight? I have basketball practice."

"You said you would."

"I didn't think you meant tonight."

"I didn't mean Christmas!"

"Sor-ry."

"Forget it. Just forget it." Allie pushed by him.

Shane blocked her way. "I said I'd do it and I will. Just not tonight. I can't. Don't get mad." He bent his head to look in her face.

"It's okay. I understand. Tomorrow, then."

"I'll call you after school."

Allie ran down the street to Mrs. Brumbaugh's house. She couldn't wait until tomorrow. She'd have to get out of the house tonight to spy on Jason Densmore.

Twelve

ALLIE THOUGHT HER FATHER WOULD NEVER FIN-
ish dinner that night. He had two helpings of spaghetti
and three cups of coffee. After doing the dishes she said
she had homework. She went up to her room. Kristi
telephoned at seven.

"How'd it go with Shane?" she asked.

Allie filled her in on all the details.

"Do you still like him?"

"I can't like anybody until I find my mother."

"I can't believe Shane said he'd help you."

"You know the trellis on the side of my house where
my mother's morning glories climbed last year?"

"Yeah."

"Would it hold me if I tried to climb down it?"

"What are you going to do?"

"I've got to spy on Jason Densmore."

"You'll get in trouble," Kristi squealed.

"You want to come with me?"

"Are you kidding? On a school night? My mother
would put me in a convent if I got caught."

Allie sighed.

"Be careful," Kristi pleaded before she hung up.

At seven-thirty, Allie pulled her bathrobe on over her clothes. She rolled up her jeans so they wouldn't show. Then she went downstairs to the living room where her father dozed in front of a Mets game on TV.

"Dad, I'm going to bed," she announced.

Her father came to with a jerk. "Huh?" His hair stood on end, and he looked worn out.

"I'm really tired, Dad. I'm going to sleep."

"You finish your homework?"

"Yeah."

"Okay. Sleep well."

In her room, Allie arranged her pillows under the bed covers so they looked like a person sleeping. Then she hung up her bathrobe, pulled on a dark sweatshirt, and tied her long hair back in a ponytail.

She shut the light. Like a blind bat, she rushed to the window. Focusing on the streetlight, she pressed her forehead against the cold glass. She took deep breaths. If she concentrated on her mother, the fear would disappear.

Slowly, she raised the window. Then, with as little noise as possible, she climbed out onto the roof. She remembered to shut the window behind her.

One careful step at a time, she picked her way across the sloping roof. Her foot slid out. She grabbed the drainpipe. Then she lowered her foot until it touched the top slat of the trellis.

Still hugging the drainpipe, she placed both feet on the trellis. It held. Her foot found the next slat. She kept going down, hand over hand, clutching the trellis.

With a shaking breath, she finally dropped to the

driveway. She waited a full minute. No one called her name. No doors opened. She was safe.

Then she raced across the driveway, down the sidewalk, and around the corner. She didn't stop until she reached Jason's street. Her side ached, and she thought her lungs would burst.

She leaned against a parked car. It was a good thing she did. A couple of kids were riding bicycles up and down Jason's driveway. Allie ducked out of sight.

Peering around the car, she recognized Jason and two guys he'd played basketball with at the playground. Across the street, Shane's garage stood open and empty. He must have gone to basketball practice. She didn't see Tim Callahan's Mustang anywhere. She was glad.

She crept closer to Jason and his friends. She crouched behind a big bush by the driveway. A chill wind blew against her face. Dark clouds moved across the sky, shutting out the moon. She shivered.

The guys rode over a jump they'd built. They talked and laughed about their attempts to outdo each other. Dumb boy junk.

Allie was ready to go home when one of the guys said, "Let's go to Bob's house."

"Shouldn't we call first?" the other guy asked.

"Naw. Not after dark. No one will see us."

"I have to be in by nine-thirty," Jason said.

"It's an easy ride up Clove Road to Victory."

They sped off down the street. Great. How could she follow them? She stared at Shane's house, willing him to come home. The streetlight shone on something metal in the garage. Shane's bike!

She raced across the street into the Schroeder garage. She grabbed the ten speed. For once she was grateful

64

for her long skinny legs as she swung her right leg over the bar of the bike.

She pedaled down the street and turned left on Clove Road. The boys had gotten a good jump on her, but on the ten speed, Allie caught up to them at Clove Lakes Park.

Careful to stay well behind them, she followed them to Victory where they turned left. A few blocks down, they veered right into a cement parking area behind a one-story apartment building with four carports under it.

Allie leaned the ten speed against the building. The boys' bikes were parked by a VW in one of the carports.

They must have gone into one of the apartments, but which one? Above the carports, each apartment had a railed-in porch. Could she climb up there?

At one end of the building, a grassy bank sloped up to the porches. Allie climbed the bank and stretched her arm until she touched the vertical slats of the railing.

She grabbed the slats and braced her feet against the building. Scraping and scrabbling, she seized the top rail. Then she pulled herself up and over onto the porch.

She crouched, panting. Sweat trickled down her sides. Splinters pained her hands. She didn't dare move. Her heart sounded like a drum. But no one came. No one looked out a window.

She crept to the first window. Her ragged breathing steamed the glass. Through a crack in the curtain she saw an old man and woman watching TV.

She sidled along the wall to the next apartment. A half raised miniblind hung in the window. Allie knelt to look in. Jason and his friends came into the room. She jerked back, banging her chin on the windowsill. Tears sprang to her eyes. She wanted to cry.

She took deep breaths. Slowly, she looked through the window. The three boys sat on the floor around a TV, their backs to Allie. They were playing Nintendo. To their right, someone sat on a couch. All she could see of him were his long legs. He wore blue jeans and white leather high-tops.

She moved her ear closer, but all she heard was laughter and snatches of words. She crouched until her knees cramped. All they did was play Nintendo and drink Cokes. Boring.

Maybe she was on the wrong track. It looked like an innocent visit to a friend or a relative.

The kid playing against Jason finally raised his arms in victory. Jason stood, looking at his watch.

The guy with the long legs headed for the window.

Allie jerked back against the wall. She held her breath. Her heart hammered like crazy. The miniblinds crashed closed.

With her hands pressed flat against the building, she waited. Nothing happened. Everything was quiet—except for her own breathing.

From below, loud voices split the silence. Jason and his friends. She heard their sneakered feet slap against the cement.

"Let me at my bike, ya jerk."

"I'll race ya home."

Allie tried not to move. She saw them just below, wheeling their bikes out of the carport. They jumped on the bikes and sped away. Their raucous voices floated back through the darkness. Then they were gone.

Allie inched her way to the railing. Her leg was straddling the railing when two guys walked into the parking area. She slammed back into the shadows. They climbed the bank to the front of the house, so close she could hear their rough breathing as they climbed.

She jumped from the porch and slid down the slope. She raced to the front in time to see the guys walk into the second apartment. A hand from inside clapped one on the shoulder just before the front door slammed shut.

What was going on? Why were these kids visiting this guy?

Tomorrow she'd find out who lived in the second apartment. She ran back to her bike and swung it away from the building.

Someone grabbed her. He wrapped his arm around her neck and pulled hard. She dropped the bike.

"Hey!" She struggled to get loose.

"What are you sneaking around here for?" He smelled of cigarettes.

"Let me go!" Allie jabbed both elbows into the guy's chest. His grip loosened. But a second guy blocked her way. She was pinned between the two of them.

"He asked what you're doing here." The one in front shoved her. He had pimples on his face.

"The same reason you're here." She swallowed.

"Oh, yeah? You're just a punk kid."

"So? I came to see Bob too."

They backed off a little. The one behind stepped in front so he could see her better. They both wore black leather jackets.

"Let's see if Bob knows you." He shoved Allie toward the bank.

"Let her go," a voice commanded.

The guys and Allie whirled. Someone tall and huge stood in the shadows of the bushes.

"I said beat it!" He moved closer.

The guys turned and ran from the parking area, not even looking back over their shoulders.

Allie grabbed up the bike. She swung her leg over the seat and started pedaling.

"Wait!" The man in the shadows lunged for her bike. He grabbed the seat. The bike slid sideways. She pedaled hard. But he held her fast.

She sobbed and looked back into his face. It was Mad Dog! His dark eyes blazed. His hair bounced wildly around his head. Allie strained until she thought her neck would pop. The driveway sloped downward. The bike rolled forward with Mad Dog clinging to the seat.

"Stop!" She felt his breath on her neck. "I want to talk to you!"

With a desperate lunge, Allie thrust forward. His fingers slipped from the seat. The bike wobbled out of control. She pedaled like a crazy person down the sidewalk. Mad Dog pounded after her.

But once on the straightaway of Victory Boulevard, he was no match for the ten speed. Allie sped away.

By the time she reached Shane's house, her legs felt like rubber, her lungs like a balloon ready to burst. She crashed in a heap on Shane's lawn. If someone had come after her right then, she'd have been dead meat.

Shane's garage door was closed. When she'd gotten her wind, she propped the bike against the garage.

Then she walked home. Everything hurt—her feet, her legs, her hands, her shoulders. She saw lights on in the front windows of her house. Was her father still dozing in front of the TV or had he discovered she was gone?

Allie climbed back up the trellis. She was so tired

68

she wanted to cry. Somehow, she made it back across the roof and into her bedroom.

The pillows still lay arranged under the blankets. She peeled her clothes off. Too exhausted to find her nightgown, she crawled into bed in her underwear.

Just before dawn, the old nightmare returned. The sound of her scream woke her up. She dripped with sweat. She jerked up against the headboard. Her hands fought off his touch. She flailed the air in front her.

"Go away," she whimpered. "Mother! Mother!"

Then she remembered. Her mother was gone. She wouldn't come. She had to face him alone.

Tonight she had a weapon. "It wasn't my fault." She stared into the darkness. "You left before I got home. Why didn't you wait? You should have waited."

Hearing only the pounding of her heart, Allie waited. Silence. The tightness gripping her chest eased. The blankets fell from her fingers. From the window, the pale light of morning crept into the room.

Allie slipped from the bed. In the bathroom, she turned on the shower. Under the spray of hot water, she laid her plans. First of all, she'd have to break her promise to her father. She'd have to ditch school. Because she'd been following the wrong person.

Thirteen

IN THE MORNING SHE HAD TO REVISE HER PLANS. Her father insisted on driving her to school. She thought she could slip out the back gate before the bell rang, but her father marched her into the office to give the secretary Mrs. Brumbaugh's phone number as Allie's official baby-sitter. Allie was *so* embarrassed.

By the time they were finished, the bell had rung, the gates were locked, and she had no choice but to go to band class. Kristi's seat was empty. How could she be absent when Allie needed her? Now she *had* to escape from school. She couldn't stay without Kristi.

While Rottenburger took attendance, Allie thought of a way. She rushed from her seat in the saxophone section, one hand over her mouth, the other holding her stomach.

"I'm going to throw up," she gasped.

Rothenberg shoved the pass at Allie. "Run to the rest room. Sandra, go with her." He pointed at the girl who was first chair clarinet.

Allie ran with Sandra behind her. Inside the toilet cubicle, she poked her finger down her throat. She gagged. She poked again. Her stomach heaved and out spewed the Froot Loops and milk she'd had for breakfast.

"You okay?" Sandra called.

Allie came out. She wiped her forehead and shook her head.

In the office, the school nurse asked if Allie wanted to go home.

"Yes. Call my baby-sitter."

The nurse spoke to Mrs. B. and said she'd send Allie home.

Mrs. Brumbaugh waited on the front porch. "You okay, Allie?"

"It's just cramps."

"Oh." Mrs. Brumbaugh opened the door. "Come lie on the couch. I'll make hot chicken soup. That's what I always did for my daughter. It will help. You'll see."

Allie shook her head. "I need to go the store. I need Kotex." She couldn't meet Mrs. Brumbaugh's eye.

"I can go to the store for you." She looked so concerned Allie almost blurted out the truth. She hated lying. But this time she had to.

"I'll be fine. First, I have to go home and get some money." Allie ran down the steps. "Don't worry if I'm gone long," she called over her shoulder.

Mrs. Brumbaugh looked worried already, but she nodded anyway.

In her kitchen, Allie paged frantically through the phone book. There were too many Madisons, and no Rick, so she dialed the playground. The phone rang and rang before a woman answered it, sounding out of breath.

"Forest Avenue Playground," she said.

"May I please speak to Mr. Madison?" Allie tried to sound grown-up.

"He ain't here right now."

"May I have his home phone number, please?"

"Gee, I don't know. He might be mad if I give it out."

"This is an emergency."

"Who is this?"

"Staten Island Hospital. Someone from his family had an accident."

"Oh, no! Are they hurt?"

"Yes. So, we need to reach Mr. Madison."

"Can't they give you his number?"

"He's unconscious. He needs surgery immediately."

"Oh, no. Just a minute, I'll get it."

Allie drummed her fingers on her cheek while she waited. The girl rattled the number off to Allie. She wrote it down.

"Does he still live on Clove Road?" Allie asked.

"It says here he lives at 3461 Castleton Avenue."

"Thanks." Then she dialed Mad Dog's number.

He answered on the third ring. Allie hung up. She grabbed a Twinkie and ran out to the garage. She wheeled her ten speed outside and hopped on.

Her legs felt stiff from last night's marathon ride. Luckily, Castleton was only five blocks from Forest Avenue. Mad Dog's address was not far from the library and Sacred Heart Church. The house was a brown duplex.

Allie watched from across the street behind an elm tree. She ate the Twinkie and hoped this was not a wild goose chase.

In half an hour, Mad Dog ran down the front steps

of the house, carrying a motorcycle helmet. He pushed a motor scooter from the garage and then drove off down Castleton Avenue. Allie shoved off after him. Thanks to traffic and stoplights at almost every corner, she had no trouble following him.

But when he turned left off Manor Road she thought she'd lost him. Mad Dog was nowhere in sight. She pedaled down the street, searching to the left and right.

Behind some bushes, metal gleamed. Mad Dog's motor scooter. She almost flew headfirst over the handlebars. She slowed but didn't dare stop until she reached the corner. She braked and jumped off her bike, propping it against the wrought-iron fence.

She peered around the corner. Mad Dog knelt by the fence. He looked through the bars like he was checking the place out.

It was an old white mansion, surrounded by acres of grass and trees, behind a tall wrought-iron fence. Everything was overgrown with weeds. It didn't look like anyone had lived there for a long time. A dilapidated barn looked ready to fall down, and two old garages needed paint. All the windows were either boarded up or shuttered. It must have been a really spectacular place when it was new. Right now, it looked spooky.

Mad Dog stood up. Then, like a cat, he jumped to the seat of his scooter, sprang to the top of the fence, and landed on the other side.

Allie crept closer. He picked his way stealthily around the whole place. He slid around corners of the buildings, tried to see into windows that were boarded up. He rattled doorknobs, pushed against heavy doors. He even raised the doors of a root cellar on the side of the barn.

What was he looking for?

Finally, Mad Dog scrambled back over the fence, wheeled his motor scooter out to the sidewalk, and headed out to Manor Road.

Allie checked her watch. It was almost three o'clock. She had to get home before Mrs. Brumbaugh called her father. She turned her bike toward home.

Mrs. B. Had a bowl of steaming chicken soup ready for her. It tasted good. Allie tried not to slurp, but she hadn't realized how hungry she was.

Tears came when she remembered how her mother would tie on a huge apron, wave a spatula around her head, and pretend to be an exotic dancer whenever she cooked dinner. If they were having spaghetti she'd sing "O Sole Mio." If they were having Mexican she'd croon "South of the Border."

"The soup too hot?" Mrs. Brumbaugh asked.

"Yeah." Allie wiped her eyes.

The doorbell rang and Mrs. B. went to answer it.

She returned, beaming from ear to ear, with Shane behind her.

"Hey, Allie." He slid into a chair across the table.

"Hi, Shane." He looked good in a red sweater and tight blue jeans. She wished she'd had time to comb her hair and put on some lipstick.

"Guess what happened to Jason Densmore?" Shane asked.

"What?" For some reason Allie held her breath.

"He got beat up."

Fourteen

"JASON GOT BEAT UP?" ALLIE'S MOUTH dropped open.

"Yup." Shane nodded. "Some guys jumped him last night and stole his wallet. They worked him over real good. I saw him this morning when I left for school. He had a shiner you wouldn't believe. His mouth was swollen to twice its size."

"This used to be a safe neighborhood." Mrs. Brumbaugh shook her head. "Now we have hoodlums and gangs."

"Jason wasn't beat up by a gang." Allie rapped her fingers on the table.

"That's what his brother was saying at school. I heard him say he was going after the goons that did it."

"I know the goon who did it." Allie nodded.

"Who?" Shane and Mrs. B. said together.

"Mad Dog Madison."

"Mad Dog?" Shane looked skeptical.

"Who's Mad Dog?" Mrs. B. looked lost.

Allie sighed. "It's a long story. I followed Jason last night."

75

"You did *what?*" Shane put his hands on his head. Mrs. B. had that worried look again.

"I'll tell you everything that happened. But I don't want my father to know, Mrs. B."

The old lady pressed her lips together. "Does this have to do with your mother?"

She nodded. "I want to find her, Mrs. B. Everyone else has given up on her. I won't."

"You're spunky, just like your mother." She patted Allie's hand.

"Promise you won't tell my father?"

Mrs. B. rubbed her chin. "How can I do that? He trusts me. I can't keep things from him."

"Please, Mrs. B., for my mother's sake and Jimmy's. It's just like keeping a secret. Please?"

She sighed. "I'll promise not to tell what you've already done." She shook her finger. "But I won't keep something from him that is dangerous for you."

"That's fair enough," Allie admitted.

"Come on. Tell us." Shane waved his hands.

Allie retold everything that happened from the minute she'd climbed out of her room last night until she followed Mad Dog Madison to the deserted mansion this afternoon.

"You could have been hurt!" Mrs. B's teeth wobbled like crazy.

"Are you sure it was Mad Dog who grabbed your bike?" Shane scratched his head.

"Positive."

The phone rang on the counter. Mrs. B. struggled up to answer it. "It's Kristi." She held out the receiver.

"Where were you today?" Allie accused.

"I've got chicken pox! Can you believe it?"

76

"You haven't had chicken pox yet?"

"Nope. My mother says I have to stay home for a week. That's the pits. I'll miss the dance on Friday."

Allie bit back angry words. Her mother was missing, and Kristi thought getting the chicken pox was the end of the world. "What a shame," she said, "especially since you had a big date lined up."

"You don't have to be sarcastic." Kristi lowered her voice to a whisper. "Did you do it last night?"

"Yes, I did."

"Oooh. I don't believe you! What happened? Tell me every gory detail."

"Can I call you back later, Kristi? Shane's here."

"Shane? What's he doing there?"

"I'll tell you later. Hope you feel better."

After Allie sat back down at the table, Mrs. B. asked, "What has this Mad Dog done? And what does it have to do with your mother?"

"I think he's selling drugs to kids, using the playground as a cover. Maybe my mom found out."

"You don't have any proof, just suspicions." Shane tilted the chair back.

"But they add up to something." Allie counted off on her fingers. "First, he was at Bob's apartment last night. Second, he grabbed my bike. Then, today, he was snooping around an old mansion. And lastly, Jason gets beat up after we saw Mad Dog arguing with him yesterday afternoon. It all adds up."

Shane's mouth dropped open. "I just thought of something."

"What?"

"The initials R. M. in your brother's diary."

"Holy cow! I forgot about that. R. M. Rick Madison."

"Where is this mansion you followed him to?" Shane sounded excited.

She described it again.

"Could that be the Vandermeer mansion?" Mrs. Brumbaugh's eyes grew big.

"You know it?" Allie asked.

"Sure. The Vander Meerhuisen family goes back to the days of the early Dutch settlers. Along the way someone shortened the name to Vandermeer. Old Bertram Vandermeer was borough president when I was married. The house was a showplace then. He died some years ago."

"Who owns the house now?" Shane asked.

Mrs. B. pursed her lips. "I read something about it in the paper recently. What was it?" She hobbled up from the table. "Maybe I can find the article. I donate my papers to the Salvation Army." She pointed to a stack of newspapers by the back door.

"We'll help you look." Allie grabbed a bundle and began paging through them. Shane did the same.

Mrs. Brumbaugh found the article. "Here it is." She pulled her glasses from her apron pocket and propped them on the end of her nose.

"This was last Thursday's paper." Mrs. Brumbaugh read out loud. "It says that Robert Vandermeer, the only surviving member of the Vandermeer family, has sold the family estate to a group that will use it for a drug rehabilitation center."

"Drugs again." Allie slapped the table. "Everywhere we look we find drugs."

"Maybe Mad Dog is using the place to stash drugs," Shane suggested.

"Let's search—er—clean up these newspapers." Allie grabbed up the papers on the table. She jerked her head at Shane, who just looked puzzled.

The phone rang. Mrs. B. sighed as she picked it up. Allie carried the papers back to the corner.

"It's your father." Mrs. B. held the phone out.

"Hi, Dad."

"I have to work late tonight, Allie. It can't be helped. I want you to stay at Mrs. Brumbaugh's until I get home. Okay?"

"Sure, Dad."

He paused, like he was surprised she didn't gripe about it. "Ask her if it's okay."

"My dad wants to know if I can stay here until he gets home, which might be late," she asked Mrs. B.

"Of course. If it gets real late you can spend the night. I have a spare bedroom."

Allie started to protest, then changed her mind. "Okay. But you'd better ask my dad." She handed the phone to Mrs. B.

While Mrs. B. spoke to her father, she turned to Shane. "Yes!" she mouthed so only he could see.

He smiled and shook his head at her.

"It's all settled." Mrs. B. hung up the phone. "You'll spend the night here if your father's real late."

"Thanks, Mrs. B." She touched the old lady's arm.

"What would you both like for dinner?" Mrs. B. rubbed her hands together like she couldn't wait to cook.

"I'm not hungry." Allie pressed her stomach.

"My mother's expecting me for dinner." Shane grabbed his books from the counter.

"I need to go to the library to get a book for a book report." Allie signaled to Shane by blinking. "But I don't want to walk back by myself in the dark."

"That's not a good idea." Mrs. B. shook her head.

"Did you say you were going to the library, Shane?" She couldn't believe he could be so dense.

He stared at her. Then he blinked. "Oh, yeah. I am. I could walk you home."

"Would that be okay, Mrs. B.?" Allie tried not to sound too anxious.

Mrs. B. stroked her chin. "Would your father mind?"

"Uh-uh. I go to the library all the time."

"Okay. As long as you're home before nine o'clock."

"I'll take care of her." Shane narrowed his eyes.

Allie almost choked over that.

Once they were outside, she steered Shane toward Clove Lakes.

"The library's that way." He pointed in the opposite direction.

"The Vandermeer mansion is this way. This is a perfect opportunity to search the place."

"You promised Mrs. B. not to do anything dangerous."

"We'll just snoop, not rob the place."

"In the dark?"

"A perfect cover. No one will see us. We can get a flashlight from your garage if you want."

"For a junior high brat, you're awfully pushy, know that?"

"So I've heard." She put her hands on her hips. "You're not chicken, are you?"

He laughed. "You got to be kidding. But something

tells me this is a dumb idea and I'm stupid for letting you talk me into it.''

''Nothing will happen. It's just a deserted old estate. What can go wrong?''

Fifteen

SHANE REACHED FOR HER HAND AS THEY WALKED toward his street. It felt good—safe and comforting.

"Shane, let's stop at Jason's house."

"Why?"

"Maybe he'll talk to us now that he's been beat up."

"I think he'll be scared stiff to open his mouth."

Nevertheless they rang Jason's doorbell. Allie backed into the shadows. His stepbrother, Tim Callahan, opened the door.

"Yeah? What do you want?" He took a drink from a can of Coke.

"Jason home?" Shane asked. "I want to ask him something about my bike."

"I'll get the jerk. Hold on."

"Whatcha want?" Jason looked awful, as if someone had used him for a punching bag. Tim stayed in the doorway.

"I want to sell my ten speed. You interested?"

"Uh-uh."

"It's a good deal. Come take a look at it." Shane started down the steps. Jason muttered but followed him across the street.

Allie joined them by Shane's garage.

"You!" Jason exploded when he saw her. "What's going on?"

"Who beat you up?" Allie scrutinized his bruises.

Jason spun around to leave. Shane grabbed his arm. "Just tell us."

"You ain't getting nothing from me." He jerked loose from Shane.

"Was it Mad Dog Madison?" she asked.

Jason stopped. "Where'd you get that idea?"

"He's been peddling drugs, hasn't he?" Shane asked.

Under the streetlight, Jason's face paled. "Let me go."

"You got beat up so you wouldn't talk, didn't you?" Shane moved closer.

"You were lucky, Jason," Allie said softly. "You only got beat up. My brother got killed."

Jason wet his lips. "Back off. I'm warning you. Or you'll end up just as dead as your brother." With those words, he ran across the street and into his house.

Neither she nor Shane said anything. Shadows moved on the sidewalk. She looked over her shoulder.

Shane blew out his breath. "Maybe we should back off. He may be right. This could be dangerous."

"No. I'm going to the Vandermeer place. I've got to find my mother." She strode down the street toward Clove Lakes Park. Shane caught up with her and they walked on in silence.

They stopped in front of the tall wrought-iron gate. Behind it, the estate looked eerie in the darkness. Huge trees and dense bushes made it seem like a jungle.

"Can you climb over this gate?" Shane asked.

"If you can, I can." Allie touched the scrolling in the center "We could step on this."

"You go first. I'll give you a boost."

She stepped into Shane's cupped hands, grabbed the bars, and climbed on the scrolling. The gate swung inward.

"It's open!" She jumped down.

"There's an open padlock on the inside handle."

"Maybe someone's in there," Allie whispered.

"Maybe we'd better leave."

"No. Let's check it out."

They circled the property, staying close to the fence. Leaves and dead brush crackled under their feet. Allie counted four buildings other than the main house: a barn, two garages, and a sloping-roofed shed.

Shane stopped short. Allie bumped into his shoulder. "Ssh." He pointed up ahead to one of the garages. Two men came out of a garage, carrying bundles. They stacked the bundles in the trunk of a car, then made half a dozen more similar trips between the car and garage. Neither man spoke. They moved very quietly.

"What are they doing?" Allie whispered.

Shane put his finger on his lips.

When the trunk was full, one man slammed it shut. The other locked the garage door. Both men jumped into the car. They drove slowly down the dirt track to the gate with the headlights off.

"They sure didn't want anyone to see what they were doing, did they?" Shane watched the red taillights.

"I bet it was drugs." Allie nodded. "They had to get rid of the evidence, because this Vandermeer guy is selling the place. They can't use it to store drugs anymore."

"Could you see who it was?" Shane asked.

"It was too dark. I bet one was Mad Dog, though."

"Let's take a look in that garage."

Standing on tiptoe, Allie peered through one of the dirty windows. All she could see were dark shadows.

"I can't get this dumb flashlight to work." Shane shook it so it rattled.

"Shane, the car's coming back!" The rumble of a car engine headed their way.

"Quick, behind the barn," he whispered. They huddled together against the barn. Allie's heart hammered so loudly she was sure they could hear it. The car stopped. Doors slammed. Feet crackled the brush.

She peered around the barn. A flashlight swept the shrubbery. She jerked back. The light moved closer.

"I don't think anyone's here," a voice said.

"Why was the gate open, then?"

"Maybe the wind blew it open."

"A big gate like that? Let's check this garage first. Then we'll check the grounds."

The voices disappeared into the garage.

"We've got to hide." Shane pulled her along the barn.

"In the root cellar," she whispered. "I saw Mad Dog open it this afternoon." She ran to the wooden doors angled against the side of the barn. Together they lifted one of the doors.

Allie descended the stone steps first. Shane lowered the door shut over their heads. A vertical door blocked their way. There was just enough room for the two of them to crouch in front of the door.

Shane gripped her hand. She could hear his breathing as they waited, motionless.

Muted voices. A pinpoint of light through the crack of the sloping doors above them. Allie held her breath. There was a scraping noise, like something was being dragged across the door.

"There, that should hold it," someone said.

"Yeah, just in case," someone else answered.

The car engine started up. Then only silence.

Allie broke the silence first. "I think they're gone."

"Let's get out of here." Shane stood in a crouch and shoved the door. Nothing. He pushed harder.

'What's the matter?" She hated the way her voice sounded panicky.

"I can't open it. They must have locked it!"

Sixteen

"DON'T PANIC," SHANE SAID. "WE'LL FIND A way out."

The close darkness surrounded her. She couldn't see. She couldn't breathe. "I can't. I've got to get out. Help!"

Shane grabbed her shoulders. "Close your eyes. Take deep breaths."

She tried, but the terror came anyway. Her stomach cramped, her legs turned to jelly, and a roaring filled her ears. She jumped up, hitting her head on the door. She flailed with her arms. From somewhere she heard a wailing sound. It was her.

A hand cracked across her face. Stunned, she fell against Shane.

"I'm sorry. Did I hurt you?" His arms encircled her.

She clutched his shirt and panted like she'd just run a mile.

"Are you claustrophobic? My mother is."

She nodded.

"Hang on. You'll be okay. Easy now. I've got you." He stroked her face with one hand and rubbed her back with the other.

Her breathing quieted. Shane's cheek touched hers. His arms tightened around her.

"Allie?" His voice sounded funny.

She waited, their faces just inches apart. His breath moistened her mouth. His lips brushed hers. Just the lightest of touches. It took her breath away.

"Shane." Her voice sounded odd.

His mouth met hers again. This time his lips pressed harder. They moved against hers. She swayed toward him. Her lips moved under his. A trembling swept through her. A sweetness she had never felt before filled her.

"You okay?" he said against her cheek.

"Yeah." She exhaled.

"We should try to get out of here," Shane mumbled into her hair. "Don't you think?"

"Probably."

They broke apart. Shane shook the flashlight. "If only I could get it to work. There. It's on."

The light blinded her. "Shine it on the doors. Maybe we can see what's holding them shut."

Through the opening between the doors, they could see a thin piece of wood.

"They must have slid that through the handles. If we had something sharp, we could work it out." Shane swept the flashlight around the floor.

"What's that in the corner?" Allie picked it up. "A hairbrush. How'd it get here?"

Shane grabbed the brush. "The pointed end will work great. You hold the flashlight."

He jabbed the handle into the crevice and slid it back and forth on the piece of wood.

"It's moving!" She held her breath until the wood was dislodged and rattled down from the handles.

"Yippee." She clapped her hands.

Shane pushed the doors open. The cold night air rushed in, fresh and welcoming. They scrambled up the stairs and outside.

Allie gulped in the fresh air.

Shane grabbed her hand. "Let's get out of here."

"Wait, where's the brush?"

"In the cellar where I dropped it. Why?"

She ran back down the stairs and retrieved the brush. "Shine the flashlight on it." She turned the brush over. On the underside of the handle was a red initial *P*.

"This is my mother's brush. She's been here!"

Seventeen

"LOTS OF GIRLS HAVE BRUSHES LIKE THAT, Allie. My sister does," Shane argued.

"I have one too. See the red *P* on the handle? I wrote that one day with my mom's red nail polish. We were always getting our brushes mixed up. I know it's hers."

"If you're positive, you better show it to the police."

"They wouldn't believe me. They didn't before. Besides, what would they do?"

"They could search this place—turn it upside down."

Allie froze. "Do you think my mother could still be here?"

"I don't know." He stared at the ground.

The way he said that made her afraid. "Do you think they killed her and hid her body here?"

"Allie, don't say—"

"Maybe they caught her snooping around. Maybe she saw the drugs in that garage."

"That doesn't mean they killed her."

"They may have killed Jimmy."

"Allie—"

"Stop trying to protect me, Shane! I want to know

the truth. I'm not a little kid who's going to fall apart. I know about death. When it comes, you can't stop it. You can't change it even though it almost kills you, too. But you go on living. It's the not knowing that tears you up."

Shane didn't say anything.

"Maybe that's why my mother disappeared. Maybe that's the reason the police can't find her. She's dead."

"They haven't found her body either."

"No. But it's the only reason I can think of right now why my mother wouldn't come home to me."

Shane pulled her close.

"What if she's dead?" she sobbed.

"Don't think the worst. We don't know what's happened to her. But I do know you've got to tell your father about all of this."

"He's not home."

"Tomorrow's Saturday. He'll be home then, won't he?"

"I guess so. But what's he going to do about it?"

"Call the police. They'll listen to an adult."

"Maybe."

"They can at least search the entire estate."

"Only if they have enough evidence for a search warrant. I've read enough detective books to know the police can't walk in and search a place without just cause."

"The only real evidence we have is the flashlight you found in your mother's closet."

"And that has to belong to Mad Dog Madison. He works at the Forest Avenue Playground."

"Maybe his fingerprints are on it."

"No, my fingerprints are on it."

Shane sighed. "Let's get out of here." They headed for the gate and climbed back over it.

Allie checked her watch. "We'd better run. It's eight-thirty. My warden awaits."

Mrs. Brumbaugh was so relieved to see them, she hugged Allie. "Your father got home five minutes ago. I was so afraid he'd come over to get you."

Allie hugged her back. "Would you mind if I went home, since my dad's back?"

"I understand." But she sounded disappointed.

Shane acted like he wanted to kiss her again when they said good night outside her house. But she was afraid her father would look out the window and see them. So she gave him a quick peck on the cheek before she ran up the steps and inside.

Her father was dialing the telephone. When he saw her, he hung up. "I was just calling Mrs. Brumbaugh."

"She saw your car, so I came on over."

"I'm glad."

"Did you have dinner?"

"I had a couple of hot dogs on the ferry."

"I can make you something if you want."

"No. Thanks, anyway."

She headed for the stairs.

"I heard you cry out last night."

Allie turned.

He stood there fiddling with his tie. "Was it a nightmare?"

She nodded.

"I didn't know if you wanted me to come to your room. Your mother always did that."

"It's okay. You don't need to."

"How was school today?" He sat down on the edge of the couch.

"I went home during second period." She was tired of lying.

"Why?" He frowned.

"Stomach cramps."

"Oh."

"Dad? Can I talk to you about something?"

"Sure. Anything."

"I think I know—" The telephone interrupted.

Her father reached to pick it up. "It's Kristi. Do you want to call her back?"

The moment had passed. "No. I'll get it upstairs." She took the steps two at a time, grabbed the hall phone, and carried it to her room. She shut her door and sat cross-legged on the bed. "I got it, Dad." He hung up.

"Where have you been?" Kristi asked.

"Looking for my mother."

"I wish I didn't have this stupid chicken pox, so I could help you."

"It's okay. How do you feel?"

"Itchy. I've got blisters in my hair, my mouth, up my nose, and in places I don't even want to mention. Forget me. Tell me what's happened."

Allie related everything she'd found out.

"I agree with Shane. I don't believe your mother's dead. She's tough and gutsy just like you. Besides . . ." Kristi hesitated.

"What?"

"Something you once told me about dead bodies."

"What? Spit it out."

"Don't they stink after a few days? Wouldn't someone have noticed?"

"You're right. You're absolutely right. Thanks. I needed to hear just what you said."

"I've been thinking about that flashlight, Allie. If it's not your family's and it wasn't there when the police searched the room, then ... then, somebody's been in your house. How else could it have gotten there."

Allie sat still. The wind outside whispered through the trees. The clock on her nightstand ticked.

"Allie? Are you still there?"

"Thanks for sharing that with me, Kristi. I feel real good about going to sleep now, knowing Mad Dog Madison has access to my house."

"It could be someone else."

"Who else works at the Forest Avenue Playground?"

"Anyone who goes there could have picked up the flashlight."

The picture of Bob Meer walking into the playground office jumped into her mind. "It's possible." Allie drummed her fingers on her cheek. "I've got to go, Kristi. My dad's calling me. Talk to you tomorrow."

Bob Meer. No. He spoke at schools. Allie flopped on her stomach. But Jason and his friends had gone to a Bob's apartment. Could it have been Bob Meer? And Mad Dog was there. He knew Bob Meer.

How could she find out where Bob Meer lived? She snapped her fingers. The phone book.

She ran to the hallway, pulled open the drawer of the phone stand, and grabbed up the phone book.

"Allie? You off the phone?" her father called from downstairs.

"Yeah, Dad." Then she scooted back to her room with the phone book.

She crossed her fingers that he was listed. Yup, he

was. Robert Meer. She gasped when she read the address. Victory Boulevard.

She dialed Shane's number. ''Guess who lives in that apartment I followed Jason to?''

''Who?''

''Bob Meer.''

''The ex-basketball player? The one who goes around to the schools talking about drugs? He used to be a drug addict.''

''You got it.''

''How did you find out?''

She told him. ''What if he's the drug pusher?''

''I seriously doubt it. I've heard he helps kids who are in trouble. Jason and his friends probably go to his house because he's a nice guy.''

''What was Mad Dog doing there then?''

''I don't know.''

''And why did those two guys grab me and want Bob to identify me?'' Allie argued.

''I don't know that either.''

''Think about it, Shane. He'd have a great cover for selling drugs to kids.''

''We can't go accusing innocent people for no reason.''

''What if the flashlight I found in my mother's closet is his? He has access to the playground.''

''Have you talked to your dad yet?''

''I'll do it tomorrow.''

''I'll call you then. Are you okay?''

''Sure. Thanks for going to the mansion with me.''

''No problem. I'll see you tomorrow.''

She paced her room after she hung up. If only they'd

been able to explore the mansion more. She was sure that the old place held the key to everything.

She tapped her cheek. Maybe there was another article about it in today's newspaper. The one they'd read at Mrs. Brumbaugh's was a week old.

She ran downstairs. Her dad was eating a bowl of cornflakes in the kitchen.

"Where's the paper?" she asked him.

"I threw it in the trash when I was done with it. I didn't think you ever read it."

"Sometimes I do." Allie fished it out of the trash basket.

Her dad rinsed his bowl under the faucet. "I'm going to bed, Allie. What about you?"

"Me too. I'll take the paper upstairs with me."

She raced up to her room. She heard her father trudge past her bedroom.

On the second page she found the article she wanted. It stated that the Vandermeer mansion had been sold to a drug rehabilitation group. Local businessmen were volunteering time and equipment to help renovate the estate. Tomorrow, a wrecking crew, donated by a local contractor would demolish a dilapidated barn and shed on the property.

Tomorrow? Then there's be no chance to search the estate. Allie jumped up from the bed, scattering the newspaper all over the floor. She bent to crumple it up when a face stared back at her from one of the pages. A familiar face with a toothy smile and thinning hair.

Robert Meer, ex-basketball star, ex-drug addict, and former owner of the Vandermeer mansion!

She grabbed the page and spread it across the bed.

The picture was the same one she'd seen on the flyer at the playground announcing the basketball clinic.

Robert Meer. Of course. Why hadn't she seen it before? The family name had been shortened once, and Bob Meer had shortened it even further. Vander Meerhuisen had become Vandermeer, and Vandermeer became Meer.

Bob Meer had owned the Vandermeer mansion—the mansion where strange things were happening, the mansion where she had found her mother's brush.

Allie read further. The basketball clinic had started today with a demonstration on the court this afternoon and a slide show talk tonight at eight o'clock.

It was nine o'clock already. No time to call Shane. She had to reach the playground before Bob Meer left. If he knew anything about her mother, she'd get it out of him!

Eighteen

ALLIE CLIMBED DOWN THE TRELLIS AND RACED to the Forest Avenue playground. She was out of breath, but she'd made it on time. Kids still hung around inside the rec building. Parents stood in groups waiting to take their kids home.

She shoved through the door and spotted Bob Meer in the middle of the rec room. He stuck out like a giant in a crowd of kids wanting his autograph. What a fake. If she hadn't been so winded she'd have rushed over and socked him in the stomach.

"You show up everywhere, don't you?"

Allie spun around and faced Tim Callahan. "What are you doing here?" she asked.

"I brought my little brother to see the superstar." Tim jerked his head toward Meer.

"Don't you like him?"

"What's to like? The kids think he's a god just because he once played for the Knicks and can hook a sky shot."

"Do you know him?"

He shrugged. "No, I don't know him."

"Do you visit his apartment like your brother does?"
She couldn't believe her nerve. But she knew her question hit home from the way he narrowed his eyes.

A heavy hand spun her around. "Hey!" she said.

Mad Dog Madison looked like he wanted to strangle her. "I want to talk to you, kid."

"Why?" Allie heard her voice shake.

"Tim, get lost. This is private." Mad Dog jerked his thumb for Tim to leave them alone.

Tim looked at Allie. "Don't let him push you around, little girl."

If he hadn't called her little girl she might have told Mad Dog to get lost, too. Instead she said, "It's okay. I've got a few questions for him, too."

"It's your life." Tim sauntered off toward Meer.

Mad Dog pulled her into a corner. "What were you doing at Meer's apartment last night?" he demanded.

"What were *you* doing there?" she retorted.

"Don't get smart. Just answer my question."

"I don't have to."

"You're not like your brother, are you?" Mad Dog's face softened.

"No. But I'm Peggy McKenzie's daughter. If you read the papers, you know she's missing. All I want to do is find my mother."

Mad Dog rubbed his chin. "Look, let me give you some advice. I liked your brother. You're probably not as cranky as you act, either. Stay away from Callahan and his brother, Jason. They're bad news."

"What were you doing at the Vandermeer mansion?" Allie watched him closely.

"What?" He moved back.

"I followed you there.'"

99

"You're gonna get hurt." Mad Dog shook his finger at her. "I'm warning you."

"Are you and Meer in this together?" she asked on a hunch.

"In what?"

"Drugs."

Mad Dog lunged for her arm. She backed away.

"Who's your friend, Rick?" Behind Mad Dog stood Bob Meer. He smiled, but it made her skin crawl.

Mad Dog seemed annoyed. "Bob, this is Allie."

"Allie. Short for Allison, right? I saw you the other day, right?"

She nodded.

"What's your last name?"

"McKenzie." Allie thought she saw a gleam of recognition in his eyes. Maybe it was her imagination.

"Do you play basketball?" Meer smiled, showing big wide teeth. A front one was chipped.

She took a deep breath. "No. I came to return a playground flashlight someone dropped in my house."

Dead silence. Mad Dog stared at her. Bob Meer stared at her. No one moved.

"You want a ride home, Allie?" Tim Callahan stood behind them with Jason. He scowled at her.

"My dad's picking me up," Allie lied. She was angry at Tim's bad timing.

He shrugged. "Your choice."

"Have you been to a doctor?" Mad Dog looked Jason over. His bruises had turned an ugly purple color.

Meer clapped Jason on the shoulder. "Jason's tough."

"Come on, twerp. Let's get some punch before we split." Tim poked Jason in the ribs. Jason winced.

"I'd go to a doctor if I were you," Mad Dog called after them. *What a hypocrite,* Allie thought.

She slipped around the two men. "I've got to go."

"Take care." Meer smiled. Mad Dog rubbed his jaw, deep in thought.

Allie hurried from the rec building and around to the back where she leaned against the rough bricks. Her heart hammered like crazy.

Were Mad Dog and Meer in this together? Did they know where her mother was?

Allie sidled along the building until she reached the window of the office. It was streaked with grit and grime and protected by bars, but she could see into the room.

She peered around the edge of the window. Bob Meer stood just inside the doorway, an angry look on his face. Someone sat by the desk. But all she could see were his white leather tennis shoes. Meer shook his fists like he was telling the guy off.

Was it Mad Dog? Meer walked to the window and stood with his back to it. She strained to hear what he said.

"No!" Meer raised his hand. "This time we'll do it my way."

She couldn't hear what the other guy answered.

Meer nodded. "The wrecking crew will do the job for us. Don't worry. There'll be nothing to point the finger at us. Tomorrow morning we'll be home free."

Meer walked to the door. "I want to shoot a few baskets before I leave."

Allie tore away from the building over to the swings. She crouched down low, until she saw Meer walk back to the courts. Then she raced for the front gate.

She ran halfway home before she stopped. She sat down on the curb between two parked cars to think.

What did Meer mean when he said the wrecking crew would do the job for them? The newspaper said heavy equipment would knock down the barn and shed. What was in them to point the finger at Meer? She and Shane had already watched them remove everything from one of the garages.

Whatever it was would be gone by tomorrow morning, crushed by the bulldozers.

She had to go to the mansion tonight. Right now.

The something in the barn could be a *someone*. What if it were her mother?

Nineteen

ALLIE CUT THROUGH CLOVE LAKES PARK. SHE ducked behind bushes and trees whenever a car drove by. A gang of toughs made her run for cover under a bridge. She huddled on a bank, her feet in two inches of water until they were out of earshot. She was freezing.

To keep warm, she ran the rest of the way to the old mansion. Dark clouds covered the stars, and a cold wind stirred the trees. It would probably rain before morning.

Allie climbed over the locked gate. She hid behind a hedge until she was sure no one had followed her. Her heart hammered like a drum. The wind rustled through the trees. A dog barked in the distance. A car drove by on the road. The wind picked up dry leaves and scudded them over the ground.

Allie wanted to run home. Instead, she drew a deep breath and pushed through the undergrowth to the old shed. The roof had caved in. Rotting timbers made the walls buckled. She peered through the gaps. It smelled musty.

Allie turned her attention to the barn. The double doors were bolted and locked. She tugged on the handles. They didn't budge. A side door was locked and barred, too. On one side, Allie found a window, but it was over her head. She needed something to stand on.

She dashed back to the shed. On her hands and knees she crawled through a gaping hole. A jagged edge of wood stuck her arm. Inside, it was pitch-black. She stumbled around, bumping her shins. Cobwebs brushed her face. Something rustled by her feet, and she gasped.

Finally she touched what felt like a wooden crate. Dragging it back to the opening, she half carried and half shoved it to the barn and under the window.

Then she searched the ground until she found a rock the size of a baseball. She climbed on the crate. Her shoulders cleared the windowsill.

She slammed the rock against the window. Glass splintered in all directions. Shards flew by her face. She crouched on the crate and waited. No one came. No one yelled. No one had heard.

She pushed the remaining glass from the windowframe with the rock. Then she pulled herself up to the sill, eased her legs over, and dropped down into the barn.

She bit her knuckles while her eyes adjusted to the blackness. Pale light filtered in the window. She saw shadows of objects stacked here and there. She forced herself to move. Cobwebs clung to her face. She gagged. A spider crawled on her neck. She brushed it off and sobbed.

She touched tools, gardening equipment, old milk crates, old furniture. A ladder. Good. She'd need that to get out again.

Dust flew up in her nose and made her sneeze. Mice scurried in the corners. Allie examined every square inch of the barn. There was nothing suspicious, nothing unusual. But there *had* to be. Meer said the wrecking crew would destroy some kind of evidence.

Then it had to be in the shed. The thought of crawling around again in that rotting place made her shudder.

She dragged the ladder across the wood floor. The scraping noise set her teeth on edge. She crossed her fingers, hoping that no one heard.

She set the ladder under the window. What was that? She held her breath and didn't move. There it was again. A faint cry. Her nose prickled. She sneezed—again and again. She couldn't help it.

There it came again. Louder this time. A voice— definitely a voice from somewhere close, but hollow sounding.

"Who is it?" Allie spun around. "Where are you?"

She closed her eyes and waited. This time a little louder. It sounded like it came from under her feet. Was there a basement?

She searched for steps, for a trapdoor. But she found nothing. Maybe an outside door led to a basement. The root cellar! Of course. There had been a door where she and Shane had hidden. And the two men they'd spied on had secured the outer doors, as if they were afraid someone might try to get out. Allie's breath caught in her chest.

On shaking legs, she climbed the ladder, maneuvered out the window, and dropped to the ground. She raced around the barn to the root cellar.

She lifted the sloping doors. A dank smell wafted from the darkness. She ran her hands over the inner door. A locked padlock hung from a metal hasp. There was no way she could open it.

"Are you in there?" She pounded with her fists. "Please, answer me."

"Help. Help." The words were faint, but Allie understood them. Someone was locked inside. And it sounded like a woman.

Sobs broke from her throat. "Mom!"

She heard an answering cry. The police would believe her now. They'd hear with their own ears that someone was in the root cellar.

Allie charged up the stone steps, smack into someone at the top. She teetered backward. He grabbed her.

"You pesky kid." Mad Dog Madison held her with a steely grip.

"Let me go!" she yelled.

"What are you doing here?"

"My mother's in there. Let her out!"

Mad Dog swore. "Why couldn't you stay out of this?"

"Is that why you killed my brother—because he knew too much?"

He sucked in his breath. "Your big mouth is going to get you killed." His grip tightened.

Twenty

MAD DOG'S GRIP LOOSENED. HE CARRIED ALLIE down the steps of the root cellar like a sack of potatoes.

"What are you doing?" she asked.

"We'll see if your mother's in there." He jingled a key ring. With one hand on her arm, he tried each key in the padlock. When one didn't work, he swore.

"Come on," he muttered. Allie held her breath. The padlock opened. Mad Dog kicked the door wide. He shoved Allie into the cellar first.

"Mom?" She waited in the dark. The dampness touched her face.

Mad Dog beamed a flashlight around the cellar.

In a far corner, Allie saw her. She lay on the floor, covered with a blanket. Her eyes were closed. For one awful moment, she thought she was dead.

"Allie?" The voice sounded weak and thin.

She rushed to her mother. Kneeling, she held her hand. "Are you okay, Mom?"

"Just weak." Allie had to bend down to hear. "He shoots me with tranquilizers, so I can't escape."

She spun around to Mad Dog. "You creep! How could you do this to her?"

"You think *I* did it?" He shined the flashlight in her eyes.

Her mother tugged on her hand. "You shouldn't have come here. He'll be back. He always comes at night."

"He's here already."

Her mother shook her head.

"Who?" Allie was confused.

Mad Dog yelped. An arm crashed down on his head. He crumpled like a rag doll to the dirt floor. His flashlight fell from his hand. It shined on a pair of white tennis shoes in the doorway.

Allie's gaze traveled up to the jeans, the Levi's jacket, the wide teeth, the thinning hair. Big hands held a gun.

"Like mother, like daughter." Bob Meer's voice chilled her. "Now you can die together."

Allie blocked her mother. "Don't shoot us."

He laughed. "Don't worry, shooting you is not my plan. You won't feel a thing when this barn comes crashing in on you tomorrow morning."

"My father will come looking for us." She gripped her mother's hand.

"No one found your mother."

"I did." Allie stuck out her chin.

"Too bad for you, isn't it?" Meer turned to leave.

"Where are you going?" she cried.

He slammed the door shut behind him.

"Don't leave us here!" she shouted.

She heard the padlock snap shut. Then only silence.

"Is that why he kept you here, Mom? So you'd die when they bulldozed the barn?"

Her mother nodded. "He can't be accused of murder that way, he said."

"But how would he explain your being here?"

"He's been pumping me full of drugs so I'll look like a druggie who didn't know what she was doing."

"Not if I can help it." Allie drummed her fingers on her face like crazy.

"He'll be back to give us the shots. Otherwise we'll make too much noise."

The way her mother said that made Allie's skin crawl. It sounded like her mother had already accepted her fate.

"How did you get here, Mom? Was it what you read in Jimmy's diary?"

Her mother nodded. "Jimmy wrote that Bob Meer was a drug supplier. He used kids to sell the drugs. Jimmy wrote that he was going to get proof the day he died." Her words were slurred when she spoke.

"What about Mad Dog Madison? Where does he fit in?"

"Is he the man on the floor?"

"Yes. Isn't he in this with Meer?"

"I've never seen him before. Just Meer. I called him that day. He said to meet him at the old Vandermeer estate. Like a fool, I went."

Allie exhaled. "I knew you didn't run way."

"I was so afraid you'd think I had abandoned you."

She kissed her mother's cheek. "It's okay, Mom. Don't talk anymore. Just rest."

"How's your father?"

"He's worried sick about you. He said he loved you," Allie blurted out.

"Your father said that?"

"Yes. He's been pretty okay. Nicer."

Her mother sighed.

"Don't talk. I'll think of a way to get us out."

Mad Dog moved. Allie felt around on the dirt until she found the flashlight. She beamed it on Mad Dog. He sat up, holding his head. "Ow," he moaned.

"Help him." Her mother pressed her hand.

"Help *him?* He's Meer's partner."

"You've got it all wrong," Mad Dog said.

"I don't think so."

"Why would Meer knock me out if I'm his partner?"

"Maybe you double-crossed him."

"Give me a break."

"Explain it, then," Allie challenged.

"I've been suspicious of Meer for a long time. That's why I was following him."

"Looks more like he followed you."

"The last few days I followed him here every night. It was hard to get close enough to see what he was up to. But last night I saw him go into the root cellar. So tonight I came prepared with a bunch of keys."

"Are you a cop or a narc or something?"

"No, I'm not a cop. My kid brother was killed eight months ago. He ran out in the middle of the Staten Island Expressway and was hit by a car and killed instantly. He was so high on drugs he didn't know what he was doing."

Allie said nothing. She knew what he was feeling. She also knew that words didn't help the pain.

"Someone in this community supplied my thirteen-year-old brother with drugs. Enough drugs to keep him hooked and loaded half the time. I was away at school and didn't know. After he died, I moved home. I vowed

110

to find the guy who killed my brother. Because in my book, it was murder.'' He slammed his fist into his hand.

"How did you catch on to Bob Meer?"

"It took a while. The only connection I had was the playground where my brother hung out. So I got the job as activities director there. I got close to the kids. I listened. I watched. It didn't take long to spot the regular drug users. The kids were really closemouthed—almost like they were scared to talk. So I followed the obvious users. They led me right to Bob Meer and—''

A key turned in the padlock.

Mad Dog stumbled to his feet.

Bob Meer entered their dungeon. Still holding the gun, he looked smug and arrogant.

"Back off, Madison.'' He waved the gun. "Sit down against the wall.'' Mad Dog obeyed.

Allie watched as Meer flicked on a lantern and set it on the floor. It cast eerie shadows. Meer drew a syringe from his jacket pocket.

"What are you doing?'' She got to her knees.

"He'll feel a little prick. Nothing more.''

"How will you explain three bodies, Meer?'' Mad Dog asked.

"No problem. You shot the girl and her mother. They found out about your nasty drug operation. So you had to eliminate them. To celebrate, you got so high you passed out in a drug stupor. Never even heard the bull-dozers. And the gun will be in your hand.''

"You're insane.'' Mad Dog pointed at Meer.

"Let my daughter go,'' Allie's mother cried. "Kill me, but let her go.''

"Shut up! All of you.'' Meer walked to Allie, but kept the gun aimed at Mad Dog. With a lunge he

111

grabbed Allie up and pressed the gun to the back of her neck.

She didn't dare breathe.

"One move out of you, Madison, and the girl dies right now."

She could feel the tension in Mad Dog. His back didn't touch the wall. His hands pressed against the floor like he was ready to spring. Allie prayed he could do it.

"You." He rammed the gun harder into Allie's neck. Cold steel. "Walk slowly over to Madison. I'll shoot you now if you try anything funny."

She moved like someone in a dream, one foot in front of the other.

"Sit down facing the wall." The gun rammed her neck. She did. He kept the gun on her neck. Allie rolled her eyes to her right, hoping Mad Dog would understand. He frowned and shook his head ever so slightly.

Allie glared at him. It was their only chance.

"Stretch out your arm, Madison. Slowly."

Out of the corner of her eye, she saw Meer, with his free hand, pull the plunger back on the syringe.

Allie signaled with her eyes again. She jerked sideways. Mad Dog sprang. The gun went off. Meer swore.

She rolled to her mother. Mad Dog and Meer thrashed in a tight clinch on the floor. With a lunge, Meer pinned Mad Dog under him. Allie ran to the lantern. She held it aloft and slammed it down on the back of Meer's head. He yelled in surprise. His head flopped forward.

She hit him again. And again. Sobbing, she dropped to her knees and kept banging the lantern on Meer's head.

"Enough!" Mad Dog grabbed her arm.

"Allie!" Her father's voice.

Someone pulled her back. "Stop it!" Shane's voice. "The police are here. Your father called them."

Allie slumped against Shane, who knelt beside her. "I found my mother. I found her."

Twenty-one

"ARE YOU SURE YOUR MOTHER'S OKAY?" MRS. Brumbaugh placed stacks of steaming pancakes in front of Allie and Shane at her kitchen table early Saturday evening. Outside, rain beat against the windows with a pleasant pattering.

"The doctor said she'll be fine once she gets the drugs out of her system." Allie poured a puddle of syrup on her pancakes. "But she'll have to stay in the hospital awhile. She slept most of the day."

"Except when she chewed you out for taking all those risks." Shane grinned, then shoved a forkful of pancakes into his mouth.

Allie made a face at him. "I wanted to stay longer, but my dad sent me home to rest. He's going to sit with her all night."

"That's good." Mrs. Brumbaugh nodded.

"Yeah." Allie knocked on the kitchen table for good luck. "I know things won't be perfect right away, but I think we can work it out and be a family again."

"I still can't believe that awful man would have left

you and your mother to die under that barn." Mrs. Brumbaugh lifted her hands in disbelief.

"We would have died, if my dad hadn't gone into my room during the night because he thought he heard me having a nightmare," Allie said.

"Your father sounded scared to death when he called me at one in the morning to ask where you could possibly be." Mrs. B. sighed. "Imagine how I felt telling him you might be with Shane looking for your mother!"

"When he called me, he was spitting smoke!" Shane waved his fork. "He threatened to sic the police on me if I didn't tell him where you were. He didn't believe me when I said I didn't know."

"So how did he know where to look?" Mrs. B. wiped her hands on her apron.

"I told him that, knowing Allie, she might have gone back to the Vandermeer estate."

"I bet he thought you were crazy." Allie laughed.

"He did. So did my parents when I left to go help your father find you." He pointed the fork at her. "You got me in a lot of hot water."

She locked her fork in combat with his. "Want to fight about it?"

"It's a good thing your father called the police," Mrs. B. said.

Shane laughed. "Otherwise Allie might have killed Bob Meer on the spot. She was beating up on him like she was Mike Tyson."

Allie clenched her fists. "After what he did to my mother and brother I wanted to kill him!"

"Did he admit running Jimmy over?" Mrs. B. set another stack of pancakes on the table.

"Not yet. But he will." Allie nodded. "Once we get all the proof together, he'll confess."

Allie looked at Shane. "What's the matter? You look skeptical."

"It was just something Mad Dog said at the hospital."

"What?" She poured another glass of milk.

"You were with your mother. Mad Dog and I were waiting to be questioned by the police. Mad Dog kept shaking his head. He said, 'I could have sworn Meer was genuinely upset when Jimmy McKenzie was killed.' "

"Did he confess selling drugs to the kids?" Mrs. B. turned off the stove and sat down.

"My dad said he did," Allie replied. "Meer insisted that was his only crime—that he never killed Jimmy and he never intended to kill my mother."

"I think he's trying to weasel out of a murder charge by admitting to the lesser rap of dealing drugs." Shane sounded disgusted.

"He couldn't very well deny it when a couple of kids came forward and confessed that Meer gave them drugs." Allie reached for another pancake.

"Mad Dog said that Meer was a sponsor for kids who were in drug rehab programs," Shane explained. "The kids could call him anytime when they felt like they craved drugs. He was supposed to help them. Instead, he gave them drugs. He told them to bring their friends around so he could get them hooked, too."

"The kids said they were afraid he'd kill them if they told on him." Allie shook her head.

"I hope they put him in prison forever!" Mrs. Brumbaugh clasped her hands.

116

"Did you hear they found Allie's mother's car?" Shane asked.

"Where?"

"In one of the garages on the Vandermeer estate."

"Good. One more piece of evidence against that terrible man," Mrs. B. said.

Allie dropped her fork. It clattered to the table.

"What's the matter?" Shane stared at her.

She closed her eyes and tried to pinpoint the elusive thought that had disturbed her. "It doesn't make sense."

"What are you talking about?" Shane asked.

"Last night when I went to the playground and spied on Bob Meer, he was talking to someone in the office. Someone who had to have known that my mother was in the root cellar, because Meer said that the wrecking crew would get rid of the evidence for them."

"What are you getting at?" Shane wiped up syrup with the last bit of pancake.

"At the time I thought it was Mad Dog he was talking to. But if Mad Dog is innocent, who was it?"

"Are you sure you heard him right?" Shane washed down his pancake with milk.

"I know I heard him say 'this time we'll do it my way. The wrecking crew will do the job for us.' We know now that he meant killing my mother."

"If it wasn't Mad Dog, who could it be?" Mrs. Brumbaugh asked, her eyes wide.

Allie held her hands up, then dropped them. "Unless . . . no . . . that couldn't be."

"What?" Shane asked.

"What if Mad Dog's lying? What if he's trying to pin everything on Meer?"

117

"What about his brother killed while on drugs?" Shane frowned.

"What if that's a lie, too?" Allie rubbed her temples. "I'm too tired to think straight right now."

Mrs. Brumbaugh began clearing the dishes. "Your father's right, Allie. You need some rest. I've made up my spare room for you. Would you like a nice hot bath?"

She rubbed her sore shoulders. "Yeah. A long hot shower. I need to go home and get clean clothes first, Mrs. B."

"I'll walk you over." Shane jumped up.

"Don't be long. I'll put fresh towels in the bathroom." Mrs. B. walked them to the door.

The rain fell in a heavy torrent. Thunder rumbled in the distance. They ran with their hands over their heads to Allie's house. The streetlights were already on.

She found the key they kept under the rosebush by their front porch. "You want to come in?" She unlocked the front door.

"I better not. My parents are waiting for me."

"Will I see you tomorrow?" She hoped she didn't sound too pushy.

Shane grinned. "Try and keep me away."

They looked into each other's eyes. Shane's blue ones brought goose bumps to her skin.

Then he bent his head and kissed her. Allie wrapped her arms around his waist and leaned toward him. He held her face with his hands. They felt warm and strong. Then he kissed her again, long and hard. His hands slipped down her back. This time the kiss lasted forever. Allie thought she might die on the spot.

Shane pulled away. "I'd better go. I love you, Allie." He ran down the steps into the darkness.

She almost fell into the house. She leaned against the door. Her legs felt like rubber. "Wow!" she exhaled. Then she danced around the living room, flipping on the lights. If she had wings she would fly.

She took the stairs two at a time and waltzed into her bedroom. She started laughing. She sounded just like her mother when she used to sing and dance around the house.

She stopped laughing. That was before Jimmy died.

Then she smiled. Now they had another point of reference. Now they could say "Before Mom was kidnapped" or "Before Allie found Mom" or "Before Mom and Dad got back together."

She hugged her arms tight across her chest. Things would be different now. They could look back on something other than Jimmy's death. They could focus on when her mother was missing and was found again. A new beginning.

"Can you hear me, Jimmy?" she whispered into the silence of her room. "It's okay now. You can rest. We found the person who killed you. You didn't die for nothing."

The telephone shrilled. She ran to the hallway to answer it. It was probably Mrs. B., wondering what was taking so long.

"Hello," she sang into the phone.

"Allie?" The raspy voice of a boy, sounding scared. For one awful second she thought it was Jimmy. Her euphoria vanished with a thud.

"Yes?"

"Are you alone?"

119

"Why? Who is this?"

"Get out of there quick. He's coming to kill you."

Her heart jumped in her chest. "Who? Is this Jason Densmore? It sounds like Jason."

"Look, I'm warning you. He'll kill you just like he killed your brother."

"Is this your idea of a sick joke?"

"You've got to believe me!" His voice rose to a whine. "He's going to kill you. Call the police." The line went dead.

Allie stared at the receiver in her hand. She dropped it back on the cradle like it might bite her.

Suddenly the house seemed too quiet, the hallway too shadowy. Slowly, she turned to the stairway.

"Hello, Allie." He stood at the bottom. He climbed toward her one step at a time.

She pressed her hands on her mouth.

"Don't be scared. I've come for the flashlight."

"Don't . . ." she whimpered.

"Was that Jason?" He smiled a horrible smile on his handsome face.

Allie shook her head.

"You're lying, Allie. He guessed I would come here. I saw it on his face. Next time I'll have to beat him up better. My little stepbrother needs to be taught a lesson."

Tim Callahan's white leather tennis shoe reached the top step.

Allie charged. She shoved his chest. He stumbled and fell to his knees. She raced through the door of her bedroom and slammed it shut.

She pushed open the window and leaped through onto the roof.

Tim Callahan banged into the room.

The rain made the roof a slippery torture. She clung to the house. Her breaths came in great gasps. Her feet slid like ice skates.

Tim made a horrible racket behind her. She lowered one foot to the trellis. His hand grazed her shoulder.

She climbed like she'd never climbed before. Halfway down her feet flew off the rung. She dangled like a limp puppet.

Tim's shoe crushed her fingers. The pain gave her strength. Her foot found the rung. She pressed down and dropped to the driveway. Pain shot through her ankle.

A great tearing noise jerked her head up. The trellis tore away from the house. It came rushing at her with Tim clinging to it, screaming at the top of his lungs.

She rolled to the side. The trellis brushed her arm. Tim crashed to the cement on his back. The sound of his head banging the concrete ripped through her.

She lay where she'd rolled, the only sound the heaving of her ragged breathing.

The trellis rose. Tim Callahan sat up. Allie could not move. He threw the trellis off him like it was a twig. "Say your prayers, kid." He struggled to his feet.

"No, you don't, Callahan." Out of the darkness, two figures grabbed Tim from behind.

"You okay, Allie?"

Shane and Mad Dog Madison.

Mrs. Brumbaugh rushed to Allie. She helped her sit up. "The police will be here soon."

Someone else came charging down the sidewalk. He stopped when he saw Shane and Mad Dog holding Callahan. Jason Densmore confronted his stepbrother.

"I'm sorry, Tim. I couldn't let you kill anyone else."

"Shut up, you stupid idiot!" Callahan lunged. But Mad Dog and Shane held him fast.

Jason turned to Allie. "I didn't know for sure, but I suspected that Tim ran your brother down. When I asked him, he said he'd kill *me* if I ever told."

"Why?" Tears streamed down her face. "Why did you do it?"

"*Why?*" Callahan threw back his head. "I couldn't let a nosy brat like your brother ruin a thousand-dollar-a-week income. Could I?"

Allie's brain spun. It wasn't making sense.

Mad Dog explained it. "Callahan, here, was Meer's middleman. Meer supplied the drugs. Callahan sold them. Oh, it was small-scale stuff compared to most drug operations, but enough to set him up for life. Callahan sold the drugs to the kids—at the high school, the playground, wherever he could. How do you think he paid for that fancy car?"

"I had a good thing going." Callahan sneered. "Then your mother came snooping around. I wanted to kill her on the spot. But after I iced your brother, Meer made me promise I wouldn't kill anyone else."

"Why did you go after Allie?" Mad Dog asked. "She didn't know you were involved."

"She found the flashlight I dropped in her house."

"Why were you in my mother's bedroom?" Allie rubbed her ankle.

"After we locked her in the root cellar, I had to make sure she hadn't left anything behind that might point to us." Callahan snorted. "You thought you were so smart mentioning the flashlight to Meer. I knew then I had to kill you."

"Because of the flashlight?" Allie asked.

"You spoiled everything. You fingered Meer. I couldn't let you get away with that. And when Meer was in the slammer, he couldn't tell me what to do anymore." Callahan started laughing.

"Shut up, Callahan." Mad Dog twisted his arm.

"How did you all get here?" Allie looked from one to the other.

"I felt there was a piece missing," Mad Dog explained. "I didn't think Meer was in it alone. And for some reason I couldn't get it out of my mind that you were in danger. You're feisty and nosy."

Shane grinned.

"Thanks." Allie made a face.

Mad Dog laughed. "If I were the killer, I'd have come after you too. You spelled trouble with a capital T. If he was going to come after you, I knew it would be soon. It was just a matter of time before Meer fingered the other guy. So I decided to watch you."

"I thought you went home, Shane," Allie said.

"I ran into Mad Dog on the way. He told me he thought you might be in danger, so I came back with him—just in time, too. I couldn't believe it when I saw Tim chasing you on the roof."

"I guess everyone knew but me." She looked at Mrs. Brumbaugh. "How'd you get here?"

Mrs. B. sighed before she answered. "I felt so responsible for not telling your father what you were up to that I watched from my window the minute you left the house. I was afraid to let you out of my sight.

"I saw you say good night to Shane and go in the house." Mrs. B. coughed to cover her embarrassment. "It seemed like you were in there such a long time. Then I saw him." She pointed dramatically at Tim.

"Where?" Allie asked.

"In the living room. I can see into your living room from my kitchen window. At first I thought it was Shane who had come back. Then I realized he was creeping around like someone up to no good. When he started for the stairs, I ran for the telephone and called the police. By the time I was on my way over to help you, I heard him scream and the trellis break."

Allie got all choked up.

"You okay?" Mrs. B. asked.

"You bet. You know how great it feels to have such terrific friends? I would never have found my mother without you guys."

Screaming sirens and flashing red lights tore down the street. Three police cars jolted to a stop in front of Allie's house.

While everyone talked at once, and the cops put Tim Callahan in handcuffs, Allie slipped over to Shane who slid his arm around her waist.

Was it only a week ago her mother had disappeared? Never had Allie felt so alone as then. But things were different now. She found out she was strong enough to face her problem alone, just like Dr. Diamond had said.

Shane's arm tightened around her. And she'd gotten back with Shane. Found a new friend in Mrs. B. Made peace with her father . . . and with Jimmy.

PRAISE FOR JOAN BAUER'S BOOKS:

"It's hard to imagine any ordinary young reader coming across a book by Joan Bauer and not feeling at least a little bit better about the world."
—Charles Taylor, *The New York Times*

Rules of the Road

★"Jubilant, strong, and funny, this is a road trip to remember."   —*BCCB*, starred review

WINNER OF THE *LOS ANGELES TIMES* BOOK PRIZE
WINNER OF THE GOLDEN KITE AWARD

Hope Was Here

★"When it comes to creating strong, independent, and funny teenaged female characters, Bauer is in a class by herself."   —*SLJ*, starred review

A NEWBERY HONOR BOOK

Backwater

"This warm, funny, patchwork quilt of a book offers a sturdy heroine, vivid characters, a touch of romance, and a final survival adventure that will keep readers turning the pages to the last."   —*Booklist*

Squashed

★"This laugh-out-loud story is a delight. . . . Ellie proves herself an all-around winner. So is Max and so is this book."   —*SLJ*, starred review

AN *SLJ* BEST BOOK OF THE YEAR

NOVELS BY JOAN BAUER

Backwater

Hope Was Here

Rules of the Road

Sticks

Squashed

Stand Tall

Thwonk

Stand Tall

JOAN BAUER

speak
An Imprint of Penguin Group (USA) Inc.

Speak

Published by Penguin Group

Penguin Group (USA) Inc.,

345 Hudson Street, New York, New York 10014, U.S.A.

Penguin Books Ltd, 80 Strand, London WC2R ORL, England

Penguin Books Australia Ltd, 250 Camberwell Road, Camberwell, Victoria 3124, Australia

Penguin Books Canada Ltd, 10 Alcorn Avenue, Toronto, Ontario, Canada M4V 3B2

Penguin Books (N.Z.) Ltd, 182-190 Wairau Road, Auckland 10, New Zealand

First published in the United States of America by G. P. Putnam's Sons,
a division of Penguin Putnam Books for Young Readers, 2002

Published by Speak, an imprint of Penguin Group (USA) Inc., 2004

10 9 8 7 6 5 4 3 2 1

THE LIBRARY OF CONGRESS HAS CATALOGED THE G. P. PUTNAM'S SONS EDITION AS FOLLOWS:

Bauer, Joan. Stand tall / Joan Bauer. p. cm.

Summary: Tree, a six-foot-three-inch twelve-year-old, copes with his parents' recent
divorce and his failure as an athlete by helping his grandfather, a Vietnam vet
and recent amputee, and Sophie, a new girl at school.

ISBN: 0-399-23473-X (hc)

[1. Divorce—Fiction. 2. Grandfathers—Fiction. 3. Size—Fiction.
4. Individuality—Fiction. 5. Schools—Fiction.] I. Title.

PZ7.B32615 Sr 2002 [Fic]—dc21 2002023876

Speak ISBN 0-14-240148-X

Printed in the United States of America

FOR EVAN, MY HERO

ACKNOWLEDGMENTS ■ Abundant thanks to: Nancy Paulsen, my editor, for her wisdom, grace, and deft handling of this story. George Nicholson, my agent, who read every draft and offered superb counsel during the writing of this book. Jean Bauer, my daughter, who told me I could and would finish this book, despite evidence to the contrary. Marjorie Good, my mother, who has given me a lifetime of inspiration. Pastor JoAnn Clark, Laura Smalley, and Rita Zuidema, who stand firm during the writing of all my stories.

Thanks to all who shared the realities and struggles of Vietnam vets, amputees, and the extremely tall: Colonel Jeffrey Thompson, M.D., United States Air Force, who provided not just medical facts, but profound thoughts on the realities of war. Twala Maresh, Clinical Instructor II, M.S.P.T., University of Central Arkansas—who taught me the day-to-day struggles, victories, and mechanics of working with amputees. Eileen R. Ascher, L.O.T., Coordinator of Rehabilitation Services at The Rehabilitation Center of Southwestern Connecticut, Inc., who showed me the power of rehab at work, and along with physical therapist Laurie Schacht, answered endless questions *and* introduced me to John DeMaio, a retired fireman and recent amputee. John's courage and heart inspired many characters in this novel. Don Shirley, a veteran and children's writer, who forwarded me useful information about VA Hospitals and Vietnam. Vicki Walker at Tall Persons Club of Great Britain and Ireland—her insights as a mother of tall children helped greatly, as did the Tall Persons Club organization. Alex Tarshis, who shared his experiences in the wild world of height.

To every thing there is a season,
And a time to every purpose under heaven:
A time to be born and a time to die,
A time to plant and a time to uproot,
A time to kill and a time to heal,
A time to tear down and a time to build,
A time to weep and a time to laugh,
A time to mourn and a time to dance,
A time to scatter stones and a time to gather them,
A time to embrace and a time to refrain,
A time to search and a time to give up,
A time to keep and a time to throw away,
A time to tear and a time to mend,
A time to be silent and a time to speak,
A time to love and a time to hate,
A time for war and a time for peace.

—ECCLESIASTES 3:1–8

CHAPTER ONE

"And *where* is home this week?"

Mrs. Pierce, the school administrative assistant, asked him this.

His brain blistered.

"Your parents didn't fill out the multiple-residence sheet that we sent to them in the fall. We need to know where you are, and when, for emergencies."

She handed him a form with multiple boxes for two home addresses, two business addresses, faxes, e-mails, cell phones, beepers.

He handed her the monthlong schedule his mother had given him—color-coordinated for each week (yellow for when he would be living with her, blue for when he would be living with his father).

When life got tough, his mother got organized.

Mrs. Pierce looked at the schedule. "Will this be changing monthly?"

He shifted. "Yes."

"You'll be getting a new schedule monthly?" She had a too-loud voice.

He nodded.

"You'll need to bring that by the office on the first of the month. *And* we need to know who is the custodial parent—your mother or father."

"They're doing it together even though they're divorced." He said this quietly.

"If your parents are co-custodians, then that's a different form."

She handed him that form.

"Is there one parent who should be contacted with all school issues?"

He sighed. "They kind of take turns."

She handed him a form for that. "If *both* parents want to be contacted on any issue, it makes it a little more difficult for us. If they *both* want to receive your report cards, we need to know that, too."

He didn't want anyone to receive his report cards. He wished there was a form for that.

Mr. Cosgrove, the school janitor, was fixing a squeaky door. He took out his little can of oil, squirted a few drops in the hinges. Opened it, closed it. Instantly fixed.

Mr. Cosgrove could fix anything.

"Is there anything else?" Mrs. Pierce shoved her reading glasses low on her nose.

He wondered if oil worked on administrative assistants.

"Oh, yes," she snipped. "*Who* will be receiving the invoice for school trips?"

2

She gazed up at him, way up.

He bent his knees to seem shorter.

"I don't know," he said.

"That can be put on this form—form C—which you can attach to form D, which covers any emergency medical care you might require when you are off school property but participating in school activities, like athletics. And if *both* your parents want to receive an audiocassette of the principal's nondenominational holiday address, they need to put an X in that box. I think that's it. The newsletter comes out quarterly and can also be mailed to grandparents and other interested parties."

"My grandpa lives with my dad."

"That saves us on postage. I'll need those back by Friday."

He looked at the forms in his hand.

There it was in black and white, just how complicated his life had become.

He stood in front of the huge white oak tree in the middle of Ripley Memorial Park. It was tall and thick with serious bark.

An oak with attitude.

He cocked his head, stretched his long arms out, imitating the tree, and froze.

He'd seen a street performer do this in New York City—the man drew a big crowd. Every so often the man would move slightly. People put money in his hat.

Mrs. Clitter walked by with her granddaughter and stopped.

He didn't move, didn't breathe.

They looked up at him for the longest time.

He moved his right hand a little.

Then his left.

The little girl giggled.

Mrs. Clitter said, "Now, where'd you learn to do that?"

He said nothing. Part of the act.

Winked at the little girl, who grinned.

He had an itch, but didn't scratch it. Mrs. Clitter moved off, laughing. He lifted his leg slightly, wiggled it.

"You say a big hello to that grandfather of yours," she shouted. Mrs. Clitter was in love with his grandfather. "You tell him I'm going to do everything I know to do to help him in his time of need." His grandfather, currently in the Veterans Administration Hospital in Baltimore, had his right leg removed just below the knee two weeks ago. His grandfather usually hid when he saw Mrs. Clitter coming. This was harder to do with half a leg, but he was working on it.

The little girl waved good-bye and crossed the bridge with her grandmother.

He straightened to full height—six feet, three and a half inches.

He was the tallest seventh-grade boy in the history of Eleanor Roosevelt Middle School.

The tallest twelve-year-old boy anyone in Ripley had ever seen.

Now you know why people called him Tree.

It had been years since anyone had called him by his real name, Sam. Jeremy Liggins had first called him Tree in fourth grade. Jeremy was one of those emperor athletes who got to do whatever he wanted. He'd stood on the baseball diamond and

4

renamed half the class, like Adam named the animals in the Bible.

Jeremy's friends got the cool names.

Fire.

Boomerang.

When it came to nonathlete nobodies, the names got harder.

Tree.

Mole.

Snot.

He'd gotten used to the name. Considered the white oak.

Some of its roots protruded from the ground—fat roots that wound around rocks.

He had studied the root systems of trees. Figured if he was going to be called one, he should at least know how they worked.

He'd learned this from his grandfather, who could fix almost anything except Tree's parents' marriage. "You've got to take a thing apart to see what it's made of," his grandpa always said.

So he learned how roots could go as deep in the ground as a tree's branches grow tall.

How they suck up nutrients from the earth like a boy slurps a milk shake through a straw. How the bark protects the tree's insides like skin protects people.

How being a tree is the best thing going in the plant world. People expect trees to be strong and steady and give good shade.

Tallness is packed with great expectations.

He picked up his duffel bag, remembered what he'd forgotten to pack.

Now that he was living every other week at different houses, he always forgot to pack something.

His warm gloves were at his mother's house.

His good sneakers were, too. He needed them for basketball practice, but it would take a lot more than sneakers to make him good at the game.

He couldn't remember if he packed underwear.

Probably not.

His personal park squirrel, Nuts, came a foot away to greet him. Nuts had half an ear, so he was easy to spot. He was more nervous than the other squirrels. Tree always wondered what happened to him. A dysfunctional childhood, probably.

"Hey, Nuts." Tree took out a bag of almonds, tossed one to the squirrel. "How's life in the park?"

Nuts shook a little, ate the food.

"You being treated okay? Because if anything's hassling you, you give me a call."

He threw the squirrel another nut.

A strong, cold wind whipped through the park. He'd been playing here, walking here for so many years. But since his parents got divorced, it felt like a different place.

Up the stairs to the north was where he'd go when he was staying at his mom's new house.

Across the footbridge to the south was where his dad and grandfather still lived.

So much had changed since the summer.

Including the white oak.

Its fat green leaves had turned red in the fall, then shriveled up. The acorns had fallen off, picked up by squirrels getting ready for winter.

It was winter in his life, too, and not just because it was December.

He started walking toward his father's house, past a lone Salvation Army trumpeter playing Christmas carols. Fished in his pocket, found a dollar, put it in the red bucket.

Mrs. Stench's dog, Fang, trotted toward him, barking mean.

"Fang, be nice." Mrs. Stench yanked on the expanding leash, lurched forward.

Fang ran up to the white oak, lifted his leg, and peed on the noble gray bark.

Tree sighed deep; cold air came out.

Being a tree isn't easy.

CHAPTER TWO

Tree sat at the computer in his father's dining room.

Typed in *heymom.com.*

Up on the screen came the smiling face of his mother. A bouncing bird flitted across a cloud that read *Thought for the day.*

The cloud morphed into *Divorce ended our marriage, but our loving family will never end.*

This was a big theme that Tree's parents were trying to get across.

A little Christmas tree appeared on the screen. An elf was underneath it.

19 Days Till Christmas appeared over the tree. *I can't wait.* The elf giggled.

Tree sighed.

This would be the first Christmas since the divorce.

The computer screen flickered.

Up popped his mother's schedule. She was in Boston for three days teaching computer seminars, but she was reachable by beeper, cell phone, and e-mail for anything he needed.

He pictured his mother beeping, ringing, and whirring all at once.

Remembered all the hours she put in when she was going to school to become a computer whiz. She'd sit at this machine, working late into the night.

Went from teaching aerobics to running computer seminars in three and a half years. Once his mom got interested in something, she'd learn everything about it that she could.

She'd done that with divorce, too.

A letter from his mother appeared on the screen.

Dear Curtis, Larry, and Tree, it began.

Curtis and Larry were his big brothers, both away at college.

I've been collecting thoughts about Christmas. I'd like us to talk about our feelings in the midst of so much change.

Tree didn't like talking about his feelings.

A wreath came up on the screen.

Then the words: *Change is part of life. It is the healthy family that learns to adapt to change that prepares each member for our ever-changing, complex world.*

And here's the first question we can discuss. **How are we all feeling this Christmas season?**

In the response section was a three-word reply from Larry, a freshman at Penn State.

I've got gas, Larry wrote.

Tree started laughing. He could see his mother's smile getting tight when she read that.

Very funny, she'd replied. *Humor is one of the ways to diffuse feelings of alienation and frustration at the holidays.*

9

Then up on the screen was a response from his brother Curtis, a sophomore at the University of New Hampshire.

I've got more gas than you.

Tree really laughed now. He knew his mom was trying to reach out, but how she did it sometimes was hard.

His mother wrote, *It's certainly nice you're learning such cogent ways of communicating at college. It's certainly nice that you've bothered to respond at all.*

Tree tried to think of what he could write back. He ate some barbecue potato chips, burped twice. Maybe *I've got more gas than anybody.*

Tree really broke up at this and wished his best friend, Sully Devo, was here. Sully had the best laugh of anyone Tree knew. Sully would laugh so hard, he'd fall off a chair and say, "You're killing me, you're killing me," then he'd pull himself together, sit down, and start cracking up all over again.

He clicked on the elf. "Deck the Halls" began to play in that computer-generated musical way.

He shut the computer down. Watched his mother's cyber self disappear from the screen.

On-line quality time, she called it.

He looked at the empty wall where the big hutch used to be.

His mother had taken it when she moved out. The shadows of where it had been remained. His dad said they were going to get a new hutch, but they hadn't yet.

His dad said they were going to repaint the downstairs so the darkened places on the walls where the pictures had hung—the ones his mother took when she moved out—would be gone.

They hadn't done that, either.

Divorce casts so many shadows.

Tree and his brothers had helped her move out.

Their old dog, Bradley, kept going up to Tree's mother to get rubbed, and every time he did, she'd start to cry. Bradley tried to climb in the U-Haul truck, but Tree's father dragged him back into the house.

Tree's grandpa spoke for everyone: "My God, Jan, I'm going to miss you like crazy."

It was like a sci-fi movie where someone is there one minute, gone the next.

Poof.

Curtis said he'd seen the breakup coming.

Larry knew Mom was going to leave Dad, too.

Tree sure hadn't. It was like watching floodwaters burst through a dam he'd always expected to hold.

Tree tried to understand how his parents went from seeming okay, but kind of bored and crabby, to living in different houses.

They'd waited to get divorced until Larry had gone to college.

Why hadn't they waited for Tree to go, too?

He stretched his long legs out. His muscles were sore, which meant he was growing more.

He wondered when he'd stop. He'd been wondering that for years.

In first grade when he sat on a stool for the class picture while the other kids stood around him.

In second grade when Mr. Cosgrove had to add another panel to the "How Tall Am I?" poster just for him.

In third grade when he got stuck in a desk and Mr. Cosgrove had to pry him out.

In fourth grade when he played a kind tree in the school play and no one had to sit on his shoulders to be the branches.

In fifth grade when he was Frankenstein at the Women's Auxiliary's House of Horrors and scared Timmy Bigelow's sister so bad, she peed in her pants.

In sixth grade when he was taller than his teachers and the principal.

And this year, seventh grade, when he just sat in the back at the table because he was too big for the desks.

The back table wasn't so bad.

Bradley padded over, put his paw in Tree's hand. Bradley understood when people needed comfort. The older and slower Bradley got, the more he seemed to know.

"Good dog."

Tree scratched Bradley's head, massaged his neck like the vet showed him.

"We've got to practice your trick."

Tree walked into the kitchen, Bradley followed. Tree got out a large dog biscuit from the canister.

"Bradley, sit."

Bradley sat.

"Good dog."

Tree got the picture he'd drawn of a sitting dog balancing a biscuit on his nose. He showed it to Bradley, who looked at it. Tree had invented this method of dog training.

"Okay, that's what you're going to do. Ready?"

Tree balanced the biscuit on Bradley's nose, put his hand out in the stay command. Bradley sat still, balancing it, as Tree timed him with his watch.

People think you can't teach an old dog new tricks, but an old dog is going to pay attention when you're doing something serious.

After forty-five seconds, the biscuit dropped, Bradley ate it.

"Good dog."

He made Bradley his dinner, put it on the floor. He made two serious submarine sandwiches with extra meat and cheese, put them in a bag.

A car horn outside.

"That's my ride, Bradley. I've got to go see Grandpa."

Bradley looked up, wagged his tail.

Seeing Grandpa was the best part of the week for just about anybody.

CHAPTER THREE

"Is that man behaving himself or being difficult?"

Mrs. Clitter half shouted the question over the phone.

Tree held the receiver, looked at his grandfather lying in the hospital bed at the VA with half a leg all bandaged up. The VA is a special hospital for people who've served in the military.

"She wants to know if you're behaving yourself."

"Tell her I'm dead."

"Grandpa ..." Tree covered the receiver.

"Tell her I have amnesia."

"She'll come and take care of you."

"Tell her I escaped." He motioned for Tree to hang up.

Tree sighed, phone to his ear. "He's behaving. But he's got to get some sleep, Mrs. Clitter."

"Let me just say good night."

Tree extended the phone. Grandpa shook his head, made snoring noises.

Tree: "He's already asleep, ma'am."

"You tell him I'll call in the morning."

Tree hung up the phone.

Grandpa raised a tired hand. "That woman needs a hobby."

"Sounds like she's got one," said Wild Man Finzolli, Grandpa's roommate. *"You."*

A loud groan from the old soldier.

Tree scrunched down in the vinyl chair that had been designed by a short person, rearranged his body to get comfortable.

Sometimes it seemed like the whole world had been designed by people shorter than him.

Airplane seats were misery.

Mattresses were never long enough.

Regular clothes didn't fit—he had to shop at the Big Guy Shop in Baltimore.

Regular shoes were out—he had to order from the Big Foot catalog.

The pediatrician had run tests to see if Tree had some kind of condition that made him so tall, like Marfan's syndrome or giantism.

He didn't.

"You're just unusually large," Dr. Flemmer said, like that explained it.

Tree shoved his long legs out.

He couldn't imagine losing a leg.

A young nurse came in to change Grandpa's bandage. "How are you, Mr. Benton?"

"It's getting harder for me to sneak up on people."

15

She laughed, unrolled the bandages down to the stump. Tree didn't want to look, but he did. The leg stump looked better than it had the first day—a big raw wound with staples. It still looked pretty angry.

But his grandfather wasn't into bellyaching.

Hadn't been since the Vietnam War, when his leg got shot up with shrapnel when he was on a night patrol in the Mekong Delta. There had been multiple surgeries to try and fix it, but like the Vietnam War, that leg just wouldn't behave.

"Take it off," Grandpa finally said to his doctor. "It's more trouble than it's worth."

And the long road back to healing began.

First, he'd be in a wheelchair.

Then, he'd get around with a walker.

Months later, he'd be fitted for a prosthetic leg—a leg specially made to take the place of the old one.

Tree's grandfather wanted that new leg bad.

The nurse put on a fresh bandage and left.

Grandpa slid to the end of the bed, sat up. His arms were strong. He nodded to Tree, who brought the walker over.

They'd been practicing this.

Good leg on the floor.

"Lean on me, Grandpa."

He did. Tree took the weight. If there was ever a reason to be a too-tall seventh-grader, it was so you could help your grandpa get walking again.

Tree's grandpa steadied himself as Tree held on tight to the walker. Slowly, Grandpa moved it forward.

"Awright, Leo," Wild Man shouted. "Reach for the stars."

"I lost my leg, Finzolli, not my arm."

Slow moving to the door and back. Grandpa plopped down on the bed.

"That's a couple miles, right?"

"At least," Tree said, smiling.

Grandpa grinned back. "You want to take apart an ugly lamp and make it uglier?"

Tree really wanted to do that.

He got the trunk out from under the bed, opened it to his grandfather's tools of the trade—pliers, wires, sockets, plugs. Grandpa was a master electrician who repaired lamps in his workshop above the garage. He'd brought this to the hospital so he wouldn't go crazy.

They worked for two hours, not counting the time it took to eat the two submarine sandwiches and the two bags of barbecue potato chips Tree had brought with him. They took the lamp apart, laid the pieces on the bed, examined the insides. Talked about how the wires had been broken and the power couldn't get to the bulb.

"When that happens, nothing works," Grandpa said. "Kind of like life."

They glued nails around the base. Grandpa searched in the trunk, held up a rubber tarantula.

"I've been saving this bug for the finishing touch." He hung it off the lamp's side.

They rigged up a little motor that rotated the lamp and shot the tarantula's shadow against the wall in creepy red light.

17

It was the best lamp in the universe.

"That," said Belle, the night nurse, "is *disgusting*."

Tree was so proud.

Disgusting is what they were going for.

Belle folded her arms across her chest. "You're not supposed to have tools in the room, Leo. You know that."

"Belle, I'm saving you grief. Let me tinker around here, or I'll get so bored, I'll start taking this hospital apart piece by piece."

"Someone already beat you to it," shouted Wild Man, looking at the peeling paint, the broken TV.

Tree couldn't wait for his grandpa to come home.

Tree's father was late picking him up at the hospital. He'd never been too punctual, but since the divorce, he was so late for everything.

Tree's mother had been the time sheriff.

It was one of the things Tree's parents always fought about.

Nine P.M. Visiting hours had been over for a half hour. Tree was getting nervous that something had happened to his dad.

Things made him more nervous these days.

At nine-thirty, a nurse going off duty said Tree had to leave.

Tree got really upset at that.

"Put on one of those patient robes," Grandpa told him. "Those awful things that flop open in the back. Sit on the empty bed and look wounded."

Tree did this, feeling strange. A hospital attendant came in at ten, stared at Tree. "I don't remember you here before."

18

"He just got transferred," Grandpa explained.

"Where's his chart?"

"On its way up," said Wild Man.

Tree slumped his shoulders, tried to look wounded.

The attendant walked closer. "Where'd you come from, soldier?"

Tree tried to think of a recent war and couldn't, so he said, "Canada."

The attendant looked surprised. "Canada?"

"It was a secret mission," Grandpa said.

"It saved the Republic," Wild Man whispered.

Tree tried to look brave and humble.

"This one's got some stories to tell," Grandpa added.

Tree sniffed. "I got a few." He'd heard a cowboy say that in a movie once.

Then, thankfully, the attendant's beeper went off and he headed for another room.

His grandpa gave him a thumbs-up; Wild Man said he seemed so much like a real soldier, he could have fooled a five-star general.

A regular-sized kid couldn't have pulled that off.

Tree's father rushed into the room like he'd driven a hundred miles an hour to get there.

"Sorry. There was a problem with the computer at the store, we had a shoplifter, my best checker quit."

He managed a sporting goods store, or maybe it managed him.

He looked at Grandpa. "How you doing, Pop?"

19

"They're going to paint my stump green for Christmas so we don't have to look at the purple lines anymore."

He laughed. "That's good, Pop."

He looked at Tree in the robe.

"What's this?"

"I saved the Republic," Tree explained, and went into the bathroom to get dressed.

"Hold this here, Dad."

They were in the bathroom of their house, putting up rails around the toilet so Grandpa would have something to hold on to when he came home.

Father and son looked at each other, wondered how the other was doing.

"You okay?" Dad asked, looking up. Tree's father was five-eleven.

Tree nodded.

"Good." Dad slapped Tree's back, relieved.

He so wanted Tree to be okay. To look at this boy, it was easy to believe he was handling things.

How could someone so big not be fine?

"You okay, Dad?"

Weak smile. "I'm just tired. Christmas, you know."

Tree knew.

Christmas for retailers was crazy—the late hours, the difficult customers.

But Tree's dad was tired down deep.

He tried to explain it with sports.

"All this change, Tree, is kind of like trying to bat left-handed when you've been a righty all your life."

Tree mostly struck out. He could barely bat right-handed, much less left.

"Divorce is like being in the fourth quarter with ten seconds left on the clock. They throw the ball to you and you get pushed back from the goal. You can't make it over. You don't make the play-offs."

Tree had always been one of those linemen anyone could get by—even a small child—but he knew that not making the play-offs was a bad thing.

Curtis and Larry were athletes. They spoke Dad's language.

Tree wanted to speak it, too. "It's like you don't get your contract renewed. Right, Dad? You get sent to the minors."

"Not *exactly*. . . ."

Dad went to bed.

Getting ready for bed, watching the clock tick off the seconds, minutes. On Saturday, Tree had taken the clock apart to see how it was made, and when he put it back together, there were two parts left on the table. He didn't trust the clock much after that.

He got into his queen-size bed, lay at an angle, covered himself with two blankets. Angle sleeping gave him more room.

He had heard that people grow when they sleep, so last year he'd tried to stay awake to stop his bones from expanding. He was so tired, he kept tripping over Bradley, who up to that time had felt safe sleeping in the hall.

A cold draft blew into the room. He hadn't minded a drafty room as much when his parents were still married, but his room seemed colder these days.

He tried to sleep. Couldn't.

Got out the cool laser pen his father had gotten him from the sporting goods show at the convention center.

Took out the insides. Put each part on the desk. Studied the laser section—it was so small to make such a big light.

There was a beauty in seeing how things worked, machines in particular.

Grandpa taught him that.

He put the pen back together piece by piece, saw the clean lines of each ink cartridge, the small tunnel for the laser beam that had to be fixed on the little battery just so. The batteries had to be put in the right way or the flashlight wouldn't work. There was no other road to take in the battery world—the negative and positive ends had to be touching.

He turned out the light and shone the laser on the wall, making circles and slashes like a space warrior.

He wished life could be simple like a laser pen—with clean lines and a clear purpose.

CHAPTER FOUR

"Men..."

Coach Glummer walked slowly across the basketball court in the Eleanor Roosevelt Middle School gym and studied the faces of his team, the Fighting Pit Bulls.

"What, men, is the purpose of basketball?"

This seemed like a trick question to Tree. Most of his school day had been filled with them.

What is the purpose of an adverb?

Why is grammar important?

Who was the thirty-second president of the United States?

Coach Glummer looked for an upturned face. "Darkus?"

Steven Darkus, who was as bad at basketball as Tree, took a wild stab. "To make the basket?"

"That's it, Darkus. The purpose of basketball, the purpose of this team, is to make the basket again and again. We have failed in that purpose—with two exceptions."

The exceptions were Jeremy Liggins and Raul Cosada, the best players.

He walked past the team. Stopped by the plaque the PTA put up after last year's pitiful season—words of encouragement from Eleanor Roosevelt herself:

No one can make you feel inferior without your consent.

Coach Glummer had always felt that Eleanor Roosevelt, a tall person, had untapped basketball potential.

"There is hidden talent on this team, and we're going to find it." He stood in front of Tree and gazed up.

"There's gold in you, kid."

"There's not, Coach. Really."

"You're a Pit Bull for a reason."

The *reason*, thought Tree, is that I need six sports credits to graduate from middle school.

Coach Glummer put the ball in Tree's huge hands. "I know talent when I see it."

And Tree so wanted to tell him that being big didn't mean being talented. Being big didn't mean extra special or superhuman or athletically gifted.

It just meant large.

Every coach Tree had ever known believed that somewhere he had athletic ability.

"Keep your eye on the ball," coaches had shouted to him over the years.

Tree tried. He focused on basketballs, footballs, baseballs, golf balls, soccer balls, tennis balls, Ping-Pong balls, but they rarely went where they were supposed to go.

"Trust your instincts," they told him.

Tree tried. But his basic instinct was to avoid sports altogether.

"Use your strength," they'd advise.

Tree knew he was strong, but he couldn't figure out how to use it. He could lift a couch by himself, but that didn't come in handy except when his mother was rearranging the furniture.

"Keep practicing," they'd shout.

Tree kept practicing and stayed mediocre.

"I'm not real athletic," he told coach after coach.

But they weren't listening. They were remembering the trophy years when Tree's brothers, Curtis and Larry, carried their teams to victory.

Tree's father came back from those games a proud man. Curtis and Larry got college sports scholarships.

Tree's dad came back from Tree's games saying, "It's not about winning, it's about playing your best."

That's what winning athletes always say to losers.

Tree hoped there were college scholarships for height.

He wished Coach Glummer could see him help his grandfather. He could steady a one-hundred-and-eighty-pound man by himself, fold up and carry a wheelchair one-handed, but that didn't count on the basketball court or in grammar or much of anywhere.

He bounced the basketball in his hands.

Bounced it again.

Mr. Cosgrove was fixing the scoreboard.

Someone had taken some letters off again. Instead of PIT BULLS it read PITS.

Last week it read BULL PITS.

Mr. Cosgrove stood on a tall ladder, added the BULL, moved the S, epoxied them in place. Held them down till the glue set. Those letters weren't going anywhere.

Nothing like epoxy to make a thing right.

Tree bounced the ball, kept his eye on the net. Shot.

Missed.

He tried five times.

Coach Glummer shouted, *"You're so close to the net, kid, how can you keep missing?"*

Because, Tree thought, *I'm not good at this.*

Mr. Cosgrove walked off, carrying his ladder; smiled so kindly at Tree. Just last week, he'd fixed the door in the library—rescued Mrs. Asher, the librarian, who'd been stuck in the media center for two hours.

Jeremy Liggins made an easy basket, smirked at Tree.

Tree wanted to make baskets, too, but even more than that, he wanted to go home.

"There are big things in store for you, boy." Tree's uncle Roger always told him this. *"Big* things."

What are they?

That's what Tree wanted to know.

VA Rehab Center. Six P.M.

Grandpa was tired, but he wasn't going to admit it. He stood at the parallel bars. There were mirrors all around. Tree put a riser in front of him. Dad was supposed to be here tonight, but there'd been a problem at the store again.

Mona Arnold, the physical therapist, wore a white jacket

and white pants. She'd been born in Ethiopia in eastern Africa, came here as a girl.

She stood alongside Grandpa. "Learning to move without that leg is going to feel different than when you were walking with an injured one, Leo. Our brains are wired to have all our limbs working. I want you to take it slow and not be a hotshot."

"Check."

Grandpa didn't like going slow. He grabbed the bars, slid forward, up on the riser and down again. Over and over. Tree watched.

"That's good, Leo. How does that feel?"

"Like the leg's still there and hurting."

He'd have sworn last night it had never gotten amputated at all.

Mona nodded. "That's called phantom pain. It's very normal."

Grandpa muttered that it might be normal, but it sure felt weird having a ghost for a leg.

"The big goal," she said to Tree, "is to get your grandpa strong so he can get his new leg. I need to teach him how to do things with half a leg that lots of people take for granted. Getting on the toilet. Taking a bath. Getting dressed. Getting in and out of a car, maneuvering around the kitchen, carrying food from one room to the next. The more you understand how this works, Tree, the more you can help."

Tree nodded, brought the walker over. Grandpa wheeled himself to an exercise pad, hopping on his good leg. Tree helped him lie down, strapped a leg weight to his stump.

Other men were exercising, too.

"Lift, Leo," Mona said. "Hold it for eight."

Grandpa struggled with this.

Luger, a huge vet who'd lost a hand, was practicing holding a cup with a prosthetic hand. He kept dropping the cup. Over and over he tried to pick it up.

"You almost got it, Luger," a soldier in a back brace shouted.

"How's that leg feel, Leo?" Mona asked.

"Like I've got a lead weight attached to a sore stump. You're a cruel woman."

She smiled. "I get meaner. Three reps on that. Then switch to your good leg. Five reps. We've got to strengthen the good leg because it's going to be taking more of the weight. All through this process we're going to strengthen the best you've got. So, what have you got, Leo?"

Grandpa looked at his half leg. It was easy to see the loss of it. He was a one-legged man; disabled.

But he wasn't going to concentrate on that.

"I've got every part of my body working except below my right knee. I've got a decent mind, a big-time stubborn streak, and a world-class grandson."

Tree smiled bright.

"That's a lot, Leo."

A few more reps, Grandpa switched the weight to his good leg. This was hard work.

Luger dropped the cup again, frustrated. He'd been a drummer. He sure couldn't do that now.

He shouted out like a drill sergeant, "*Men*, are we having fun yet?"

"No, sir!" the vets cried out.

"*Men*, are we going to fight this like soldiers or fools?"

The vets looked at one another, grinned.

"Like fools, sir!"

Everyone laughed.

Luger dropped his cup again, but this time he kicked it hard across the room.

"I can still kick!"

And everyone in rehab worked a little harder.

Tree took it in, thinking about his oral report he had to give tomorrow on the Vietnam War.

Tree hated oral reports.

Jeremy Liggins smirked at him, made him forget things. Once Jeremy held up a sign when Tree was giving a report on wolves.

BEHEMOTH BOY, it read.

Tree forgot a whole section of his report that day.

"Gargantuan Gargoyle"—that was Jeremy's latest name for Tree.

Tree took the names apart. Decided Jeremy had his species confused—he could be either a boy or a gargoyle, not both.

Tree wasn't going to look at Jeremy tomorrow.

He'd look at Sully, who would seem interested even if he was bored stiff. Sully wore a hearing aid and *never* turned it off when Tree was giving a report.

That's the kind of friend he was.

Tree had never worked so hard on a report in his life.

He hoped he could change Mr. Pender's C-minus opinion

of him as a public speaker. He always got a C minus from Mr. Pender.

"More energy, Tree." Mr. Pender always said this. "Make eye contact. Make that delivery snappy. Show us you care. Make *us* care."

CHAPTER FIVE

"What is the purpose of war?"

Tree said this loud to the class; tried to make eye contact, nervous as anything.

"Sometimes the answer is clear. In the Revolutionary War, the United States wanted freedom from taxation from England. In the Civil War, the country fought over slavery. In World War Two, countries came together to stop Hitler's invasion across Europe. But the Vietnam War was different. To many people, the purpose of that war is still unclear."

Tree felt his mouth get chalky; he looked at Mr. Pender, who actually looked interested. Sully leaned forward in his seat.

Tree turned to the first poster he'd made—showing antiwar demonstrations and soldiers fighting in the jungle.

"Our country was divided about Vietnam. Some people believed the war should go on and some people felt it was wrong. It was a new kind of war, too, because people could see it on their TV screens and watch people die in battle. It was a different kind of war because of the military weapons that were used."

Another poster. This one of unusual words.

"The Vietnam War had its own language. A 'Bird' was a plane. A 'Big Boy' was a tank. 'Bug Juice' was insect repellent."

The class laughed. Tree felt strong, way above C minus.

" 'Greased,' " Tree said solemnly, "meant killed."

He talked about the U.S. presidents who oversaw the war—Eisenhower, Kennedy, Johnson, Nixon, Ford. He talked about President Jimmy Carter, who gave amnesty to the draft dodgers, men who left the country instead of fighting in a war that they didn't think was right.

He talked about how so many vets felt like unwelcome strangers when they came home because the country had changed while they were gone.

He showed them pictures of the Vietnam Veterans Memorial in Washington, D.C., which had every name of every soldier who had died carved into a wall.

He talked about putting a wreath by his grandfather's good friend's name.

"When you go there, you can see your reflection in the black stone of the wall," Tree explained. "It makes us all part of the experience."

Tree held up a photo of Leo looking sharp in his uniform. "My grandfather served in Vietnam. He was wounded in battle. I asked him what he thought kids should know about the war."

Tree pressed PLAY on the tape recorder. Grandpa's voice boomed through the classroom.

"The people who went to fight that war, for the most part, did their best to fight an enemy that was harder to figure out and more dangerous than any of us knew. Most of us were kids—nineteen, twenty—I was twenty-five. We thought we'd kick butt and everything would be over fast. We'd win. We didn't win. I think we stayed too long and made some really bad mistakes. But we did things right, too. I think important things are worth fighting for, but there's nothing glorious about battle, nothing cool about holding a gun. It's scary and lonely, and too many people die young. Never be a person who wants war—hate it with everything you've got. But if you've got to fight to protect people, try to do your job the best you know how. Protecting people is the only reason to ever fight."

Everyone was quiet after hearing that, even Lucy Pulaski, who had the biggest mouth in the whole seventh grade.

Tree forgot the quote he was going to use at the end. So he just said, "That's my report."

Mr. Pender led the applause.

Sully whistled loud and Mr. Pender glared at him, but he kept clapping.

Jeremy Liggins yawned and stretched.

Tree sat back in his seat, shaking from the stress.

Glad it was over, proud he'd stood the test.

A

Fat and red. It sat there on Mr. Pender's evaluation sheet of Tree's report.

Tree felt like shouting.

Then the VA said Grandpa could come home on Friday.

What a great week.

Tree was going to make this the best homecoming ever for a Vietnam vet. Grandpa said he hadn't felt too welcome when he got back from the war.

"I was at the train station in my wheelchair, wearing my uniform," Grandpa had told him. "A woman stormed up to me and said, 'Was it worth it?' I didn't know what to say. She kept shouting that Vietnam was an unjust war; we had no business being there. She walked away like I smelled bad. I had plenty of friends who served and some who went to Canada to avoid the draft. But I've just learned to throw the circuit breaker on all that. Let the whole mess go dark."

Tree tucked his right knee back and hopped through Dad's kitchen as Bradley followed, confused. He was remembering what Mona Arnold had told him.

"Think about everything you do each day, and then think about doing it with a disability."

It was hard to hop in the house without falling.

Sully was at the dining room table, researching sedimentary rocks on the computer for their earth science report. Sully looked up. "What are you doing?"

Tree made it to a chair, eased himself down like Mona Arnold was teaching Grandpa to do.

"Butt down and slide," she instructed.

Butt sliding was a big part of rehab.

"That's what my grandpa's got to do when he gets home, Sully."

Sully nodded. He didn't know what it was like to have half

34

a leg, but he knew what it was like to have bad hearing. You have to try harder to understand what people are saying; watch what they do, not just what they say. Sully adjusted his hearing aid.

Tree looked around the room, thinking.

Homecomings should be fun.

He saw it in his mind. The best ideas are simple.

He grabbed a piece of paper, drew a clothesline on a pulley hung from the kitchen to the living room. A big basket suspended from the line, delivering food to wherever his grandpa was sitting.

Sully glared at the computer screen. "Who cares if sediment is mechanical, chemical, or organic? Knowing this will not help us later in life."

"Unless we drill for oil. I'll be right back."

Tree raced through the kitchen, into the garage, past the bikes and the lawn mower, past the old Chinese gong that used to hang on the back porch. His mother would ram it with a mallet to call him and his brothers in for dinner.

That sound shook the neighborhood.

It was out of commission now, like a warship in dry dock.

On a shelf he found a pulley, an old clothesline.

He grabbed his tool kit, too, ran back inside. Lugged forty feet of line past Sully, who shouted, "*What* are you doing?"

Tree was on a step stool, pulling rope through the pulley, when Dad came home with Chinese food.

"I can explain," Tree said. He and Sully tugged on the rope to make sure it was tight.

35

"Good." Dad stared at the clothesline stretched from kitchen to dining room.

"Dad, do we need the hanging lamp in the living room?"

"I'm kind of fond of it." Dad speared a dumpling with a chopstick.

"Can I just try something?"

"You should let him, Mr. Benton. This is more educational than homework."

Dad raised an eyebrow.

Tree took the hanging lamp off the hook, handed it down.

He fastened the pulley to the hook. Checked the weight, balance. "Grandpa won't be able to reach it here. It's got to be lower. Untie the rope, Dad."

Dad walked over, chewing, untied it.

"If I bolt it on the beam, Dad, it will be steady. Okay?"

Dad laughed. "I'm a sport."

"This is going to be so cool, Mr. Benton."

Bolt screwed in, pulley and rope adjusted.

Dad watched, smiling.

Tree ran to the kitchen, stuck a package of Mallomars in a basket, clamped the basket on the rope.

"This is how we can deliver food to Grandpa when he gets home, Dad."

Swoosh.

Tree pulled the rope through the pulley. The basket made a low loop in the dining room—he'd have to fix that—Bradley tucked his tail low and slinked away. The basket stopped right over the couch.

Bradley barked.

Tree beamed.

Dad grabbed it, laughing. "Terrific!"

Sully gazed respectfully at the invention. "My mother would croak if we tried that at my house."

Tree and Dad nodded.

Occasionally something awful, like divorce, can have a good side.

It was late. Dad was asleep.

Tree stood in the driveway in front of the basketball hoop. The air was cold; his breath rose like steam.

He bounced the ball.

Tried to rise up on his toes like Curtis taught him.

Took a shot.

Missed.

Another.

Almost.

He dribbled the ball up and down the driveway.

The neighbors couldn't see how bad he was at night.

He wasn't graceful like Curtis, who could dribble a ball past anyone to make the basket.

He wasn't easy with himself like Larry, who could pick up a bat and hit a home run on the first pitch.

He wondered why he was not like his brothers.

Curtis and Larry were coming home on Friday, too.

Curtis took time to do things with Tree. They'd play basketball together. And unlike his coaches, who always told Tree what he was doing wrong, Curtis shouted out what he was doing right.

"Good move on the hands."

"Good bounce on the ball."

"Good focus, you almost had that basket."

Larry was a pain. "Giant tree sloth," that's what he called Tree.

Tree tried to take the insult apart, find the good. *Giant* he could live with, but *sloth* didn't have an up side.

He got out the can of deicer, sprayed the front steps, watched the ice evaporate. The ice had to be gone so Grandpa wouldn't fall when he came home.

He wondered if deicer would work on Larry.

Then he remembered.

Everyone was coming home, but he was supposed to stay at his mom's next week.

Curtis and Larry got to stay at Dad's for their whole winter break. Mom was supposed to turn her attic into a bedroom for them, but she couldn't yet. Money was tight.

Tree threw the can down.

He *had* to be there when Grandpa and his brothers came home.

CHAPTER SIX

Tree's mother . . .

In workout clothes.

At the kitchen counter.

Typing on her laptop computer while studying fabric swatches for the couch.

Looking up occasionally to make eye contact with Tree.

Uttered the Big Question: "Honey, what would you like most to happen on Christmas Day?"

What Tree wanted most was for it to be the way it had always been.

He didn't know how to say that.

The Christmas Schedule: "Your dad and I have worked it out. You and your brothers are going to be there for Christmas Eve, and then early in the morning he'll bring you all over here."

There and here.

It sounded so easy when she said it.

"I'm going to make apple, pecan, and pumpkin pies and

roast beef and get those dinner rolls you like. The tree will be up and it's going to be okay, honey. It's going to be fine."

Tree looked down.

He wasn't sure about *fine*. He knew it was going to be different.

A blur of memories flooded Tree:

Grandpa's Christmas lights strung around his house in Baltimore—the house looked like Santa Claus himself lived inside.

The blinking sign on the roof—MERRY CHRISTMAS, EVERYONE!

The crowds walking by.

Bradley's reindeer outfit that one year. *Bad* idea.

The Christmas the stove broke and they had to eat at that all-you-can-eat buffet.

The Christmas Larry threw up on their grandmother's lace tablecloth and they finally figured out he was allergic to turkey.

The Christmas Mom broke her leg and lay on the couch, shouting instructions for *where* each ornament was to be hung properly on the tree.

Mom had stopped typing. "If I could, honey, I would fast-forward us all to a few years down the road when we'll be more comfortable with this, even though I'd be older." She laughed, looked at the fabric swatches on her lap. "Green, I think. Stripes get tired."

Tree didn't understand how stripes could get tired.

His mother used mysterious words when she decorated.

"Curtis and Larry are coming home on Friday," he said.

She smiled. "I know." She was clipping coupons now.

"Grandpa's coming home then, too."

She looked up. "So soon?"

Big breath. "And, Mom, you know, I promised I'd help when Grandpa got home. He's going to need a lot of help."

She knew that. She loved Leo, too.

"It's not that I don't want to be here." He looked down; didn't like lying.

"It's just that you want to be *there*," she said flatly.

She wished she hadn't said it that way.

"I'll come visit, Mom. I promise."

She threw down the coupons. "I don't *ever* want you to feel like you're just visiting me. I'm doing everything I can to make this house our home."

Tree looked at the freshly painted light green walls.

The yellow curtains at the windows.

The scented dried flowers that would make his father sneeze.

Conan, the little gray terrier she got after the divorce, was barking with irritation.

"I'll let him out, Mom."

"He's just saying hi."

Conan looked like he wanted to kill someone.

Mom smiled weakly. "Hi, baby. Hi."

Tree tried to feel at home, but there weren't any memories here.

The rooms were cramped, the ceilings were low, the dog was too small.

He'd walk through the door and divorce would hit him in the face.

He stood up, cracked his head on the low-hanging ceiling light.

"Oh, honey." His mom checked the cut. "Let me put something on that."

The pain stung.

She dabbed the cut with cotton and peroxide.

He didn't know the house well enough to remember where to duck.

Ducking is a key survival skill for the too tall.

Tree and Conan were standing in Ripley Memorial Park in front of the great white oak. Conan didn't appreciate this tree like Bradley, who would lie down in front of it in dog reverence. People said this oak had been there close to two hundred years. Just growing all that time.

Trees never stop growing; he'd read that somewhere.

To most people, that's an interesting fact. To him, it was grim news.

"We're going to have to raise the roof if you get any taller," Uncle Roger always said.

Having to raise the roof was one of Tree's greatest fears.

He touched the wound on his head, remembered the story Grandpa told him about the USS *Constitution*, a battleship. The ship had been made from wood of the white oak. That wood was so hard, cannonballs bounced off it during battles at sea.

Old Ironsides, the boat got named.

Tree would like to be made of such tough stuff.

His grandpa sure was.

No matter what happened to him, he kept on going.

When his wife died of cancer seven years ago.

When he had to sell his electrical business because his leg got so bad.

Tree had heard the big story so often—the one about Grandpa in the hospital in Vietnam when his leg had been shot.

So scared.

Sure that leg was going to go.

Men dying all around him.

"I wasn't strong enough to handle it," Grandpa said. "Then a chaplain came over, asked how I was doing. I told him. A nurse was calling him to come quick to the bed of a soldier hurt worse than me. But he grabbed my hand and said the shortest prayer: 'Lord, let this man's best years be ahead of him.' He ran to the other soldier's bed. But that prayer just stuck. I couldn't shake it. I got home a month later. I've never had much luck with the leg, but I say that prayer close to every day."

A cold wind blasted through the park. Tree pushed up his hood, shivered. Conan whimpered.

Tree took out the blue-and-yellow schedule his mother made for December.

Blue was for Bradley and Grandpa.

Yellow was for Conan the Crab.

Blue was when he got to feel real.

43

Yellow was when he didn't fit.

Curtis and Larry were too old to have plasticized sheets. Too old to be told where to go, where to sleep.

When you're twelve, everyone tells you where to go, what you need.

He wanted everything he cared about under one roof.

What Conan wanted was anybody's guess. This dog was barking weird.

"You want to walk some more?"

Conan wouldn't budge.

"You want me to rub you?"

Conan backed away.

"You want to be a famous, rich dog on television?"

Conan moaned, couldn't take the cold. Tree picked him up, stuffed him inside his coat, his little head sticking out, and walked back to his mother's house.

House.

He turned the word over in his mind.

I'm going to my house.

I'm going to my mother's house.

House was a word he'd always taken for granted.

He knew there was a big difference between a house and a home.

Chapter Seven

Mocha pecan frosted brownies wrapped in cellophane with a plaid bow. Sitting on Mom's kitchen counter.

Grandpa's favorite.

Tree knew she was going to let him stay at Dad's.

"Give these to Leo," Mom said. "I know this is an important week for all of you. I called your grandpa. We had a good talk. We hadn't talked for . . ." She started to cry, stopped herself.

"Thanks, Mom. I'll come and—" He was about to say *visit*. "I'll come over and tell you how everyone is doing and Curtis and Larry will come, too, and maybe Bradley even." He looked at Conan, who couldn't care less.

She touched his arm. "I know you have things to do to get ready."

"I love you, Mom."

"I love you, too."

He looked down; she looked up. She was five-nine.

He bent down to give her a hug. Took the brownies, almost dropped them.

Clutched the tray, walked carefully out the door.

He didn't see her fold her arms tight, lean against the re-frigerator, and start to cry.

Curtis and Larry barreled into the house, tossed duffels in the hall.

"You look old enough to go, you might as well have one." Curtis threw a University of New Hampshire sweatshirt to Tree.

Tree put it on, beaming. "Thanks." Smiled at Larry, who looked upset. "Hi."

"Hi." Larry stood extra tall, didn't smile back. "Did you grow more?" Larry was five-eleven.

Tree shrugged. "Probably."

"You're the little brother now." Curtis laughed, poking Larry.

"Shut up," Larry snarled.

Curtis, six-one, looked at Tree: "How tall will he become? Stay tuned for the late-breaking news."

Tree slumped a little. "Come on, you guys."

Dad came racing home in the Kramer's Sports Mart van and they all headed to the VA to pick up Grandpa.

But Grandpa couldn't get in the van—it was too high.

Curtis and Larry tried to lift him. Grandpa cracked his head on the door.

"I'm going to need more surgery and I'm not home yet."

Tree, on hands and knees, a human step. Curtis and Larry lifted Grandpa up on Tree to the passenger seat. Curtis stepped on Tree's right hand. Larry stepped on Tree's left hand, and Tree shrieked right there in the hospital quiet zone.

"We're going to grab hold of the first rule of electrical power," Grandpa hollered. "You need a negative charge and a positive one to get something moving. We've got the negative; we're going to find the positive if it kills us."

Swoosh.

Tree had just put a submarine sandwich in the basket and let it ride to Grandpa in the living room. Curtis timed it.

"Thirteen and a half seconds," Curtis shouted.

Grandpa laughed. "You could earn money with this rig!" He pulled the rope from his end, shot the basket back. "You forgot the chips," he yelled.

Tree grabbed the basket that was racing toward him, stuck chips inside, hurled it back.

"I can get used to this," Grandpa shouted.

Curtis and Larry took over, trying to get the kitchen–to–living room run down to ten seconds.

Bradley stayed in the hall.

A knock on the door. Mrs. Clitter walked in, holding a basket; gave Grandpa a lovesick smile.

"Leo, this must be such a difficult time. I'm here to help in any way I can."

"Hello, Dorothy," he said miserably.

Swoosh.

She looked up, saw the ropes, the basket hurtling toward her.

47

"Duck," Grandpa ordered.

She did.

The basket flew by, stopped by Grandpa's arm.

"What *is* that?" Mrs. Clitter held her basket tight.

"State-of-the-art in-house food delivery by an up-and-coming genius." He sent the basket back.

Tree was so proud.

She stayed low. "I brought . . . *cookies.*"

"That's kind of you, Dorothy. You want to see my scar?"

"Actually—"

He leaned down to unroll the bandage. "It's still pretty ugly. It might be oozing pus or something worse."

"I'll come back later, Leo." She left the basket on the table, raced out the door.

Bradley barked.

Everyone laughed, ate the cookies.

Grandpa tried to get comfortable on the couch. Couldn't.

Tree could see the pain in his face.

"Are you okay?" Tree kept asking.

"I'm okay," he kept answering over the next few days as he did his exercises, practiced with his walker, strengthened the parts that were weak and were strong.

"How much time do I have left?"

Grandpa asked it, huffing and puffing on his exercise mat in the living room. He was doing his abdominal exercises twice a day like Mona Arnold told him.

Tree checked the stopwatch. "Ten minutes."

"I've been doing this for half a day."

48

"It's been two minutes, Grandpa."

Tough soldier face. Sucked in his gut, kept going; picked up the hand weights on the table.

Tree wished there were exercises to help you get strong after your parents got divorced.

He and his brothers could use them.

Larry was hardly ever home—when he was home, he'd just lie on the couch, watching TV.

Curtis didn't seem to want to do much.

They hadn't gone to a movie yet.

Hadn't practiced basketball together.

Tree wondered if divorce was like war and always had a lasting effect on the people who went through it.

CHAPTER EIGHT

Sophie Santack was standing at the popular-eighth-grade-girls' table in the Eleanor Roosevelt Middle School cafeteria, determined to make a point. She looked smack into the beautiful face of Amber Melloncroft.

"I'm not here to make trouble. I just want to know how come, ever since I showed up at this school, you look at me like I fell off a garbage truck."

A gasp rose from the popular girls assembled as Amber, their leader, looked at all of them like she *couldn't* believe this. . . .

Sophie gripped her tray. "I just want to get one thing clear. You're not any better than me. I'm not crawling with bugs or have green slime running down my neck. I'm a person just like you."

Amber made a shocked noise of disgust and all the other girls made the exact same noise.

"I've moved around a lot. What's at this school isn't all that different from other places. We don't have to be friends, but we don't have to be enemies, either."

And with that she walked off and sat at the back of the lunchroom by herself.

It was near the table where Tree sat with Sully Devo and Eli Slovik—far away from Jeremy Liggins, who used to "accidentally" spill chocolate milk on Tree.

Sophie was looking at her lunch and, it seemed to Tree, trying not to cry. A mean laugh rose from the popular-girls' table, followed by whispers, giggles, and stares at Sophie. Tree hated it when girls did that. He thought Sophie had been brave. Tree knew that Amber would get back at Sophie every chance she got. Sophie had started at the school a few months ago and didn't have any friends.

Tree knew what that was like. Sometimes it felt like every seat in the world was saved for somebody else.

He looked at Sophie and said something he'd never said to a girl. "You want to sit with us?"

Sully and Eli looked shocked because, first of all, they were seventh-graders, and a seventh-grade boy never sat with an eighth-grade girl. And second of all, Sophie was weird.

Sophie shook her head.

"We're not crawling with bugs or have purple slime running down our necks." Tree surprised himself by saying this.

Sophie half smiled. "It was green, the slime I mentioned."

"Slovik's got green slime on his neck, but he's done eating." Eli punched Tree in the arm. "So, you want to eat with us?"

"Okay, well . . ."

They only had seven minutes before the bell rang, but in that time Sophie told them close to her whole life story.

"Okay, so the last place I lived was in the Bronx—we were there for three years—and then my aunt Peach and my mother decided it was cheaper to live here, so we moved, and we're all living in an apartment, which is torture, over by the railroad station—me, my mom, my cousin, my aunt, six cats, and my iguana, Lassie. There should be a law that makes trains be quiet so people can get their sleep. When I'm a lawyer—if that's what I do—I'm either going to be a lawyer or have my own talk show. I haven't decided. But, one way or the other, I'm going to take care of problems. We don't know what the future's going to bring, but I figure law and talk aren't going away. And I was just born with a big mouth—my aunt Peach tells me that all the time—so I guess I'm going to use it. They named me Sophia because it stands for wisdom. I usually say what people are thinking and don't have the guts to say." She took a bite of her sandwich. "This is the worst food of any school I've ever been at. We should do something about this. Demand justice. People have more power in this world than they think."

Tree had never heard anyone talk like this.

Sully and Eli hadn't, either.

"Okay." Sophie was moving her head back and forth in a kind of rocking motion, like she was listening to music that only she could hear. "So, here's how it is. Here's my motto: Speak your mind and ride a fast horse. There's just one problem."

"You don't have a fast horse," Tree guessed.

"You got it. What's your name?"

"Tree. That's what they call me."

"What's your motto?"

Tree thought about that. "I don't have one."

"You've gotta have a motto."

Tree looked at Sully and Eli. They didn't have mottoes, either.

"How do you know what you're about?" Sophie slurped down the last of her milk.

Tree, Sully, and Eli weren't sure how to answer.

That's when the bell rang.

Sully and Eli got up gratefully.

Tree said to Sophie, "I'll think about it . . . the motto thing. . . ."

"Dad, do you have a motto?" Tree had been thinking about this most of the afternoon.

"Well . . ." Dad looked at the coffee mug he was holding from his store: *Kramer's Sports Mart: We Will Not Be Undersold.* "I've got a slogan, does that count?"

"Not really."

Curtis and Larry weren't home to ask.

Grandpa said, "I always liked what the POWs held to. Return with honor."

"That's good, Grandpa."

Tree went into his room, sat at his desk, took out paper and a pen. Wrote the mottoes he knew.

Speak softly and carry a big stick.

The buck stops here.

You can't teach an old dog new tricks—Tree knew that was a lie; he wasn't sure if it was a motto.

Do unto others as you would have them do unto you.

That was a decent thought, but it didn't sound cool like *Speak your mind and ride a fast horse.*

Tree tried to edit the words, make them better.

Finally he came up with *Treat people the way you want to be treated.*

He wondered if that was good enough to be a motto.

He looked at the *Tyrannosaurus rex* model on his desk. He'd put it together with Grandpa when kids were teasing him about his size in fifth grade. Tree related to dinosaurs, but wasn't too thrilled about the extinction part.

"They died off because they were too big," Jeremy Liggins would taunt him. "They died because they were slow and stupid and they needed too much food."

Tree remembered gluing all the teeth into place, how Grandpa sanded the pieces of the tail when Tree told him what Jeremy had said.

"So, how do you want to be treated?" Grandpa asked.

"Just like I'm regular. Like I'm not so big."

"The problem is, you're not a regular size. How do we work around that?"

Tree didn't know. He just wanted to be regular.

"How about wanting them to treat you with respect, even though your size makes you stand out?"

Tree nodded.

"How are we going to get them to do that?"

"I don't know."

"I think the only way it can happen is if you try to treat them with respect first." Grandpa fastened the last tail part on with glue, held it down with his thumb.

That wasn't the easy answer Tree was looking for.

"You've got to just think of yourself as a farmer laying down seeds. There might be some storms and weeds that choke what you're trying to grow. But you'll get a crop eventually. I guarantee it."

Tree looked at his motto sheet, underlined *Treat people the way you want to be treated.*

He wondered if dinosaurs had mottoes.

Probably *Eat your enemies before they eat you.*

"So, I guess people say a lot of stupid things to you about your height."

Sophie said this to Tree in the hall when he was slurping deep from the drinking fountain. He was so surprised, he half choked. She threw down her flute case and punched him on the back.

"Breathe, or I call 911."

Tree waved her off, coughing.

"You know why people do that?"

Tree coughed. "Do what?"

"Say stupid things."

"I'm not sure."

"My aunt Peach says they say them because they don't know better, and if they do, it makes them feel like they've got one up on you."

Tree hadn't thought of it that way.

"So, what do they say?" Sophie was looking up at him.

"They say, 'How's the weather up there?' "

"That's dumb. What do you say?"

"Usually nothing."

"Spit on them. Say, 'It's raining.' "

Tree laughed. "They ask me if I take a lot of vitamins."

Sophie was shaking her head.

"They ask if my parents are tall, what size my shoes are." She looked at his substantial feet. "What size are they?"

"Sixteen double E."

"So, you've got a presence. You show up, people notice."

Tree smiled. "I guess so." He liked thinking about it that way.

"There are worse things." She picked up her case. "I've been playing the flute since I was eight. I'm close to being a musical genius except for when I've been blowing for an hour and my mouth gets full of spit."

That's when Laurie Fuller and Char Wellman, two popular eighth-grade girls, walked up to Sophie, snickering.

"So, did you?" Char asked Sophie, and she and Laurie giggled.

"Did I what?" Sophie held her case tight.

"Fall off a garbage truck?" Laurie asked, and they both exploded in laughter. "Is that how you got here?"

Sophie looked right at them. Tree felt his whole body go stiff.

"I got here in a Chevy," she said quietly.

The girls ran off, triumphant. The dirty deed done.

Tree stood there, shocked.

"I gotta go," Sophie whispered.

And she went.

Chapter Nine

Tree stood in the same place in the hall by the drinking fountain for so long, it seemed like he'd grown roots. He was thinking of all the things he could have said to defend Sophie, but none of them were any good.

He remembered how Jeremy Liggins once said that Tree was "a giant freak that shouldn't have been born." Tree knew this wasn't so. He knew his parents and grandpa loved him. But some words and the way people say them are like grenades exploding on a battlefield.

"Never try to outrun a grenade," said Grandpa. "Just leap away from it, hit the ground, and pray you're far enough away."

VA Rehab, 0800 hours (8:00 A.M., military time).

Grandpa came here three times a week to work with Mona.

"I'm just a little concerned, Leo, with you playing Santa Claus this year."

The Trash King, one of Grandpa's best friends, said it. He

ran a trash pickup business. They'd served together in Vietnam. He'd driven Leo and Tree here in his truck.

Grandpa cranked hard on the arm machine. He'd been Santa Claus every year at the children's hospital when the Vietnam Vets Association did their annual show.

"Kids are going to want to crawl on your lap, Leo. You handled it last year, but I knew you were hurting."

"Santa Claus knows no pain." Grandpa said it tough; a stab of pain hit his leg.

King studied his old, stubborn friend. "You could branch out. Be an elf."

"I don't want to be an elf."

"You could be a reindeer."

"Mona," said Grandpa, "I've kicked butt on this machine. Give me something harder."

She laughed. "Take a break, Leo."

"Why?"

"Because you're making me tired."

Tree laughed, helped Grandpa get off the machine. He didn't need as much help as last week.

Of all his grandpa's Vietnam buddies, Tree liked the Trash King best. He worked for him sometimes, moving old, busted furniture like couches, lamps, and tables. King would sell them to "people who had vision."

"You give me a person with vision," he'd say, "they can take the most broken-down piece of junk and turn it into something beautiful. They don't let a few scratches worry them. They see to the heart of the piece."

Tree pushed the wheelchair in place. Grandpa plopped down, chuckled. "Santa Claus in a wheelchair could start a new trend."

"You could get hurt, Leo."

"Mona," Grandpa shouted, "tell this man what disabled people can do."

Mona Arnold folded her arms, shouted back, "Just about anything."

Luger, who'd gotten decent at holding a cup, grabbed it with his mechanical hand and raised it high.

King knew when he was outnumbered. "All right, Leo. You're on deck. But the elves are watching. If you can't handle it, they're moving in like Green Berets."

"Men . . ."

Coach Glummer walked slowly before the Pit Bulls. "I've been given a revelation that will have a lasting effect on this team."

The Pit Bulls looked concerned.

"Basketball is like a dance, men. We need to find the rhythm of the game, flow more as a team. Move from side to side like you're dancing."

Tree had never danced. Most of the Pit Bulls hadn't.

"Like you're dancing with a girl, you know. Going across the dance floor."

Tree didn't know. He'd never danced with a girl.

He tried to picture the basketball like a girl, but no girl he knew would appreciate being dribbled.

"Try some flowing movements." Coach Glummer began to sway back and forth.

Tree moved an inch.

"Throw your body into it."

Tree didn't want to do that with his body.

"Ballroom dancing," Coach Glummer announced. "It'll teach you balance, how to move across the floor with a partner, how to trust your body, and ultimately"—he looked at the basketball net—"how to win on this home court and beyond."

The Pit Bulls turned to stone.

"My cousin Sheila is starting a class at the Y. Tuesday nights from seven to nine. Maybe you got the flier."

All the Pit Bulls had gotten the flier. They had thrown them into the garbage in a great show of team unity.

"I want you to sign up. That's an order. You'll thank me for this in the weeks and years to come."

He blew his whistle. They were dismissed. But they all stood there desperately trying to think of why Tuesday nights couldn't work.

"I take allergy shots on Tuesday and, you know, Coach, I can puff up," said Petey Lawler.

"Tuesday nights I've got to watch my little sister," Ryan Trout pleaded.

Colin Renquist had the best line. "Dancing makes me puke."

The Fighting Pit Bulls exploded in laughter.

Coach Glummer was unmoved. "Bring a bucket, Renquist."

■ ■ ■

Tree's father had been carrying a bucket since he got home from work, sure he was coming down with the stomach flu. Sure he was going to start heaving any moment.

Tree was worried about him. "Is there anything I can do to make Christmas easier, Dad?"

He put the bucket down, looked monumentally sad. "We're just going to get through it."

Tree had hoped for more than that.

Dad touched Tree's shoulder. "I'll be okay, buddy. I've just got to work things out."

"I think Mom made a big mistake when she left." Tree had never said that out loud before.

Dad leaned against the wall. "It wasn't just her, Tree. I could have done a lot of things better. I could have tried to understand her more. I wasn't too good at that."

"Do you think you guys could . . . maybe . . . decide this isn't a good idea?"

Dad half smiled. "Your mom thinks the divorce is a good idea."

Tree looked down.

"It takes time," Dad said, "to get used to all this."

How much time, Tree wondered.

It was midnight. The sounds of handball echoed in the basement.

Thump.

Thwack.

Tree hadn't heard those sounds in a long time. His dad had

been a handball champion back when he lived in New Jersey. But he was too busy to play these days; too tired.

Tree headed to the basement to watch.

Thump.

Dad hurled the little handball against the basement wall; stepped back to cup it in his right hand as it bounced toward him. The best thing about this house was the high basement ceiling.

Thwack.

The wall had ball marks on it. The marks had always bothered Tree's mother, who wanted to paint the wall yellow.

Handball walls are gray.

Any guy knows that.

Thump. Thwack.

There's a rhythm to handball.

Tree sat at the top of the basement stairs and watched. It seemed to Tree that his dad was always happier when he was moving. Tree was happiest when he was taking things apart.

It's funny how life gets so complicated, you don't get to do the thing that makes you happy. You have to concentrate on the things that are expected.

His dad should have been a coach.

Run a sports camp for kids.

Thump.

His dad had helped Curtis and Larry all through school athletics. He'd tried to help Tree, too, especially in football.

"Size-wise, Big Man, you've got the potential to be one mean defensive lineman."

"I don't know, Dad."

"Just crouch down and hold your arms out. There's no finesse required."

If Tree could have changed one thing about himself, it would have been that he was better at sports and shared that with his father.

He looked at the glass case on the other side of the basement. Curtis's and Larry's sports awards were there: most valuable player certificates, athlete of the year trophies, Larry's medal for most home runs in a season.

Tree had never once won an award.

The little handball spun off the wall. Dad made a low catch. Gently threw the ball on the wall with English. Looked up, saw Tree watching him. Did his famous triple ball bounce off two walls and caught it behind his back.

That move used to drive Tree's mother bonkers. She'd run to the basement door and shout, "Is everyone all right?"

Funny the things you miss when you don't have them around anymore.

Dad threw the ball easy to Tree, who missed the catch.

It bounced off the stairs and rolled beneath the washing machine, where handballs go to die.

"Sorry, Dad."

Now the thunder of older brothers racing down the basement stairs. Older brothers who were good at handball. First-string.

"Come on," Dad said to Tree.

"I'll just watch." He didn't want to look stupid.

Dad served. Larry caught it low, spun it on the wall. Curtis caught it between his legs, returned the bounce strong.

Thump.

Pow.

Thwack.

Larry went all out for every ball; grunted, groaned.

Curtis had more confidence, but Larry played harder.

Larry could lie on a couch for hours looking half dead, but put a ball in his hand and he'd catch fire.

They were having so much fun.

They wouldn't, probably, if Tree joined in. He always felt he slowed things down.

He felt like a woolly mammoth in a world of tigers and antelopes.

A giant sloth moving slowly up a tree when all the squirrels and monkeys had gotten there first.

He sat at the top of the stairs like he'd done most of his life.

He acted like he didn't mind.

But he did.

CHAPTER TEN

"Choose how you'd die," Sully said. "Shark attack, alien abduction, or"—he shuddered—*"ballroom dancing."*

It was the first night of ballroom dance class. Sully, Eli, and Tree were standing behind the big bush near the entrance to the Y. From the front, Sully and Eli couldn't be seen; Tree poked out like a giraffe in a necktie.

"Not dancing," said Eli, who'd offered his parents half of his $123 life savings if he didn't have to take this class.

"Maybe an alien," Tree said.

Sully loosened his tie; his mother had yanked it tight like a noose. "I'd take the shark. But I'd need to have a heart attack first."

Cars were pulling up to the entrance. Girls in dresses got out excitedly. Boys in badly fitting suits slumped in misery toward the front door.

"It could be worse," Sully said. "We could be dead."

"We could all just not go," Eli suggested. "Who'd know?"

"Okay," said a familiar, tough voice from behind. "You guys

going in or what?' 'Cause the sooner we get started, the sooner it's going to be over. Those were Aunt Peach's parting words to me."

Tree turned around, and there was Sophie looking very pretty in a purple dress, her hair done up in a barrette, and her black eyes flashing total attitude, which is exactly what you'd want in a dance partner.

Coach Glummer's cousin Sheila looked at the eighty-seven seventh- and eighth-graders assembled in the gym of the YMCA. Her teacher's heart fluttered with care for her students. She wanted to become a trusted person in their lives, a teacher not just of the fox trot, the waltz, and the tango, but a role model of enduring memory.

But Sheila knew that eighty-seven seventh- and eighth-graders could turn on her at any moment. So she stood on center court and shouted, "I'm the law in this room. That means what I say goes. If you disobey, you're out, and I keep your parents' money. *Do we understand each other?*"

Eighty-seven heads nodded grimly.

"Ballroom dancing can be one of the most fun things you'll ever do. For that to happen, you have to listen like your life depended on it. Are you still with me?"

They were.

"We begin dancing like we begin most new things—by taking a risk. I'm going to demonstrate a simple step that will get you through most wedding receptions. This is as easy as life gets. Watch. *Right foot forward, left foot matches, right moves back and left detaches.* You try."

The Fighting Pit Bulls looked at one another glumly. Tree glanced over at Sophie, who was looking at the ceiling.

"Right foot forward, left foot matches. Right moves back and left detaches."

No one got it right.

They moved into dance circles. Sheila's Romanian dance partner, Lazar, who swayed constantly even when there wasn't music playing, worked with the boys.

"Okay now, young mens." Lazar tossed his head, swaying. "I'm gonna teach you how, you know, to go with it."

Lazar did a few slow steps. "You see from that? You see to just move and go with it? Okay, mens, let's slide."

The Pit Bulls were particularly bad at sliding.

The evening went downhill. Sully and Eli were sticking their fingers down their throats, pretending to vomit.

"We're going to put some of these steps together."

Partner time. The popular boys raced for Amber and her friends.

Sully said he was sick.

Eli said he had to get a bucket for Sully.

Tree hoped that dancing with someone would be better than dancing alone.

He walked slowly up to Sophie, who was studying the floor.

Cleared his throat.

Waited.

She looked up. *"Well?"*

"I'm here," Tree said.

"And?"

"I was going to ask you to, you know . . ." He looked around. "Dance."

"You need to say the words. Would you like to dance?"

"I would," Tree said.

"*No*—you ask *me*."

"Right. Would you . . . like to dance?"

She took his hand, smiled bright. "I'd be delighted—and I'm not just saying that."

They walked onto the middle of the floor. Tree was absolutely the tallest person in the room. Lazar and Coach Glummer's cousin Sheila locked into position, which seemed easier for shorter people.

"Good posture," shouted Sheila. "If you get lost, just watch me and Lazar."

Tree bent down to reach Sophie's waist. Her head came up to his chest. He took her hand gently; didn't want to squish it. He wasn't sure his left foot could detach at this angle.

He could either dance or have good posture—not both.

Sophie laughed. She had a good laugh. Solid, not tinkling. "You look like you're at a funeral."

"I'm sorry."

"Aunt Peach dragged me here by my nose hairs, but it's not as bad as I thought."

Tree nodded.

Dumb music started playing.

Tree took the deepest breath of his life and forgot everything he'd been practicing for the last ninety minutes. Sophie was right there with him, messing up.

Tree had no idea how this would help him in basketball or in years to come. But it sure was nice to be so close to Sophie.

"It's weird here now, huh?"

Tree took his tie off and said it to Curtis, who was lying on the couch at Dad's with an empty pizza carton over his face.

"I mean, with Mom and Dad and everything. . . ."

"It's weird," Curtis agreed, not moving the carton.

Tree flopped into the chair.

"I'm here *all* the time." Tree wanted to make this point. He felt like a soldier that had been fighting a battle on his own, just waiting for fresh troops to come in and give him a hand. "Sometimes I'm not sure what to think."

"I'm not, either." Curtis took the carton off his face, looked inside, ate the last bit of cheese. "We went to Mom's house tonight. Me and Larry. Larry called it Munchkinland."

Tree nodded.

"We helped her trim the tree." Curtis sighed. "She told the ornament stories. This one we got on that Christmas farm in Iowa. This one we got in Bermuda."

He didn't mention it was like being at a funeral, remembering the dead.

Didn't tell Tree the next part, either.

How Mom kept asking them, *"Are you all right?"*

What do you say?

"No," Curtis had said finally. "I'm not. I'll be all right. But this is hard, Mom."

"Why did you buy this house?" Larry asked her.

69

"It was the only one I could afford!"

"Why did you get this dog?" Larry wouldn't let up.

"Because I wanted company! You're blaming me for this divorce, and that's not fair!"

Tree took his shoes off, studied his big toe sticking out of his sock. Looked at Curtis. "Why do you think they got divorced?"

Curtis crushed the pizza carton. He wanted to get back to school, where things seemed normal. Tree looked kind of pitiful to him. As the oldest, he'd seen and heard more of the fights. The ones about his father's job were always loud.

"Why," Mom would shout at Dad, "are you content just running a sporting goods store? You have so many gifts that you've never developed."

"I *like* sports."

"That's not an explanation."

"Not everything in life has to have an explanation!"

And she would storm off saying that *she* wasn't going to just settle for whatever came. *She* was going to improve herself.

"Go for it," Dad would yell.

The next morning, they would be in the kitchen with faces like cement.

Curtis sighed. "I don't know how it happened. They just changed. They stopped doing things together that they used to do. They stopped laughing. They began to have really different lives. Dad worked mostly; Mom worked, went to school, and rearranged the furniture."

Tree half laughed. "Remember that time Dad came home

and sat where his brown chair had always been, and fell down and started shouting?"

"I thought he was going to punch a hole in the wall."

"And then I'd meet him at the door when he came home and tell him if Mom had changed stuff around while he was gone."

Curtis nodded. "You were always good at things like that."

They looked at the scrunched-up pizza box.

"Do you think," Tree asked, "they'll change their minds? I mean, if Dad learned to understand her more, they could get back together maybe. It's not like they hate each other."

"I don't know, Tree Man. I don't think so."

"I wish they'd waited till I was in college."

Curtis smiled. "They might have killed each other by then."

"Do you know the secret to fighting a war?"

Grandpa asked Tree the question as they were folding the laundry. Grandpa always dove deep doing laundry.

Tree didn't know.

"You've got to hold on to the things you know to be true, set your mind to a higher place, and fight like a dog to keep it there. War can be so fierce, you can forget the good. Forget what you're about in this world, what's really important. There's always going to be somebody who wants to try to make you forget it. Don't let them."

Tree wasn't sure how you do that in seventh grade.

He folded a towel and remembered the day his mom moved out.

August twelfth, a bright, sunny day. A day where you wouldn't think anything bad could happen. He'd just come back from helping her move. There in the dryer was a full load of her clothes she'd forgotten to take. He gathered the clothes in his arms, started up the basement steps, couldn't handle it. He dropped the pile and ran into his bedroom, crying.

A knock on Tree's bedroom door.

He was madly drying his face with his sleeve. Grandpa came in.

"You okay?"

"Yeah."

"Convince me."

Tree told him about the clothes.

"I would have cried, too, if I'd seen that." He limped over—his leg was so bad—sat on the bed. "It's the things we don't expect that just rip the scab off."

"She was supposed to pack everything."

"She meant to. It's been a hard day. People do all kinds of things they wouldn't normally do when they're fighting each other. I'll help you fold that laundry, then you call her, let her know it's here."

Tree walked to the basement steps, gathered up the clothes.

His mother had used fabric softener. Her yellow robe was soft and smelled nice. He half buried his nose in it like Bradley snuggled his old towel.

He lugged the laundry to his room. He and Grandpa folded each piece like it had cost a fortune. Tree called Mom at her new house, and she started crying. She'd come over and get it, she said. She hadn't meant to leave it.

Tree hoped he wouldn't think about this every time he did the laundry.

"It's tough around here now, I know." Grandpa held up five unmatched socks, looked in the hamper for the others. "We've all lost a piece of ourselves. War does that—it blows things up and leaves an empty place where something important used to be."

"Is that how you feel about your leg, Grandpa?"

"Yep. Is that how you feel about your mom and dad?"

Tree looked down. "Kind of."

"I'll tell you something about empty places. They don't get filled in right away. You've got to look at them straight on, see what's still standing. Concentrate on what you've got as much as you can."

Grandpa dug around the hamper, couldn't find the missing socks. He started laughing. "I don't need a pair of socks. I just need one. Doing the laundry gets easier when you're not so particular."

Tree laughed, too.

You've got to love a man who can teach you to laugh at war.

CHAPTER ELEVEN

"Okay, Aunt Peach, so this is my friend Tree."

Tree was standing in the hallway of Sophie's apartment. It was cramped and dark.

Piles of laundry all around.

Lassie, the iguana, in a cage on the dining room table.

Cats on the couch; cats in the hall.

Aunt Peach was chasing one of the cats that had just clawed the drapes.

She stopped, gazed up at Tree, way up. "You're a big one."

Tree slouched a little.

Aunt Peach ran off. *"Dimples, I'm going to break your furry neck!"*

Tree and Sophie were going to take the bus to the Midas Muffler shop in Baltimore where her dad worked. She was going to give him her Christmas present.

She knew he wouldn't have anything for her.

"He's not so good at presents," Sophie said.

"He's not so good at life," her mother added from behind the bathroom door. "Don't expect much, Sophia."

Sophie put on her coat, tucked a little wrapped present in her backpack. "I expect the bus'll get us there, Ma. I expect it'll be cold outside. That's it."

A flush. "Don't take the wrong bus."

"I've done this before."

Running water. "Don't stay long."

"He gets a fifteen-minute break."

Bathroom door opened. Sophie's mother stared up at Tree. She looked just like Sophie except for being older and rounder. "If he asks about me, tell him I'm dating three movie stars."

Sophie laughed.

"You deserve a better father."

"But he's the one I got." Sophie pushed Tree out the door.

The Midas Muffler shop was packed with people drinking coffee from Styrofoam cups and checking their watches. Sophie pointed to a big man with his head inside a car engine.

"That's him. The big guy. You've got something in common already."

Sophie's father seemed satisfied with what he'd done; he motioned for another man, who got in the car and drove it out. He walked toward the glass door—didn't smile, didn't frown—pushed it open.

Sophie got nervous, her hands went in every direction. "Okay, Dad, so this is my friend Tree."

Sophie's father looked at Tree. "How old are you?"

"Twelve."

A snort. "You think I'm stupid?"

"No, sir. I'm really tall for my age."

"You're tall for *my* age." He stepped closer. *"You know how old she is?"*

"Dad—"

"No, really." Tree grabbed his wallet, got his seventh-grade ID. He had a copy of his birth certificate, too. His mother made him carry it.

Sophie stepped in. "Okay, so we know you're busy, Dad, and we don't want to mess up your schedule here."

Sophie's father studied the ID, handed it back.

"I brought you a present, Dad, on account of it's Christmas soon." She handed it to him.

"I left yours at home." He always said that. He lit a cigarette, blew smoke rings out slow.

"I recorded some Christmas music for you on my flute. I got your favorites. 'God Rest Ye Merry, Gentlemen' and 'Jingle Bells.' " She's talking faster, too fast. "I call it *Sophie's Greatest Christmas Hits.* The last half of 'O Little Town of Bethlehem' got cut off 'cause my cheeks were getting exhausted from all the blowing."

"I'll play it in the car."

"I hope you like it."

"You still got that flute, huh?"

"Yeah. I practice a lot."

He put the cigarette in his mouth, gave her a good pat on the shoulder.

"Vinnie!" Another man shouted it. "You on vacation or what?"

He looked at Sophie, softer this time. "I gotta go."

"Sure," she said quietly.

"Hey, Soph, we'll get together."

"Anytime, Dad."

He patted her shoulder again. Shook Tree's hand. He had a killer handshake.

"Size matters, kid. Wear it proud." He pushed through the glass door.

Tree stood straight.

Sophie's mother was right.

She deserved a better father.

"He can take a muffler out faster than any man alive," Sophie said. "They had a contest here last year and he won by three whole minutes."

"It was nice, what you gave him." Tree didn't know what else to say. He couldn't imagine having a father like that.

"I'm glad you think so, because it's the exact same thing you're getting for Christmas."

"My dad doesn't know how to love people," Sophie explained. "He drove my mother crazy."

The bus was late. They stood there shivering.

Tree clapped his hands together to stay warm. "I guess my parents drove each other crazy, too."

Sophie marched in place so her feet wouldn't freeze. "I got sent to a therapist about it. She told me I had hidden anger at my father and it was coming out when I was with other people. I told her no way was there any anger hiding in me. 'Open your eyes,' I said. 'It's all here on the surface.' But I figure I've got it better than a lot of kids. At least I know where my dad is."

Tree had never once thought of that.

The bus pulled up. She climbed inside.

"You coming or what?"

Tree got in the bus, hit his head.

She laughed. "You need a bus with a sunroof so you can stick your head out."

Tree didn't think that was funny.

Sophie elbowed him. "You've gotta laugh. If you don't, you'll cry."

CHAPTER TWELVE

Getting Grandpa in the Santa suit reminded Tree of the time when his mother had bought an outfit for Bradley—a sweater, hat, and booties—and Tree had to put it on him.

"Standing's not an ability I've got right now!" Grandpa tried to steady himself as Tree tried to pull the big red pants over his legs.

"It would help," Tree said, "if you'd stop moving so much."

"It would help if I had two working legs."

"Let's go with what we've got, Grandpa!"

Finally the pants were on. Grandpa looked at the floppy pant hanging loose over his half leg.

The Trash King adjusted his elf cap, cigar in his mouth. "You could say a reindeer chewed it off." King put on his pointy elf shoes, struck a pose. "Am I hot or what?"

"Scorching," said Grandpa. "But lose the cigar."

"It's not lit."

"You've got to be a role model."

King put the cigar in his pocket. "And you've got to be

careful, Leo. We tell the kids you've got to save your strength for Christmas Eve, when an angel's gonna come down from heaven, touch you with a magic wand, and your leg's gonna grow back."

Grandpa looked in the mirror Tree was holding up, put rouge on his cheeks, fastened the big white beard. "We're going to ruin this holiday for hundreds of children."

King picked a cigar leaf from his teeth.

"Ho, ho, ho," said Tree halfheartedly, folded the wheelchair, and carried it to the truck.

"The thing about Christmas," the Trash King said, driving his truck to the children's hospital, "is how I didn't understand what it was about until I got to Vietnam. You remember Christmas in Nam, Leo?"

Grandpa sighed. "I was in the hospital."

"That's right. You didn't get to see the show." King turned the corner. "They brought in a big show from the States with singers and dancers. There were hundreds of us out there watching. A couple guys had made a Christmas tree out of bamboo and painted it green. I was feeling sorry for myself because I wasn't home.

"And then we started singing. Just singing the songs. 'Silent Night,' 'Jingle Bells,' 'We Wish You a Merry Christmas,' 'Hark, Those Herald Angels Sing.' And I could have sworn—and a few guys in the Signal Corps would back me up on this—that there was a star in the sky a little brighter over where we were. And I thought, We get these holidays all wrong. We think it's what we get and how we feel and how warm and cozy we are, but Christmas came to all us slobs that night and most of those guys weren't expecting it. Some of us hadn't even washed. Now, I'll tell you how this helps me in trash. . . ."

King pulled up to the hospital parking lot. Grandpa groaned. "Save it, King, for the ride home. We've got a job to do."

Tree got the wheelchair from the back, placed a red throw blanket over it. Carefully eased Grandpa out of the truck and into the chair.

"Santa has landed," said King.

"You bet your boots, Elf Man."

Grandpa adjusted his beard, waved them forward like a lieutenant leading a platoon into battle. "Let's take this hill."

He grabbed the chair's wheels with his strong arms and pushed through the emergency doors that swung open at the miraculous power of Christmas.

"Ho, ho, ho," Grandpa bellowed to young and old who looked up excitedly.

"The Big Guy's here!" the Trash King shouted. "We're going to party tonight!"

Tree laughed and waved and shook all the hands of all the kids who came up to him. Down the hall they went with the ho-ho-hos booming. Kids in wheelchairs were following them. Tree handed out candy canes; King had a bag of toys over his shoulder. They turned the corner, saw three vets dressed like reindeer. Luger marched forward dressed like a toy drummer, beating a snare drum with his good hand.

Rat tat tat.

Rat tat tat.

Rat a tat. Rat a tat.

Tat tat.

A doctor took them into the rooms of the children who were too sick to come out.

One little girl had an IV in her arm and looked gray. Her mother was sitting in a chair by her bed. When Grandpa rolled in, that child lit up like a Christmas star.

"Santa," she whispered.

"You've got it, kid."

"You're in a wheelchair."

"Life isn't perfect, is it?"

King pulled a stuffed bear out of his bag, gave it to her. She hugged it, smiled at Tree.

"Santa, would you tell me a story?"

"Sure."

"Would you tell me 'The Night Before Christmas'?"

"Sure. Where's the book?"

She looked concerned. "Don't you know it?"

Grandpa looked at Tree and they both looked at the Trash King, who sniffed and said, "He knows it."

Grandpa desperately tried to remember the poem. The little girl hugged her bear and smiled.

"Okay, here goes. . . . 'Twas the night before Christmas, and all through the house, not a creature was stirring, not even a mouse." He stopped dead.

"The stockings," the little girl said.

"Were hung by the chimney with care," said King.

Grandpa grinned. "In hopes that Saint Nicholas soon would be there."

Silence.

Tree whispered about the kerchief, the cap, and the nap.

They got through it, helped by the little girl and her mother, and they had to call in two nurses to get the names of the eight reindeer right. King insisted the front reindeer were Dasher, Dancer, Prancer, and Nixon.

"Vixen," shouted the older nurse.

"Jeez. They named a reindeer *that?*"

They didn't miss a room that night.

Didn't miss a child.

Dozens of children lined up to see Santa. First in line, a boy in a big leg brace. He looked at Grandpa's half leg. "What happened to you?"

"I had an operation."

"Does it hurt?"

"Sometimes."

"Mine hurts, too. I wouldn't want anyone to sit on it."

So he stood next to the wheelchair and told Santa how he wanted a complete model train set, *not* like the one he got last year, like the one *Billy Buckley got* with the cool engine and the miles and miles of track.

Grandpa motioned to King. "Take that down."

"I didn't bring any paper."

"Elves," said Santa, shaking his head.

They had a party in the cafeteria for the kids who could get there; everyone sang Christmas songs. Only a few stalwart believers sat on Santa's knee, and he managed. Then a little girl climbed up on Tree's knee and told him that she wanted her lung to get better for Christmas.

Tree didn't know what to say.

Then she whispered, "I know you can't really give me that. I just wanted to tell you."

And she hugged him like he was the genuine article.

It made Tree feel about a foot taller, which was really saying something.

CHAPTER THIRTEEN

Tree didn't need much more of Christmas to happen after that.

Except it would have been nice if Larry stopped yelling at Bradley, who, according to Larry, wasn't moving fast enough to get out of his way.

"Take it out on somebody your own size!" Tree shouted.

"Like you?" Larry shouted back.

Tree stood tough. "I'm bigger than you!"

Larry's face darkened. "Maybe I could do something about that!"

But he never did. Larry was a screamer, not a fighter.

Twice he'd come home at night really late. His voice sounded different, he swayed when he walked. Grandpa said he'd been drinking. Larry got grounded, but he snuck out again anyway. When Larry staggered into the house at 2:00 A.M. with beer on his breath, Grandpa said, "What you're doing isn't making the hurt go away."

Larry stood there, quiet.

"Booze doesn't help. Talking does. Time. And I'll do whatever I can to—"

Larry shouted at him to mind his own business.

Grandpa said that anything that had to do with Larry *was* his business.

Larry raced up the stairs, flopped onto his bed. A few minutes later, Bradley pushed the door open and stuck his old snout on Larry's arm.

"Get lost!"

But Bradley wouldn't. He just sat there with his big trusting eyes waiting to help. Finally Larry hugged Bradley around the neck, buried his head in that good, old fur, and cried his eyes out about his parents' divorce.

Right after that, he sank to his knees in front of the toilet and vomited up beer until his insides felt raw.

Eight P.M., December 24.

Tree, Curtis, Larry, and Grandpa looked at the half-bare living room.

Tree hadn't realized how important Christmas trees were until he didn't have one.

Larry said, "Some Christmas."

Curtis said, "Shut up."

They'd been at each other all day.

Grandpa grabbed his walker, struggled up. "We're going to change things here. We're going to form a squad—tough and unified. And don't tell me it can't happen. I saw it happen in Nam. Saw different people with nothing in common work together to a common goal and become strong friends. So strong, you'd do just about anything to make sure your buddies stayed alive."

He rolled the walker to the middle of the living room. "That's what it comes down to sometimes—forgetting how you feel; being brave in front of your friends."

Curtis, Larry, and Tree were quiet.

Bradley, who understood about friendship, trotted in from the hall.

"We need a Christmas tree," Larry said finally.

Grandpa nodded. "That would help."

"We could get one at the store," Tree suggested.

"The stores," Curtis snapped, "are *closed*."

Grandpa grinned. "Guess we'll have to steal one."

In the car.

Curtis driving too fast, yelling at Tree to scrunch down in the backseat.

"You try scrunching down back here!"

Curtis screeched into the parking lot of Kramer's Sports Mart. Dad was just about to close the store down. Curtis stopped fast. Tree's head hit against the driver's seat.

Wheelchair out. Too many arms to help Grandpa.

"Wait," said Larry, "I lost my grip."

"Dear God . . ." said Grandpa, sliding butt to the door.

Wheeling toward the store. Tree ran ahead, opened the doors.

Their father at the cash register, trying to clear out for the holiday. He looked up, shocked.

"This is a stickup," Grandpa boomed cheerily. "Just hand over the tree and nobody gets hurt."

"What?"

Grandpa pointed to the Christmas tree in the middle of the store, complete with lights and ornaments.

"You're closing. You don't need the tree. We do."

"Pop, it's not my tree. It's the store's tree."

"You're the manager." Grandpa motioned to the boys, who started unplugging the tree, arguing about the best way to get it out.

I need it back on the twenty-sixth when we open.

Grandpa looked around. "We'll take that wreath and that fake holly."

Tree got the wreath. Larry got the holly.

"Pop . . ."

Grandpa wheeled himself toward the door.

"It's Christmas, Bucko, we're going to start acting like it."

Tree lay across the seat with the tree placed over his body. Sports ornaments dangled in his face.

"Drive carefully," Grandpa ordered Curtis, "or he'll be scarred for life."

Tree groaned all the way home to make the point.

They got the tree up.

It filled the empty spaces of the living room.

Dinner cooking. Dad and Grandpa in the kitchen, getting in each other's way.

Huge steaks. A dozen fat tomatoes. Three loaves of bread.

Four tins of pound cake. Frozen strawberries. Endless cans of whipped cream.

Bradley looked longingly at the tree.

"Don't even think about it!" Curtis gave Bradley a push out the door.

Then Dad remembered he left his presents for everyone at the store, and Tree remembered he left his presents for everyone at Mom's house, and Curtis and Larry remembered that they should have gone shopping, but didn't. And Grandpa said they didn't need presents, they just needed to let Christmas come natural, like the first one.

Bradley started barking at the front door. Tree let him in. Bradley headed right over to the Christmas tree, lifted his leg, and peed and peed.

"See," said Grandpa, "if we had presents under there, they'd be ruined."

And Bradley slept soundly in the hall.

CHAPTER FOURTEEN

"Pommerantz!" shouted Mom. "Don't eat that. *Bad dog!*"

She ripped a celery curl with chutney cream cheese from Pommerantz's tiny teeth.

Aunt Carla, Mom's sister, came over to defend him. She and her dog were visiting from Florida for the holidays.

"He's not a bad dog, Jan. He just doesn't understand. Do you, Pommie?"

This was almost more than Tree and his brothers could stand.

Conan started barking. His territory had been invaded.

You learn the flexibility of the human spirit when you have two different Christmas experiences in less than twenty-four hours.

"How's your ... father?" Mom asked in that edgy way.

"Okay," Tree, Larry, and Curtis said together.

"Grandpa?"

Same response.

She looked at the Serenity Fountain, a gift she had given to herself. Gentle, gurgling water cascaded over small, peaceful rocks. This is what her life would become. Someday.

She was trying now to be conversational with her sons. "How was your Christmas Eve?"

"Pretty good after we stole the tree," Curtis offered.

"What?"

Tree hit Curtis in the arm, told her the story, tried to make it light. He left out how he had to lie underneath the tree in the car.

"Your dad loves to do things last-minute."

She looked at her decorated kitchen with the little wreaths of basil over the sink, the Christmas music playing softly, the three kinds of vegetables, the perfect pies. Last night she had finished decorating the house with garlands, pinecones, and blue and white bows.

She'd strung popcorn, for crying out loud.

She'd pictured everyone smiling and happy, but instead her sons seemed distant and sad. "Let's talk about our feelings."

"That's a good idea," Carla chirped.

Three distinct male groans.

Mom wiped away a tear. "We all know it's different this Christmas. We're still in the fresh pain of the divorce, the awkward parts of how to be with each other." She looked at her sons. "Don't you think?"

Tree nodded.

Curtis and Larry didn't commit.

"We can make this work if we talk. If we don't talk, we'll never know what's going on." She grabbed the supersize bottle of Motrin she kept by the sink, gobbled three pills, looked at the gurgling Serenity Fountain. "You can tell me anything, and I promise I will listen. I love you guys more than I know how to say. There is no wall between us, and there never will be. I want to know all that's happening in your lives."

Three pairs of shuffling male feet. Larry looked up finally.

"I'm kind of flunking two courses, Mom."

Apron flung off, gums back like Conan. *What are you saying to me?*

"You wanted to know what was happening!"

"You'll lose your scholarship!"

"I can't concentrate. I don't know."

"Flunking? Not even a D?"

"Yeah! I get up every morning and say, 'How can I really screw up today?' "

Larry stormed out of the room.

Carla said, "He's acting out his feelings of frustration and anger, Jan."

Mom turned in fury to Tree and Curtis.

Curtis had overdrawn his checking account again, but he was taking that news to his grave.

Tree thought about mentioning how he'd taken apart the blender a couple of weeks ago and there were two parts missing and he wasn't sure it worked, but his mother was standing in front of it now with a handful of walnut halves—she put them inside the blender and everything in Tree wanted to shout, *Don't.*

She flipped on CHOP.

Nothing.

She checked the plug, tried again. The blender made a sound like a sick duck. Dark fury came over her face. She turned to Tree.

Tree was famous for doing this.

He took the answering machine apart when his mother was looking for work.

He took the remote control apart when his father's commercial was running during the Army-Navy game.

"You will *never* do this again."

Tree gulped. "I promise."

"I think a fire in that pretty new fireplace would be nice," said Carla, running from the room.

Mom furiously chopping the walnuts by hand.

Then concern hit her face.

"Was the flue up or down?"

"I think we've got a problem here!" Carla's voice was an octave higher.

"No!" screamed Mom.

They all ran into the newly painted living room and watched as billows of black smoke blew into the room while the logs crackled in the fireplace.

"Guess it wasn't open," said Curtis.

Tree grabbed a broom from the closet, knelt down by the fireplace, breathing smoke, coughing as his lungs filled with it. He shoved the broomstick up to where the flue should be. Shoved four times, finally felt it pop open.

"Open the windows!" Mom screamed. *"Open the door! Open everything!"*

Larry ran down the stairs. "What happened?"

"Doom," Curtis said solemnly.

"Oh, God, Jan, I'm so sorry!" Carla was opening windows, batting smoke from the air.

Pommerantz was barking pitifully in the kitchen.

"Oh, poor Pommie. He must be so scared."

Pommerantz ran into the hall, stood shaking on the little yellow-and-white hooked rug, and puked up the celery stick with cream cheese.

"Pommerantz," screamed Mom, *"sit on a tack!"*

"I think that's excessive, Jan."

It was then that the smoke alarm in the kitchen went off.

Mom stood on a stool by the freshly baked pies, trying to turn it off; the siren blared.

She yanked it from the freshly painted ceiling.

Ripped out the batteries.

And finally, quiet came upon them.

Except for the gurgling drips from the Serenity Fountain.

Mom crumpled on the floor in a woeful heap. The aroma of perfect roast beef wafted from the oven.

"Smoke alarm works," said Curtis, who was known for having a firm grasp of the obvious.

Tree, Curtis, and Larry half laughed from relief.

She didn't think that was funny.

Tree scrunched down next to her, put his arm around her shoulder. "You've got to laugh, Mom. If you don't, you'll cry."

CHAPTER FIFTEEN

"My little sister is allergic to Fred."

Eli Slovik told Tree this on the phone. Fred was his parrot.

"She's got some feather allergy and Fred has to be out of the house until they test her and see if there's medication. Can I bring him to your house? Just for a little bit?"

Tree wasn't sure how Bradley would handle a parrot.

He wasn't sure how anybody would.

"He could keep your grandfather company, Tree. Just ask. *Please?*"

"Back off, Buster."

Fred the parrot said it to Grandpa, who said, "Back off yourself. I'm going to teach you some manners."

Bradley looked at the parrot and barked loud.

"I really appreciate this, Mr. Benton." Eli was holding the big cage with Fred inside. "He gets kind of excited sometimes."

Grandpa stared at Fred, who stared back.

"I've got to go, Mr. Benton. Thanks." Eli looked in the cage. "You be good, Fred."

"Back off, Buster."

Eli looked pained. "My uncle taught him to say that."

Bradley backed out of the room.

"You're certainly looking handsome today, Leo." Grandpa had his walker close to Fred's cage. "Go ahead, bird, say it."

Fred looked back.

They were getting used to each other.

Grandpa tried again. "You're certainly looking handsome today, Leo."

Nothing from the bird.

"That'll get you a whole lot farther in the world than 'Back off, Buster.' "

"Back off, Buster," Fred announced.

Grandpa sighed, headed back to the couch.

The white oak stood like a skeleton covered with snow. It was hard to look at it and remember how full and lush it had been in the spring, how its leaves had turned to wine in the fall. That's the thing about winter—it's so easy to forget the other seasons—it never seems like it will end.

Tree stood in front of the leafless white oak. He could see every branch, all the textures of the gray bark.

Tree wanted it to be spring, but dealt with the reality.

He picked up an acorn. It was so small, so compact—the seed of a new tree just waiting to be released in the earth.

With his boot, he dug a little hole in the cold ground, put the acorn in it, covered it with dirt and snow.

He liked the idea of planting a new tree.

He thought about his grandpa's new prosthetic leg, which was going to be coming soon. Mona Arnold said Grandpa was going to have to learn to walk a whole new way and it wasn't going to be easy.

They'd gotten through Christmas.

Curtis and Larry were back at college.

It was January now.

And Tree still hated his mother's house and the teeny rooms, he still hated the frozenness he felt sometimes as the fresh divorce kept coming at him in the strangest ways.

Like at night, when he would suddenly get a bad stomachache and feel scared for no reason.

Like at Eli's house, when he felt so sad when Eli's dad kissed Eli's mother.

Like at school, when Sophie told him she'd call him as soon as she got home. She said *home* like it was permanent condition.

"Where are you this week?" she asked.

The every-other-week color-coded schedule had started again.

"My mom's."

"You've gotta stop saying it that way. You've got two houses. There are worse things." Sophie mentioned living with six cats who all had their own kitty-litter beds.

"I think the stress is getting to Lassie. She's not crawling on her branch as much. She used to go crazy when I'd play 'The Ash Grove' on my flute, but now it's just another song. I'm getting worried."

Bradley was getting slower, too.

Tree tried drawing pictures of happy dogs running and jumping, but Bradley just looked at the pictures, sighed, and took a nap.

He was napping a lot these days.

Then Bradley started pooping on the hall rug.

Tree would clean the mess up as best as he could. But Bradley kept having accidents.

"We're going to have to do something about this, Tree," his dad said. "Bradley's getting old, too old maybe to have a decent, productive life."

Tree's whole body went cold. He remembered when Sully had his dog put down.

"I'm a good guy," Dad added. "I try to give everybody a break, but Grandpa can't get around the way he used to and you're only here every other week."

"I'll teach him to do better, Dad, *I swear.*"

Tree was on his knees, patting the back half of Bradley. Patting as much life into him as he could.

Dad grabbed his pounding head. Went to the basement to do his laundry. He'd been recycling dirty socks all week.

Tree cleaned up the mess.

"Bradley, this is serious."

Tree took paper, drew a rug with dog turds on it, put an X through it, held it up.

"This rug is a no-poop zone."

Bradley listened intently.

"You poop outside." Tree drew a porch with steps and the

98

big evergreen in the front lawn with a pile of turds under it. *"Got it?"*

Bradley cocked his head. He liked being talked to.

Tree wasn't a great artist, but he could get an idea across.

Tree was in his ski jacket, sitting on the front steps with Bradley. He looked at his old dog—half sleeping, breathing deep.

A squirrel scurried by. Not so long ago, Bradley would have chased it.

"It would help if you chased something, especially when Dad's watching." Tree drew a so-so squirrel being chased by a dog. Held it up. "It looks like a mouse, but it's a squirrel."

He had showed Dr. Billings, the veterinarian, his method, but the vet said dogs don't learn that way.

Dr. Billings was a good vet, but not too creative.

The front door opened.

Dad stood on the cold porch. "What I said about Bradley ... I know that scared you. I'm sorry."

A loud car honk sounded. Bradley didn't move. He used to bark when those things happened.

"We just have to figure out what's best for him."

Tree nodded.

McAllister, Mrs. Clitter's ugly cat, was slinking across the lawn.

Bradley opened one eye.

He didn't like McAllister. No one did, except Mrs. Clitter. McAllister crept closer.

Closer.

Too close.

The old dog barked, rose to his feet.

Tore after McAllister.

Bradley trotted back when McAllister was off the property. Lay back down on the porch.

Tree's father shook his head, laughing.

"Yes!" Tree shouted.

There was life in that old dog yet.

CHAPTER SIXTEEN

"Awright, Pit Bulls!" Coach Glummer shouted from the side-lines. *"Let's come alive out there!"* He clapped his hands. *"Let's see some mad-dog hustle!"*

But it's hard to find energy and hustle when the scoreboard reads

VIKINGS 43
PIT BULLS 4

That score stood stark like a tree without leaves.

Halftime. Coach Glummer clinging to hope.

"Forget the first half. Forget that all but two of you played like sheep. The past is gone!"

The Pit Bulls weren't sure what that meant.

"Think of yourselves as blank sheets of paper, and write on that paper a winner's story!"

In the bleachers, Tree's dad leaned forward.

"That huge kid's a joke." A father sitting a row back said it to another father. "All that height, not a clue how to use it."

Furious, Tree's dad stood up, applauding. *"Let's go out there!"*

Back on the court. Tree tried to think of himself as a winner.

Not missing a shot.

Awesome in power.

I am a tree.

He stepped in front of an average-size Viking, held his huge arms out. Snarled briefly.

The Viking looked for a way to pass the ball, but this is hard to do when a tree is in front of you.

The ball dropped.

Tree grabbed it. Felt a sureness as he dribbled down the court.

Tree's dad cheering him on.

Coach Glummer shrieked, *"Give me the slam dunk of a winner!"*

Tree aimed.

Missed.

Jeremy Liggins got the ball on a rebound.

Made the basket.

"Now, that kid's got the moves," the father a row back said.

Just one basket, Dad thought. *Let him get one lousy basket.*

Liggins made six more points before the game was over.

Tree never scored.

But somehow, Tree felt pretty good.

Almost like a winner.

But you know how it is with coaches.

They want the win, not the concept.

"I'm sick of most of you guys not trying," Coach Glummer snarled in the locker room. Looked at Tree when he said it.

Tree got so angry at that.

Jeremy Liggins sauntered up to Tree: "You're a joke out there."

But something in Tree rose up.

"No, I'm not." He squared his shoulders and looked down at Liggins, who looked away first.

February brought bad weather.

The temperature shot up and the rains came with a fury.

February brought more business travel for Tree's mom. She had less time at home, which meant Tree only stayed with her a few days every other week.

He was glad to spend the extra time with Bradley and Grandpa.

He checked heymom.com every day, though.

Clicked on *What We're About* to read reminiscences of him and his brothers growing up.

Clicked on *The Road Ahead* for at-a-glance thoughts on how divorced families heal and grow *(Trust + Time = Tenderness)*.

He never clicked on *Just Between Us* or *Hugs*.

The computer can take you just so far with your mother.

But one kid's snack is another kid's dinner.

He showed Sophie the website. She scrolled down the page, amazed.

"Your mother does all this for you? You don't know how good you've got it."

■   ■   ■

"You're a genius."

Bradley cocked his head as Grandpa looked at Fred the parrot, who looked back.

"You're a genius. Say it, Fred. Come on."

Grandpa had given up on Fred ever saying, "You're certainly looking handsome today, Leo." Tree's dad suggested that Grandpa could call Mrs. Clitter, and she'd come over and say he was handsome.

He needed the bird's respect.

"You're a genius," Grandpa tried again. "Say it, Fred. Make me glad you're here."

Fred ruffled his emerald feathers and squawked.

The rain kept coming.

Grandpa was looking toward May and the Memorial Day parade. His new leg was supposed to be delivered any day now, but it got held up because of the weather.

"Where's my leg?" he kept asking Mona.

"It's somewhere in Chicago, Leo."

"What's it doing there?"

"The plane it was on had to land because of the snow."

"I've got to be marching strong by May."

"Leo, I can't promise you'll be marching anywhere by May. It takes *time* to get this right."

He held up his hand, didn't want to hear it.

"I want you to push me hard, Mona."

"I'm not going to push you any harder than makes sense."

The next day:

"What's my leg doing in Miami, Mona?"

Grandpa half shouted it on the phone.

"United Airlines put it on the wrong plane, Leo, and now they're not sure where it is in the airport."

"Maybe we should send in the paratroopers to get it back. I'm going to be a genius at this walking business, and my leg is seeing the country."

CHAPTER SEVENTEEN

"Leo," said Mona Arnold, grinning, "meet your new leg."

She handed him a flesh-colored leg cut off below the knee.

Grandpa held it. "Look at this miracle, will you?" He felt the weight. "It's heavier than I expected."

"Once you get used to it, it takes your weight and gives you a nice fluid movement."

Grandpa studied it.

"If you just sit down over here, Bill will show you the next part."

Bill, the leg man, brought out the stump sock, the liner sock, showed Grandpa how to put them on. He fitted the leg on the stump, showed how the mechanism clicked tight.

Tree and his father were there to meet the new member of the family.

Grandpa worked for two hours, practicing.

Standing on the leg.

Taking it off.

Walking so carefully a few steps, a few more.

Tiring, focused work.

Every step counts. Every step teaches something.

"Swing your leg out more, Leo. That gives you an even step."

"Try to put equal weight on both legs now. This'll take some time since the good one has been taking so much of the weight."

"If you go too far too soon, you're going to get redness and swelling. Easy does it. This isn't a race."

He sat down, took the leg off, held it in his lap.

"You can put it on the floor," Mona said.

"No way. We're bonding."

"Vietnam wasn't our war. That's what the bigwigs in Washington told us."

Grandpa had been thinking about that the last few days. Every so often he'd take the war apart to try to make sense of the experience.

He was sticking his leg on, practicing walking in the house with Tree.

A couple of faltering steps.

The first steps of the day are the hardest.

"There we were on the battlefield, getting shot at, dying, but it wasn't our war. That was so confusing." He looked at Tree. "You ever feel like that?"

Tree wasn't sure. "Sometimes I feel I'm in the middle of Mom and Dad's divorce. They're fighting each other—not me—but I'm there."

"You learn to duck. That's what I did."

Tree laughed. "I know about ducking."

Three more steps.

Step, drag the leg. Step . . .

Grandpa gripped a chair for balance. "I ran for cover a lot, too. And I tried to remember the things I had control over so I wouldn't feel like a grunt."

"Like what?"

"Like how I responded to people. How I kept my weapon clean and ready. How I always wore my helmet. I protected my head come hell or high water. Guys would kid me about it." He laughed. "Figures I'd get shot in the leg."

Grandpa stood in front of the full-length mirror in the hall. Looking in mirrors helped him see if he was standing right.

He straightened up a little, smiled at Tree.

"I think you and I have a lot in common. We're both learning to walk a different way, and we're both going to be geniuses at it."

More than anything, Tree wanted to be like his grandpa.

Grandpa shouted to Fred the parrot in the living room, "You're a genius. *Say it, bird.*"

"Back off, Buster."

Grandpa shook his head. "You think I can walk a few blocks in this thing next week? I've got something I need to do."

"Put them down there."

Grandpa handed Tree a new deck of playing cards in a plastic bag. Tree put it near a wreath of flowers and a baby picture that were soaked from the pouring rain.

Grandpa reached up to touch a name on the Vietnam Veterans Memorial in Washington, D.C.

Private Elmo P. Hothrider.

Grandpa and Tree had driven here with the Trash King.

"Elmo was a fine card player. He got shot up bad outside Da Nang. His eyes were bandaged shut when I went to see him in the hospital. And you know what he wanted? He wanted to play cards. So I played for him and me. Elmo won three hands out of five, and he accused me of cheating."

Grandpa touched the name again. "Rest well, friend. Don't take any wild cards up there."

He limped to another section of the wall that stretched long and black across the mall in Washington, D.C.—an hour's drive from Ripley.

"That's the place."

Tree put a bottle of hot sauce near Sergeant Nick Marconi's name.

Candles, flowers, family pictures, a big bottle of Hershey's Syrup. Anything can hold a memory.

He placed a letter in a plastic bag and put it on the wet ground for Corporal Michael Diggins. Grandpa stood by Corporal Diggins's name for a long time as the cold rain beat down.

"Diggins always said the jungle was crazy. You think you're going the right way, but you're really going back the way you came. It changes color with the sun and the clouds. You're waiting to fight, and you start thinking the shadows are going to come get you. Then you realize that war is as much about your mind as anything else. Is what you're seeing real, or is it made up?"

The Trash King reached up, touched Calvin Merker's name. Merker dragged six injured people to safety before he was shot himself.

King stood there like he was waiting for something.

Tree had heard enough about the war to know that a big part of it was about waiting. Soldiers waiting for their marching orders, pilots waiting to fly their missions. Everyone waiting for it to be over.

"So many," Grandpa said, limping from end to end as rain poured down.

Tree tried to imagine what some of these soldiers looked like; he never could. He didn't know if they were tall or short, fat or thin. A name on a wall didn't tell you that. But Tree knew that all the names here and the people who came to remember them were connected with a special kind of courage.

Grandpa alongside him now, struggling on that new leg. "Every friend I lost, I still carry in my heart. The paratroopers do it right. They put out an empty boot when one of them dies—no one can fill that shoe.

"We hear about casualties on the news—114 dead. Two murdered. Over three thousand killed. Numbers don't tell the story. You can't measure the loss of a human life. It's all the things a person was, all their dreams, all the people who loved them, all they hoped to be and could give back to the world. A million moments in a life cut short because of war."

CHAPTER EIGHTEEN

Tree wished there was a memorial wall for divorce.

If there was one, he knew what he'd leave in tribute.

The photo of his parents laughing on the beach.

He kept it in his sock drawer, but that didn't cut it as a memorial.

"More rain expected today, folks."

That's what the weatherman said on TV. Tree was at his mom's house.

"Thunderstorms continue throughout the week." Weather laughter. "It's not my fault, I swear." The northeast section of the weather map showed storm clouds, lightning flashes, and blinking raindrops.

"They started sandbagging the levee in Burnstown." Mom said it, sipping coffee. Burnstown was three towns away. "Don't be late for the bus."

Tree got his slicker, bent down so Mom could kiss him on the cheek.

"Stay safe out there, sweetie."

Conan yipped.

And Tree headed out into the cold, wet world.

The bus was late again.

Tree stood waiting for it in his iridescent slicker, pummeled by wetness. He felt like some giant glow-in-the-dark road marker.

Other kids were waiting, too.

No one spoke.

Endless bad weather makes you not care much about anything.

Sully, who'd lost two raincoats last week, showed up completely covered by Hefty bags. He stood morosely next to Tree.

"Can you see?" Tree asked him.

"No."

"You want me to make your eyeholes bigger?"

"No."

The bus pulled up, splashed water on their legs, sloshed it in their shoes. Thunder boomed.

Tree helped Sully onto the bus.

From inside the Hefty bags, Sully spoke.

"Close the school. We're too wet to learn." He raised a bag-wrapped fist.

Students nodded.

The bus lurched through the storm.

Outside the middle school orchestra room, Sophie was unwrapping ten layers of plastic bags from around her flute.

"Aunt Peach says if the flute gets ruined, I don't get another one. I told her it would be a real loss to the music world. I've got this big tryout and I've got to play dry. I want this solo bad, Tree."

Flute sounds came from the orchestra room.

"That's pretty," Tree said.

"*That's* Sarah Kravetz playing." Sarah Kravetz was Amber Melloncroft's best friend. "She wants the solo, too. She can't even hit a high C."

Tree listened some more. "She's not as good as I thought."

The flute music stopped.

"I get mucus in my throat when I'm nervous." Sophie cleared her throat like a truck driver, spat into a tissue.

"You'll do great," Tree offered.

Sarah Kravetz walked out, looked Sophie up and down like she'd fallen off a garbage truck. Didn't even look at Tree.

Flounced off.

"So, okay, I'm next."

Sophie cleared her throat loud as Sarah looked back, amused; Amber joined her, whispering.

Sophie on her knees, searching through her book bag for the music.

"I had it this morning."

Giggles.

Tree wanted to punch a hole through the wall and shove them in.

"Okay. Wait." Sophie held Poldini's "Dancing Doll" high so Amber and Sarah could see.

And with that, Sophie Santack cleared her throat, spat big,

and marched into the orchestra room to show what a tough kid could do with a tender instrument.

I GOT IT!!!!!!!!!!!!!!!!!!!!!!!!!!

That's what Sophie's note said on Tree's locker.

He looked for her in school. Walked though the packed halls, towering over the heads of students, but he couldn't find her.

Sully lumbered by on his way to the principal's office, sent there for turning his hearing aid off in social studies.

"Haven't seen her," he said glumly.

I GOT IT!!!!!!!!!!!!!!!!!!!!!!!!!!!!

She held up a sign when he was at basketball practice.

Tree grinned at her, focused on the net, and actually made a basket.

He tried to act like he did that all the time, but inside he was soaring.

Sophie stomped on the bleachers.

"I got it!" she said excitedly when he came out of the locker room. "I got the solo at assembly *and* I got the solo at the Memorial Day concert after the parade. I'm going to be a soldier of yesteryear and play this medley of war songs I've never heard before, but I'm going to know them in my sleep by May. It's going to be a lot of pressure, but I think I'm up to it. Mr. Cloud said I had true feeling for the instrument."

Tree beamed. "That's great."

"And I needed this, Tree, 'cause people don't always get

114

where I'm coming from. Those eighth-grade girls don't get it."

"I know."

"I'm going to bake brownies and bring them to school tomorrow. We're going to *celebrate*."

CHAPTER NINETEEN

She smelled it before she saw it.

Couldn't figure out what the awful odor was.

She turned the corner, holding the plate of brownies.

She'd fixed her hair extra nice, too, with that purple barrette.

Sophie was feeling as good as she'd ever allow herself to feel.

But then she saw it.

Trash bags with smelly garbage hanging from her school locker, piled around the floor, spilling the stinking mess everywhere.

Tuna cans.

Coffee grinds.

Broken eggshells.

She dropped the brownies.

Tore the barrette out of her hair.

Stood there frozen. Kids walked past her, holding their noses at the smell.

"I didn't do this, okay? I didn't bring this here!"

Then she saw the sign—in pink block letters.

GARBAGE GIRL

She tore it down just as Tree ran up.

"Who did this?" he shouted. But he already knew. "We'll clean it up. Sully, Eli, and me. You won't have to—"

Teachers were coming now.

Students saying it was awful.

The bell rang.

They stood there.

Mr. Cosgrove pushed a Dumpster into place; moved quickly. Took down the bags, threw out the garbage.

"They're going to explode someday from all the garbage inside them," he told Sophie, but it didn't make her feel better.

She grabbed a smelly tuna can and stormed off.

"Sophie," Tree shouted.

She kept walking.

Tree ran after her. "Where are you going?"

"I've got someone to see." She was almost running, holding that can.

Pushed into first-period geometry—her class—stormed right up to Amber Melloncroft and Sarah Kravetz, who looked away, trying not to smile.

Mr. Pelling, the math teacher, said, "You can't walk in here like that."

Sophie slammed the can down on Amber's desk.

"If you and your friends ever do that to me again, you're going to be sorry!"

Amber shouted, "I don't know what you're talking about, and take your lunch off my desk!"

Sophie picked up the can, shoved it under Amber's upturned nose. "This is a smell you know real well."

"That's enough!" Mr. Pelling shouted.

"She's threatening me!" Amber wailed.

"No." Tree stood tall. "She's telling the truth about what you did. Now everybody knows." He stepped closer. "I want to know *why* you did it."

"Get away from me, you overgrown freak!"

"What made you think you had the *right?*"

"In the hall!" Mr. Pelling pointed at Tree and Sophie.

He marched them to the principal's office.

"Threatening a student," he told Mrs. Pierce, the administrative assistant.

The principal was on the phone with the superintendent.

They had to wait.

"Dr. Terry," Tree said to the principal, "Sophie didn't threaten anybody. Those girls have been mean to her for a long time."

Dr. Terry leaned back in her chair. "Several teachers told me what happened with the locker. It was an awful thing to do. I apologize to you, Sophie, on behalf of this school. That is not what we're about. But you should have come in here to talk to me as soon as it happened."

"I never think about principals when I'm mad."

Dr. Terry smiled. "I understand."

"I don't know if you do, Dr. Terry. You didn't see it."

"Sophie, something like this takes time to fix. I'm going to talk to Amber and her friends. I'm going to talk to their parents and to this school community at large. There is zero tolerance for cruelty at Eleanor Roosevelt. I'll call your parents, too, so we can work this out together."

Sophie looked down. "I don't think I want to come back to this school."

Tree's heart just broke for her.

Dr. Terry leaned forward. "I'm asking you to give me a little time to make this right."

"I'm in eighth grade, Dr. Terry. Unless I flunk, you haven't got much time."

Aunt Peach arrived at the school, folded her considerable arms, and eyed Sophie like a prison guard.

"What are we going to do about your temper?"

"They put garbage on my locker, Aunt Peach!"

"That was a cold, cruel thing to do."

"And I let them know it. Sometimes you've got to shout the truth and wake people up."

"Sophie, I like to think that truth doesn't need to be shoved down people's throats."

"In eighth grade, Aunt Peach, truth needs all the help it can get."

CHAPTER TWENTY

"I told Aunt Peach I'd rather eat dirt for a week than come to ballroom dancing, but she said it's going to help me socially." Sophie folded her arms tight. "Like there's hope."

Sophie stood miserably in a red dress near the wall of the YMCA gym, as far away from Amber Melloncroft and Sarah Kravetz as possible.

Tree stood next to her.

Sully and Eli were out front, hiding in the bushes.

Coach Glummer's cousin Sheila tossed her head; Lazar tossed his.

They stood cheek to cheek, arms extended, knees bent.

"The tango," Sheila said, "is making a comeback, and I want you to experience it."

They rotated dramatically, not smiling. Lazar bent Sheila back.

"The tango is about *passion*."

The boys started laughing, especially Jeremy Liggins. The girls giggled.

"The tango is about despair and emotional power. It was born during a time of great economic hardship. People danced it to express the sadness in their hearts."

Sophie looked at Tree, who knew he wasn't up to this.

"Don't be afraid of passion and despair," Sheila shouted. "We all have deep rivers running through us. This dance will help you find them."

"I'm there." Sophie grabbed Tree's hand and marched onto the dance floor.

After sixty minutes of tango practice, Tree had found despair.

He was too tall for this dance.

To look directly into Sophie's eyes, he had to bend low.

To fully extend his arms with Sophie's, she had to grab his elbow instead of his hand.

He almost dropped Sophie when he had to lean her back.

And the worst part was, Sophie loved it.

"Okay, we're going to connect to our deep rivers of despair, Tree, and get so sad, we can hardly stand it. We're going to let all the garbage that's been thrown at us come out and show these people what's what."

Tree was absolutely certain he couldn't do that.

But Lazar picked Tree and Sophie and Amber and Jeremy to demonstrate.

They walked to the middle of the dance floor.

Amber looked at Sophie, held her nose.

"Mr. Cosgrove should have put *you* in the Dumpster," Sophie snarled.

"You are *so* pathetic!"

"You think so?"

Tree stood tall, stared at Amber. "Stop it!"

Amber looked away.

Silence from Jeremy.

"Together with the eyes," Lazar shouted.

Sophie's dark eyes fixated on Tree.

"Okay. From that, young peoples, we find our sadness!"

Hands on hips, Sophie stepped defiantly past Amber, who was having trouble finding anything. Sophie tossed her head, posed with pain.

A big part of the tango is posing.

She did a little twirl around Tree, who almost went in the right direction.

He stood there like a stage prop, trying to keep his deep rivers to himself.

Sophie stomped her foot, her red skirt flared up. She glared at Amber, who looked down.

"You see from that?" Lazar shouted. "The girl, she becomes the dance."

Painful music swelled.

And Sophie Santack owned that dance floor.

She didn't really need a partner, but Tree wasn't giving up his slot. She came close: "We're going to try that cheek-to-cheek thing and pray to God we don't mess up."

Tree prayed.

Bent down to reach her cheek.

"Stand tall," Sophie told him. "Wear it proud."

They danced cheek to chest, which was a whole lot easier.
Tree bent her back for the finish.
The music ended.
But not the pain.
That's the point of the tango.

Chapter Twenty-one

The only thing the continuous rain was good for was Eli's little sister, Rachel, whose feather allergies got better, and the doctor said Fred could come home.

Grandpa had complicated feelings about this.

He hadn't once gotten the parrot to say he was a genius.

"Back off, Buster" was all he got. That bird was stuck like an old record.

He'd hoped to bring Fred to a new level of communication, but it wasn't meant to be.

"I would like us to begin a new level of communication."

Tree's mother said this on the speakerphone in her kitchen to Tree's father, who was at work.

Tree was in his mother's living room, listening.

Mom scrolled down her computer screen. She'd typed out exactly what she wanted to say.

"I think we're strong enough to do this now, Mark. I know it will be important for the children."

Silence. She geared up for the next line:

"I know that we are forever linked to each other because of the kids. We need to be able to talk together and make decisions together without all the old stuff getting in the way."

Tree's father didn't say anything because his stockperson had just dropped a box of golf balls and the balls were rolling everywhere.

"Are you still there?" she asked.

"Yes." Dad stopped a golf ball with his foot.

"Did you hear me?"

"I heard you."

"It would be nice if you at least acknowledged you heard me."

"I heard you." Dad stopped three balls with a hockey stick. He didn't like talking about important things on the phone.

Mom lived on the phone. *Well?*

This, thought Tree, is the old stuff.

Mom and Dad decided to talk about it next week at dinner. At Dad's house, so she could say hello to Grandpa.

They said good-bye in that edgy way.

Tree wondered if they would ever talk to each other easily again.

He walked into the kitchen.

Tree wasn't sure he should confess. But he did.

"I kind of overheard, Mom."

"Your dad and I don't want to let our problems stand in the way of doing the best for you and your brothers."

Tree nodded. That was nice.

"I'm not going to let years of misunderstanding stand in the way of being a forgiving adult."

She wasn't done.

"Your dad and I shared important moments. I'm not going to let them get buried." She said that pretty fast.

"It's good you can talk," Tree offered.

She turned off her computer, sighed. "It's going to be hard for me to go to the old house."

"I know, Mom."

"I haven't seen Grandpa and Bradley for . . ."

"They miss you. We all do."

Her eyes teared up. "I'm crying so much these days. I'm sorry. I see a baby and I cry. I see a kitten and I can hardly stand it. I see a commercial with a happy family eating vegetables and I fall apart."

"Maybe we should stop eating vegetables," Tree offered hopefully, handing her a box of tissues.

She blew her nose. "Should I bake something for next week? Anything you'd like?"

Tree laughed. "You should probably bring the whole dinner, Mom."

Twisting the tissue. "Your dad said he'd take care of dinner. I don't want to insult him."

"Your mother's coming for dinner."

Tree's father said this at six o'clock.

Tree was shocked. "I thought she was coming on Thursday."

"We changed it." Dad checked his watch. "She'll be here in thirty minutes."

Tree looked around—no food on the stove, in the oven. "What are we eating?"

"I don't know." Tree's father wrung his hands.

"Sophie's coming over, Dad. Remember? We're going to watch that TV show on lizards since her TV's broken. You said it was okay."

"It's okay." Already Dad regretted this whole evening.

"But *Mom's* coming."

"That's okay, too."

He picked up the phone to order pizza.

For men, there's always a simple solution to dinner.

"Well . . ."

Mom sat at the dining room table, looked at the empty walls, the shadows of where the hutch had been.

Remembered how they'd fought about who got the hutch.

Studied the clothesline and pulley system on the ceiling. Felt a tightness in her chest.

"It was an experiment, Mom."

"I'm sure it was."

She smiled at Tree, looked kindly to Grandpa, patted Bradley's old, loyal head. Bradley hadn't left her side since she'd walked through the door.

"We haven't sat at this table together for a long time," Mom said quietly.

Dad moved a can of motor oil off the table to make room for the pizza.

"Sausage or veggie?" he asked too loudly.

Mom's smile grew thin. "I don't eat sausage. I never have."

"Right." Dad cut into the veggie pizza, slapped a huge piece on a paper plate, looked at his ex-wife. "We've got salad."

"Please."

Salad plopped on the plate. Too much dressing.

Lightning cracked in the sky; the hanging light over the table flickered just like in a horror movie.

Mom turned sympathetically to Grandpa. "How are you, Leo?"

"Sausage or veggie?" Dad asked Grandpa.

"Whatever's easy."

Dad froze. He needed facts.

"Give him one of each, Dad." Tree said this miserably. "I want sausage. No salad."

"You should have salad," Mom said.

"I'm not hungry, Mom."

"Give him some salad."

A teaspoon of salad dropped onto Tree's plate.

Dad made a pizza sandwich—slapped two pieces of sausage pizza together facedown; took a huge bite.

Mom looked away. She hated it when he did that.

Grandpa asked, "How's it been going for you, Jan?"

She picked at her salad. "I'm traveling a lot. Teaching more seminars. We've been streamlining the curriculum. I have to do a three-day workshop in a day and a half now. I'm not sure everyone is learning what they need. It's frustrating. Not as frustrating as what you're dealing with, Leo."

"I handle it. I'm walking in the mall. You know how much I love shopping."

She laughed. "I didn't think anything could get you in the mall."

"Only raw courage, rehab, and rain, Jan."

She laughed. "Leo, I haven't been by to see you because... well—"

He held up his hand. "It's been a tough time. I'm just glad to see you now."

She took his hand.

The doorbell rang.

"I think that's my friend."

Tree went to the door, opened it to Sophie, who stood there, drenched, holding something big and square covered in a plastic bag.

A car horn. Shouting voice: "Two hours, Sophia. That's it."

"Okay, Ma."

Tree waved at the car. Rain poured down.

"I brought Lassie. I wanted her to see this."

"Boy, that's real nice you guys can have dinner together without killing each other."

Sophie stood by the table, holding Lassie's cage. "We've had a lot of divorces at my house. My aunt Peach got a restraining order against her second husband. If he comes closer than thirty feet from her, she'll have him arrested. She carries one of those snap-up rulers to keep things legal. We don't mess around in my family."

Mom stared at the cage, not a lizard lover.

"This is Lassie, my iguana. I named her that 'cause I'm

working up to a dog. I wanted Aunt Peach to get used to the idea. She's pretty upset these days."

"Your aunt Peach is upset?" Mom asked.

"Lassie's upset." Sophie shoved the cage in Mom's face. "See how she's not moving much? She used to have a good personality. Her head would go up and down when I talked to her. I think the weather's got her depressed."

Booming thunder in the distance.

"The weather's doing that to all of us." Mom pushed her chair back, wondering where this young woman came from.

"Your show's probably on," Dad said weakly.

Sophie checked her watch, sat at the table, put Lassie in front of her. "We've got a couple minutes. I just wanted to say that you guys do this divorce thing right. When my parents split up my mother said, 'Your father's a moron. I'm kicking him out.' "

Tree stood fast, grabbed Lassie's cage, and headed for the television.

The doorbell rang.

Tree got the door, holding the cage.

It was Mrs. Clitter holding a basket.

"Now, how is that man—"

She stopped dead, stared at Lassie.

"It's an iguana," Tree said.

"But she's under a lot of stress," Sophie explained from behind. "She's missing other lizards, so I brought her over here."

Mrs. Clitter looked confused. "There are other lizards over here?"

"There's a nature show on lizards starting. I'm going to let her watch it. The vet says iguanas are exotic animals and won't examine her for less than seventy-five dollars. My aunt Peach says hell's gotta freeze solid before she gives a vet that much money to take an iguana's pulse."

"I baked bread," Mrs. Clitter half shouted. "Have I come at a bad time?"

Grandpa kept his mouth shut on that one.

Mrs. Clitter sat at the table and joined the party.

The lizard on the screen was creeping up a tree limb, bobbing its head.

"See, Lassie, that could be your sister," Sophie said.

Lassie was sitting on her rock, watching Bradley instead of the TV lizard.

The doorbell rang.

Mom got up, opened the front door.

The Trash King stood there holding a salami. He grinned. "Are you kids back together?"

"We're *just* having dinner."

Dad closed his eyes.

"Well, you never know what these things can lead to, Jan. Just be open to the world of second chances." He winked. "That's what keeps me in business."

He walked into the dining room. "Leo, I brought a salami."

"And I brought bread," said Mrs. Clitter.

"Okay," Sophie shouted from the next room. "Lassie's doing the dance."

Lassie was bobbing her head like the TV lizard.

"She just needed a role model. She needed to know she wasn't the only lizard in the world."

Sophie's bobbing now, too.

The Trash King got out his Swiss army knife, cut hunks of salami, handed them around.

From the dining room he could see Sophie bobbing. "Do the dance, Lassie. Do it."

"Who's that kid?"

"That's what we're all wondering," said Dad.

Grandpa reached down, took off his prosthetic leg. It was hurting him. He put it on the table. "I like her. She's got her own style."

The Trash King looked at the leg. "Leo, if you ever decide you don't want that leg, I could sell it to a person who has vision."

"You could turn it into a lamp," Mom suggested.

"Or hang it over the fireplace," Dad offered.

Bradley trotted in, took one look at the leg on the table, lowered his tail, and backed out of the room.

Mom and Dad smiled at each other and laughed.

It was a sound Tree hadn't heard from them in the longest time.

He sat on the couch, listening to his parents' laughter.

CHAPTER TWENTY-TWO

Seven A.M. Tuesday morning.

Dad's house. Tree's alarm went off.

This always caused Bradley to at least rise to be let out.

But this morning, Bradley just lay there and looked pleadingly at Tree.

"What's the matter, boy?"

Tree jumped out of bed. "Come on, get up."

Bradley didn't move.

Tree tried to lift him to his feet, but Bradley fell back down.

"Dad!"

Tree knelt by Bradley's side. Bradley's head was down, his breathing forced.

"Dad!... It's okay, boy." Tree tried to sound soothing, but the lump of fear in his throat was so big, he could hardly speak. Dad was in the doorway with shaving cream on his face.

"What's wrong?"

But as soon as he said it, he knew.

Dad bent down by Bradley's old, tired body and put his

hand over Bradley's stomach, which was heaving hard with every breath. He did what Tree had done, tried to get the dog up.

"Aw, Bradley." Dad wiped the shaving cream from his face onto the T-shirt he was wearing. "We've got to call the vet. I think he had some kind of a stroke."

Tree couldn't move.

"I'll call, Tree. You stay with him."

Tree was trying not to cry. He reached in his drawer, got out a dog treat. He stuck it under Bradley's nose. "You want a biscuit?"

Bradley didn't want one.

Dad was back. Hand on Tree's shoulder. "The vet said we need to bring him in. Tree, you understand how old Bradley is."

Tree croaked out, *"Can I call Mom?"*

"Of course."

"Can she be there? 'Cause she loved him—"

"And he loved her."

Tree carried Bradley to the car, wrapped in a Baltimore Orioles beach towel. Grandpa followed, moving better on his new leg. They drove to Mom's house. She got in the backseat and started to cry.

This helped all the men to be stronger.

They rode to the vet's with Tree saying "Good dog" and Grandpa saying "It's going to be okay, buddy," just like he'd said to so many buddies in the war. Dad forgot the way to the vet's because Mom usually took Bradley, and she had to give him directions, which seemed like old times with a sad new twist.

Dr. Billings brought them right into the examining room. Tree put Bradley gently on the table. Bradley shivered; Tree covered him with the Orioles towel, even though Bradley was more of a Red Sox fan. Dr. Billings looked in Bradley's cloudy eyes, felt around his stomach, listened to his heart. Did what Tree and his father had tried to do, get him to stand.

"He can't," Tree said.

The doctor sighed. "His heart doesn't sound too bad, but I think the rest of him just gave up. He's old. You need to decide what you want to do. I know how hard this is."

Mom put her hand on Bradley's head and wept.

Tree just let loose all the sobs he'd been holding in. Grandpa bent over sadly; Dad lost it, too.

They tried to discuss what to do.

Would they stay when the doctor gave Bradley the shot? Yes.

Did they want to bury him or have him cremated?

"It doesn't matter," said Dad.

"Buried," said Mom.

Did they understand that the shot would be given and after a few minutes it would go into Bradley's heart and cause it to stop?

Yes, they understood that.

Did they want a few minutes alone first to say good-bye? Yes. They really did.

. . .

Tree didn't know how to say good-bye to a dog he'd known all his life. The sadness of it just washed over him, and because he was big, he had more sadness—at least that's how it seemed. So he stood there with Mom, Dad, and Grandpa and just patted Bradley and said he was a good dog, which is what everyone else was saying. That's when the doctor's cat came into the office. Bradley looked at Tree; their eyes met. And Tree knew Bradley had chased his last cat.

Not even McAllister could save him now.

The doctor came in with his needle, started filling it as the cat walked back and forth, loving the power. Tree wanted to kick the cat out. It wasn't fair to have a cat at Bradley's end. The vet walked over, rubbed Bradley's neck.

Tree stamped his foot at the cat. *"Just go!"* The cat jumped out of the room. Tree looked at Bradley, half dead on the table.

He didn't know he had this many tears inside.

"Well," said the vet, moving closer.

Tree bent over the back half of Bradley, held him tight.

Didn't want him to go through this alone.

"Okay now, Bradley," said the vet. "Okay."

Bradley opened one eye.

Gave half a bark.

Barked for real now.

Shook his head.

Stretched his front paws.

Struggled up like a great old wolf.

Faced the cat, who'd slinked back in.

Tree's mother froze right there.

There are plenty of stories about old dogs who die in their owner's arms, but this isn't one of them.

"Hold on," the vet said, shocked. "Can you put him on the floor, Tree?"

Tree cradled Bradley, lowered him gently down.

"Come on, boy," Grandpa whispered. "Come on."

Bradley walked shakily forward.

The cat scurried into the other room.

Bradley turned slowly, came back.

"I've never seen this happen," the vet said, stunned. "It's your decision, folks. I can't promise how long, but I think this old dog's got some life in him yet."

Tree laughed from sheer relief.

"All right now!" Grandpa shouted.

Dad shook his head, amazed.

Mom couldn't speak.

Bradley looked at Tree, who said, "You want to go home, boy?"

Bradley lay down.

"Home is this way." Tree headed for the door. Bradley got up, walked slowly after him.

The whole town was buzzing with Bradley's near-death experience.

"He probably saw a light going through a tunnel before he turned around," said Mrs. Clitter, who brought over some homemade dog biscuits to celebrate.

137

She said she'd let McAllister slink by more often to keep Bradley on his toes.

That cat was so irritating, he could keep anything alive.

In the days following Bradley's resurrection, the animals of the neighborhood seemed to come by more to celebrate their friend's return. Tree made sure he always had biscuits in his pocket for any dog who wanted one.

"This is from Bradley," he'd say.

Tree knew it wouldn't last forever, but he decided to focus in full on whatever time was left.

CHAPTER TWENTY-THREE

The basketball season was winding down and Coach Glummer had developed irritable bowel syndrome, which seemed to reach heightened intensity whenever the Pit Bulls were losing by more than twenty points, which was close to always. They were moving down the court in a more unified manner since ballroom dancing; Tree had made some okay handoffs, but it wasn't enough.

Coach Glummer was holding his stomach, shouting that *no one* was paying attention out there. *No one* on this team cared.

Tree stepped forward. "I don't think that's right, Coach. I care. I was paying attention. I know that Petey was trying, and Ryan, and all the guys."

The Pit Bulls, emboldened by this declaration of courage, said yeah, that was right.

Coach Glummer stammered, said they could do better.

"Maybe," said Tree. "But the Huskies were state champs three years in a row. And the last two years they beat us by much bigger point spreads."

The Pit Bulls growled in agreement.

"And we all went to ballroom dancing like you said, and we've been trying to get better."

Tree knew from his grandpa that hard things take time. He decided to not mention this.

Coach Glummer stormed off.

There are two kinds of coaches in the world—those that listen and those that don't. Jeremy Liggins stood back as the Pit Bulls circled Tree, slapped him on the back, and told him, "Way to go, man."

Way to go.

No team had ever told Tree that before.

Helping Grandpa take a shower wasn't easy.

Grandpa was embarrassed he needed help getting in and out of a wet tub, but it was so easy to slip, he needed a spotter, at least for now.

Tree was standing by the tub. Grandpa sat on the plastic stool, using the shower hose to spray the soap off.

That's when they heard the siren.

At first the sound didn't register.

Then a voice on a loudspeaker blared the news:

"This is an evacuation. Move immediately to the Eleanor Roosevelt Middle School. The Burnstown levee broke. Floodwaters are heading toward us."

Tree couldn't believe it. Wasn't there supposed to be more warning than this?

The siren grew louder.

"Okay," said Grandpa. "We move quick and smart."

Tree let Grandpa lean heavily on him to get out of the tub. "Throw me that towel. Get me my leg."

Tree's whole body was shaking. He knew how long it took to get his grandpa dressed.

Dad was working at the store.

It was just them at home. He didn't know how they'd get to the school.

"Get my pants. Get my shirt." Grandpa said it strong, but urgent. "No panic."

Pants on, socks; stump liner; leg clicked into place.

It was going to take forever to walk him down the stairs.

"Call your dad."

Tree raced to the phone. It was dead. Picked up the cell phone. Dialed. No answer.

Dialed again with shaking hands.

Nothing.

"Mom's out of town, Grandpa."

"Call the neighbors. We'll find somebody."

Tree's mind went blank. "I can't remember—"

"Johnsons on the left, Nagels on the right."

Another siren.

"I'm going to call the police, Grandpa. Tell them we need a ride."

He punched 911.

Circuits busy.

CHAPTER TWENTY-FOUR

The front door opened.

"I'm here!" Tree's father shouted.

"We're upstairs, Dad!"

Dad took the stairs three at a time. "We've got to get out fast. Pop, can you move?"

"Slowly. Sorry to be a bother."

"You're no bother. Tree, hold him under the arm." Tree did. Two men trying to carry a third. Too much confusion.

"I've got him, Dad. Grandpa, just hold on."

Tree bent down, slung Grandpa over his shoulder. Felt his muscles sag under the weight.

"I feel like I'm in Vietnam again."

Sirens louder. Dad grabbing food, boots, coats.

"In the car. Come on. We've got to beat it."

Rain lashing outside. Wind railing.

Tree, scared frozen. How could a flood be coming when they hadn't seen it yet?

There wasn't time to go back, to get more clothes, anything

important. Tree thought of his tools and his books and his computer.

In the car Tree remembered Bradley.

"I've got to get Bradley!"

Tree ran back into the house as the sirens grew louder. He found Bradley scared half to death in his room; carried him to the car. Dad trying to drive up the hill. Not easy with the sloshing. Tree looking forward, looking back at the house and wondering what, if anything, would be left. Bradley lay as still as Tree had ever seen him.

The car didn't seem like it could make the hill, started sliding.

Grandpa: "Okay, steady her to the left and crawl it up, that's right, just loose the clutch a bit, ram her forward now."

Inch by inch they slid, slipped, up the muddy hill.

Buses, cars making the trek, packed with scared people. For some reason Tree thought of the photo of his parents laughing. He wished he'd grabbed it. He buried his face in Bradley's fur.

"Good dog," Tree said. "That's a good dog."

It's hard to understand the power of nature when it's unleashed on you like that. Man can walk on the moon, orbit Mars, and cure so many diseases, but no one can stop a raging river once it decides to flood its banks.

At the middle school. A policeman at the door told Tree the impossible.

"No animals in the school, son. I'm sorry. They're being kept at the football field."

"But he'll be scared!"

"They've got some tents. It's the best we can do right now. We've got to get the people inside."

Lightning crashing, rain falling sideways.

Bradley shaking like he's going to explode.

A volunteer fireman asked Tree if he wanted to leave Bradley with him—he'd get him to the shelter.

"No. I'm taking him myself." Tree looked pleadingly at his father, who was helping Grandpa inside.

He gave the fireman Bradley's leash. "Can you hold him just a minute?"

Tree helped Dad get Grandpa into the gym.

They got him settled. Dad took Tree aside. "I don't think I've told you how much help you've been with Grandpa. . . . I don't know what I would have done without you."

"Thanks, Dad. That means a lot."

More people were streaming in.

People shouting if anyone had seen so-and-so as the lightning flashed outside and the thunder sounded like a nightmare. Tree looked up at Eleanor Roosevelt's words carved below the basketball hoop:

No one can make you feel inferior without your consent.

Grandpa was doing his best to help the people around him, like the little girl crying for her mother. Her father kept telling her that Mama was going to be coming through that door any minute, but the little girl kept crying anyway.

"Well, darlin'," said Grandpa. "What color hair does your mother have?"

"Brown." The child sniffed.

"And what's her name, other than Mommy?"

Small voice. "Carol."

"I just happen to know a story about a mother with brown hair named Carol who got stuck in a flood, but she was so smart, she helped a dozen people to safety."

The little girl's eyes were wide.

"You want me to tell you that story?"

"Yes!"

"I've got to take Bradley over to the field, Dad."

"I want you right back."

Tree ran out the door; Bradley was cowering near the fireman's feet.

"Okay, boy, it's okay."

Tree tugged on the leash. Bradley dug his heels in, wouldn't move. Tree bent down to pick him up, saw Mr. Cosgrove walking fast, wearing a big slicker, carrying a flashlight.

That's when Tree got the idea—as clear and clean as taking apart a laser pen.

"Mr. Cosgrove, could we keep some animals in the basement in those storage rooms?"

Mr. Cosgrove stopped, looked at Bradley.

He thought for a moment, then motioned Tree to the back door.

"Thanks." Tree picked up Bradley, carried seventy-four pounds of old, wet dog through the darkened hall.

Mr. Cosgrove unlocked the storage room. "Put those news-papers on the floor and pray we don't get caught."

Tree pictured the vet's office with all those animal cages. If they had cages, they could have more animals in the basement. Tree looked around the big room. It had lots of tall steel file cabinets. He opened some file drawers—they were empty and deep—almost like cages. But he'd need a top so the animals could breathe and not get out.

A loud siren blasted in the distance. Mr. Cosgrove and Tree ran upstairs.

More people were pouring in.

Dad walked over.

"We need to stay together."

Tree told him about Bradley in the basement.

"He'll be all right, Tree, I—"

A little boy let out a huge wail. "But they'll drown! They can't be outside. They can't!"

His father was holding a cage with two white rabbits.

Tree whispered to Mr. Cosgrove, "They've already got a cage."

"Do you know what a pension is?" Mr. Cosgrove snapped.

"Sort of." Tree knew it involved money.

"You know what this could do to my pension?"

The little boy was crying hard.

"*Just* the rabbits and the dog. No more."

Tree carried the rabbits downstairs, told Bradley he had two roommates. Told the rabbits, "This is the greatest guard dog in the universe."

The rabbits looked on, unconvinced, as Bradley slept.

"Tree!" Mr. Cosgrove was holding McAllister, who looked like he'd been drowned nine times. "Some woman said this cat can't stay on the field—it's too sensitive."

McAllister shook, hissed.

Tree: "I can make a cage for him if we have some chicken wire."

"I've got that."

Deep hissing.

Mr. Cosgrove deposited wet, crabby cat in Tree's arms.

Bradley opened one eye.

"No, Bradley."

Bradley rose, barking.

"Bradley, no!"

McAllister arched his back, big meow.

"You guys have to get along."

But certain animal ways are bigger than floods.

CHAPTER TWENTY-FIVE

"What are you doing?" Sully stood at the storage room door.

"Saving animals." Tree put newspaper in a file drawer, lowered McAllister in, covered the top with wire netting, attached it with screws.

"He's not too happy to be saved," Sully observed as McAllister hissed.

"That's the *last* animal." Mr. Cosgrove put the cat in another room.

But more animals were coming.

Tree was running ragged, making cages. He and Sully tried to keep Mr. Cosgrove calm.

"These are just a couple of kittens, Mr. Cosgrove."

"Look what we've got here . . . a ferret."

And the big challenge . . .

"How do you feel about farm animals?"

Three chickens clucked in a cage. "They have arthritis," Sully explained.

News of the flood came sporadically. Radio signals went in and out. Tree was wondering about everything.

Will the house survive?

Will anyone be hurt?

Where in the world is Sophie?

He'd called her house endless times on Dad's cell phone; no answer.

Over and over they heard the warnings: Never stay in your car during a flood. It only takes two feet of water to carry you off.

Amber Melloncroft and Sarah Kravetz shuddered in a corner, blankets over their shoulders.

Tree remembered Grandpa saying how in Vietnam it didn't matter how much money you had, how good you'd been on the football field, how smart you'd been in school.

War is the great equalizer.

Jeremy Liggins stood in the doorway, holding a cage. A policeman told him to bring it outside. Jeremy wailed, "Hamsters can't be in the rain. They're desert animals. *They'll die.*"

Tree walked over. "I might have a safe place for them."

"Where?"

The policeman helped an old woman inside; Tree led Jeremy downstairs.

Mr. Cosgrove stopped when he saw them. *"No."*

"Mr. Cosgrove, Liggins's hamsters will die if they have to be out in the rain."

Mr. Cosgrove took a hard look at Jeremy. He'd heard him say plenty of mean things to Tree.

"You can keep them down here, but *only* because Tree asked. I hope you appreciate a friend like him."

Jeremy looked down, nodded.

"Mr. Cosgrove, you're going to get a medal for being a hero."

"That won't mean much on unemployment."

"This reminds me of Vietnam, Leo." The Trash King huddled under a Red Cross blanket. "Those tropical storms, we'd never get dry. Everything smelled like jungle rot."

"I'll take this over Nam any day."

"Me, too." King's wife, Betty, leaned against his shoulder. "You think there'll be any junk left when we get home, babe?"

"There'll be junk in our lives till we're dead."

Tree watched Grandpa massage his bad leg. King waved an unlit cigar. "A flood like this makes you think. Maybe I should branch out. Get into something current, like hazardous waste."

"You've always been a trendsetter," Betty observed.

Tree's dad came by. "I talked to your Mom in Philadelphia. She's fine. She can't get back yet because of the weather. She sends her love." He smiled. "Her house will probably be okay. It's on a hill. She's worried enough for all of us."

He didn't sound edgy at all when he said it.

Dad's house wasn't on a hill. Tree wondered what that meant.

"I told her how well you've been handling all this, how you're helping out everywhere." Dad grinned. "I told her I was so proud of you, I could bust."

Tree beamed. "Thanks, Dad."

Mayor Diner came in at this point, windblown and wet. She took her slicker off, looked at the horde of people in the gym.

150

Walked to the free-throw line, smiled sadly.

"Ladies and gentlemen. No one expected to be here tonight."

The people nodded, that's for sure.

"The weather bureau says we could get a lot more rain. That could wipe things out by the river. The sandbags haven't held the way we'd hoped."

Worried looks.

"It's going to be a long night, folks. Whatever you've learned about getting through hard times, I hope you'll share it with the people around you. I've seen so much today that's encouraged me. The bravery of the rescue workers, neighbors helping each other get to safety. It's easy at a time like this to remember all the things we've left behind, but what this town has—the most important part of it—is sitting right here in this place.

"I don't know why these things happen. But I'm asking you to hold on. We'll keep you updated. We'll keep praying. We'll keep looking for it to be over."

Mayor Diner nodded at Inez, the ministry intern at Ripley Presbyterian Church. "Would you lead us in prayer?"

Inez smiled weakly. This flood had her scared stiff. She'd rather have a braver person pray.

But she took the hands of the little girl and the old man next to her; closed her eyes.

"We feel scared, Lord—give us courage. We feel lost— stand beside us. We feel weak—give us strength."

■ ■ ■

Mrs. Clitter had just visited McAllister in the basement. She didn't much like the makeshift cage, but she knew her cat was safe. She had thanked Mr. Cosgrove, gave him some of the homemade fudge that she kept frozen in blocks in her freezer. She'd grabbed pounds of it when the sirens first blared.

You just never know when someone might appreciate something homemade.

A squawk in the hall.

Eli Slovik, completely drenched, was holding a large cage with Fred the parrot inside.

"Back off, Buster," Fred shouted to the policeman who was telling Eli he had to take Fred to the shelter.

"He can't get wet!" Eli screamed.

"There are parrots in the jungle," the policeman shouted. "It gets wet in the jungle!"

Fudge extended, Mrs. Clitter stepped forward.

The officer crumbled, took the bribe.

Mr. Cosgrove ran by; Mrs. Clitter grabbed his arm tight. "Could we ask you to help just one more of God's creatures?"

Eli was praying Fred wouldn't say "Back off, Buster."

"We're full up."

"Not even for this beautiful, rare bird?"

"No more."

Mr. Cosgrove looked at Fred, who looked back and said the words that would save him.

"You're a genius."

Mr. Cosgrove's eyes went soft.

"Now, isn't that something?" Mrs. Clitter marveled.

"You're a genius." Fred made sincere eye contact.

Mr. Cosgrove, struck by the parrot's depth, said, "The bird stays. Make sure he's warm and dry."

"You're a genius," Fred repeated.

"Get him some food. Whatever he wants."

Mr. Cosgrove ran down the stairs, feeling smarter than he had in years.

One man sows, another reaps.

They slept on mats brought by the Red Cross.

They slept in corners wrapped in blankets they had brought from home.

They slept and woke and wondered when it would be over.

Sophie hadn't shown up yet, and Tree was so worried about her, he couldn't sleep.

Cell-phone batteries were out.

Phone lines were down.

Grandpa rigged up a generator so they could watch TV news. The TV cameras captured the mostly flooded town.

"A flood is like a war," Grandpa observed sadly, "because it can take so much with it."

Chapter Twenty-six

The rain stopped Wednesday morning.

The sun, bright and full, announced the new day.

Streets were flooded, cars were overturned.

They'd been in the shelter for two days—living in a time warp.

We just want to get home, the people said.

Home to what?

That was the question.

Grandpa, the Trash King, and Tree were working hard to make sure some of it would be positive.

The sign.

That's the first thing people noticed. It made up for the smell, which was rank and persistent and hung over Ripley like foul gas.

Mildew. Piles of yuck.

It rose from the streets, infiltrated the nostrils.

But the sign.

Grandpa lugged parts of it from his workshop over the

garage; wired it. The Trash King stood on the ladder and balanced it on the roof of Temple Beth Israel—a roof most people could see coming back from the middle school—it overlooked the park, too.

Rabbi Toller turned on the generator.

Tree held the ladder as King fixed the big sign in place.

"Plug her in, Rabbi."

"Let there be light," Rabbi Toller announced.

Pow.

WELCOME HOME, FOLKS
WE'RE GOING TO MAKE IT

People were honking their horns in their trucks, cars, and vans when they saw it.

The Trash King, Tree, and Grandpa grinned as the photographer from the *Ripley Herald* took photo after photo of that sign.

"Why'd you do it?" the reporter asked. "What made you think of it?"

The old soldiers smiled. "We wanted to encourage the town," Grandpa said. "Give people something good to come home to."

They didn't mention the most important part.

You've got to welcome people back when they've been through a war.

Nobody understands that more than a Vietnam vet.

The shock of loss was everywhere.

A flooded-out house is a ghastly sight.

Especially when it's yours.

They'd called the insurance company.

Turned off the electricity.

Tree, Dad, and Grandpa stood on the muck-covered hall carpet wearing white masks passed out by the Public Health Department.

No one spoke.

The couch was soaked and dirty, the stereo was turned upside down, lamps lay broken on the floor, tables upended.

Brown watermarks three feet up on the first-floor walls. Lower kitchen cabinets opened, soaked cereal boxes, broken dishes, piles and piles of what could never be used again.

Tree's clothesline invention hung untouched from the ceiling, casting shadows.

Tree stepped across the mushy rug. He could hardly stand the fumes.

He'd lived in this house most of his life. And now this, too, was going to be a memory.

Grandpa said, "We rebuild with what we've got left."

But there wasn't anything left except the second floor.

The basement windows had popped out.

Five feet of murky water sat in the basement with dirty clothes, empty paint cans, basketballs, and footballs floating on the surface.

Grandpa steadied himself, Old Ironsides.

But Tree wasn't built of such strong stuff.

He couldn't take any more.

He leaned against the dining room wall and started to cry.

CHAPTER TWENTY-SEVEN

"I know what you're thinking," Grandpa said.

Tree sniffed. It's hard to cry when you've got a white mask over your face.

"I bet you're thinking this whole house will have to be torn down."

Tree shrugged. He was, sort of.

"I can see why you'd think that, having never built a house before." Grandpa studied the wall. "See, floods leave clues. We can see how high the water went on the first floor. Everything above the waterline is okay. The mirrors, the hanging lights. We've got a whole second floor in mint condition. Now, inside the wall . . ." He put an arm on Tree's shoulder to steady himself and kicked a hole in the wall with his good foot. He stuck his hand in, pushed past insulation. "We can see that the plumbing pipes still look solid. I'll have to rewire where it got wet, but we haven't lost the farm. Not by a long shot."

"We haven't?"

Grandpa handed Tree a hammer. "Ram that there."

Tree hit the wall, made a hole.

"Rip it out."

Tree did.

"Stick your hand in there until you feel the frame."

Tree pushed through the insulation. "I can feel it."

"Knock on it."

Tree rapped strong. It was solid.

"We're going to lug this mess out of here, strip this Sheetrock down to the frame, and build her back up again."

Tree sighed. "You make it sound so easy, Grandpa."

"It's not going to be easy. It's going to be worth it."

They stayed in a hotel that night. Bradley, too.

Tree was so tired and sore from cleaning up.

Dad called Curtis and Larry at school. Both wanted to come home in a few days to help.

They sure could use the extra hands.

Then Tree called Sophie's house and finally got an answer.

He almost shouted for joy when he heard her voice.

"I tried to call you, Tree, for the last three days, but I couldn't get through. Aunt Peach got us a room at a motel. We were all shoved in there with cots and cats. It was torture. But the apartment's fine. The flood didn't touch us. I guess there's something good about a fourth-floor walk-up."

He told her about Dad's house and how hard they were working.

"I'm sorry you lost out. But it's good you're not average

size, Tree. It's good your dad and grandpa have a really big guy to help take care of business."

Tree squared his shoulders at that one.

Two of Grandpa's friends brought an electric pump to drain water from the basement.

Dad and Tree picked through the kitchen and garage, finding what could be saved.

They worked like machines while they still had daylight, wearing big rubber gloves. Floodwater is infectious.

Lugged trash to the Dumpster in the driveway.

Every house on Tree's street had one.

Tree shoveled out piles of junk from the first floor into the Dumpster, smiling bravely at other neighbors who were doing the same thing.

Tree worked till he couldn't anymore. Then the momentousness took over.

There was too much to do. How could they *ever*—

"The first rule of rebuilding is to find something positive and concentrate on that," Grandpa said.

Tree looked at the flooded, smelly mess. "I haven't thrown up yet."

Grandpa laughed. "That's a start."

The basement water had been drained, leaving rank, thick sediment that covered the floor and walls.

Sophie threw ruined books and sports equipment into garbage bags. She'd come to help Tree with the cleanup.

Tree looked at the broken trophy case lying open on the muddy basement floor—Curtis's and Larry's sports certificates were all ruined. Some of the trophies were cracked.

They'd seemed so important when he was growing up.

Tree knelt down to touch a frame with smashed glass. He remembered his mother framing Curtis's award for basketball. Remembered being in the high school auditorium when Curtis got it. Tree had applauded so hard, his hands hurt.

Tree picked up Larry's brass home run medal and Curtis's athlete of the year trophy, dripping mud.

All that glory covered in sludge.

Tree put them in a box.

"I'm going outside before I puke," Sophie announced, lugging a bag up the stairs.

The Trash King picked through the rubble of what was left in his junkyard—so much of it had been ruined by the flood.

"You look at this red wagon," he said to Tree, who'd come to help him move some of the heavy pieces. "Why did it survive? It should have been sucked up by the wind—carried down the river. But it's here. That tells me it can take the heat. I'm not going to sell it for peanuts. I want some real cash for a tough piece like this."

He walked over piles of rusted metal, lifted an old weather vane from the heap. Stuck it in the ground; the vane pointed north. "Still working," he declared, "after all we've been through. You can look at this yard of mine, think there's nothing left worth saving. But trash is here to remind us all that the old's not so bad—it's got life in it yet."

He looked toward the sun, scratched his chin. "I'm going to put that in the brochure."

The giant oak tree began to bud five days after the flood.

Birds were chirping in its branches.

Not one limb was out of place.

Benches were upended, lesser trees snapped in two.

It makes you appreciate a serious root system; roots planted so deep in the ground, holding steady against the storm.

Tree stood in front of the tree with Sophie. Every day at Dad's they were making progress. A huge dehumidifier was in the basement now, drying things up. They'd ripped up the carpet, lugged it out to the street.

"I know this is a special park for you, Tree. I like nature, but too much of it makes me nervous." A tear rolled down Sophie's cheek.

Tree bent down. "What's wrong?"

"I didn't tell you 'cause you had so much going on, but Lassie ... she didn't make it."

"Oh, no."

"It happened at the motel. She was crawling so slow. Then she just froze on the branch. I tried to get her to do the dance, but she couldn't do it anymore." Big sniff. "I told her, 'I know what it's like to not have anyone like you around. You feel like giving up sometimes.' "

Tree took her hand.

"I told her that, as a pet, she'd been true. She didn't fetch or do tricks, but she gave back as much as a reptile can. She fell off the branch, hit the floor of the cage." Sophie lowered her head. "I buried her in the Dumpster in the parking lot. I said, 'Thanks, girl, for everything. You could have been a dog if you'd had better luck.' "

"You were good to her," Tree said. "You gave her a good life."

Sophie nodded. "God knows I tried."

Tree looked across the park to the roof of Temple Beth Israel, where the sign was still welcoming people home.

Just then, Nuts the squirrel showed up, nervous as anything.

"Hey, Nuts. You made it." Tree threw him a peanut; the squirrel grabbed it, studied Sophie.

"You know this squirrel?"

"Kind of." Tree felt stupid.

"He looks like he's got a lot to deal with."

Nuts shook a little, scampered off.

"So are you sleeping in the park or what, with your dad's house all messed up?"

Tree grinned. "Actually, my mom's house made it through fine. She invited us to stay with her until Dad's house gets fixed."

Sophie snorted. "Your dad, too?"

"Even Bradley. She said it was going to take a lot of work to get the house right, that no one should have to sleep in a hotel, and that she and Dad were adults and could handle this. We're going there tonight."

Sophie looked at the white oak. "You've got a strange family, Tree."

Tree didn't say it, but he thought this was a very good sign. Maybe his mother wanted to work things out with his father.

He wondered if something awful, like a flood, could have a good side.

CHAPTER TWENTY-EIGHT

Dad, Tree, Grandpa, and Bradley stood on Mom's front porch.

They had been working hard at the house. They looked and smelled it, too.

Dad rang the bell. "Okay," he said nervously. "This is going to be fine."

Tree bit his lip, hoping like crazy.

Mom answered the door, looking really pretty in a blue sweater and skirt.

Her hands went up. "You're *early*."

Bradley went right to her.

Dad croaked, "You said come before dinner."

"I *said* come *after* dinner."

"We can come back," said Dad.

"No, just come in. Tree, wipe your feet. Leo, how are you?" They came inside. "This is going to be a little complicated, but we're all adults."

I'm twelve, Tree thought. *I just look older.*

The doorbell rang.

Mom smoothed her skirt, announced shrilly, "I have a date."

Her first date in twenty-three years.

"Oh," Dad said strangely.

Doorbell again.

"And that's him. So we're all just going to deal with it."

She smiled too bright, opened the door to Richard Blunt, an average-size, average-looking person.

"Richard," Mom said.

"Jan, you look lovely."

Grandpa sniffed.

Tree coughed.

Dad shoved his hands into his pockets.

Conan spoke for them all—hurled himself in complete fury at Richard Blunt's ankle with a clear purpose: tearing it to shreds.

"Bad dog!" Mom grabbed Conan, handed him to Tree.

Good dog, Tree thought as Conan flailed.

"Are you all right?" Mom asked. "He's never done that before."

Richard Blunt nodded warily.

"Richard, this is my son Tree."

Hand extended. "You're back from college?"

Tree shook it. "I'm in middle school."

Richard Blunt looked up.

"And due to the flood, I have some houseguests." Mom glared at Dad, who was dank and damp and looked like he'd slept in the park. "Richard, this is my ex...this is my former... *this is the father of my children.*"

"How's it going?" Dad said.

Richard Blunt nodded.

"And *this*," Mom said, "is my former father ... I mean ... in-law ..."

Grandpa took a lurching step forward, shook hands.

Not to be forgotten, Bradley walked to Mom's side.

"And *this*," Mom shouted, *"is my former dog."*

Bradley's cloudy eyes looked up in undying loyalty.

There is no such thing as a former dog.

It was a toss-up as to which was worse.

The introductions, or when Mom and Richard Blunt tried to leave.

The front door was stuck. And Tree, trying to help, made the mistake of putting Conan down, which caused Conan to go back to his original idea of tearing Richard Blunt's ankle to bloody shreds, which caused Mom to shriek, *"Remove that animal!"* as she raced out the door.

Tree, Dad, and Grandpa stood there. No one knew what to say.

Then, finally ...

Dad: "That guy's a real turkey."

Grandpa: "He has sneaky eyes. I don't trust him."

Tree didn't say what he was thinking.

He couldn't believe his mother would go out with anyone except his father.

He couldn't believe he'd thought that all this togetherness was a good idea.

They cooked pasta in the kitchen and ate it silently.

They waited at the kitchen table until she came home.

She walked into the kitchen, saw the dirty dishes.

"You could have at least cleaned up," she snarled at Dad, who said nothing, which never helped.

Then Dad unfolded the new sleep-away couch too hard and busted the spring, and it sat there, half opened—a huge, broken thing. He lugged the mattress onto the floor.

"I'll leave in the morning, Jan. Get a hotel room."

"Oh, yes," she shouted, "make *me* the unreasonable one."

"You don't need any help with that," he muttered.

Tree was listening from the kitchen, doing the dishes. Grandpa had gone to bed. Don't fight, he thought.

Too late.

"How *typical*," she shouted, "to use sarcasm."

Dad said sarcasm was better than hair-trigger emotion.

"You always need the last word, don't you, Mark?"

"Whatever you say, Jan."

Tree wanted to march in there, tell them they were both wrong.

Stop fighting. He wanted to shout it.

Just for tonight, can't you stop fighting?

Slam. That was her bedroom door.

Dad got the last word.

But Mom got the last sound.

CHAPTER TWENTY-NINE

Curtis and Larry showed up the next day and bunked in sleeping bags at Mom's.

Dad was at a motel.

Grandpa stayed at Mom's, too, with Tree and Bradley, but this afternoon he was out with the Trash King getting building supplies.

"How bad is it?" Curtis asked Tree.

Part of Tree wanted to say, "It's awful with Mom and Dad," but he knew Curtis didn't mean that.

Tree tried to find the words, but you've got to see for yourself what a flood can do.

Curtis and Larry walked around the muddy lawn, kicked debris away, looked in the broken basement windows.

They went inside the house, came out gagging.

Larry swore, hit the Dumpster, stormed off to get away from the sight.

Curtis went after him. Motioned Tree over. Put one arm

around Larry, one around Tree, and they stood there looking at the old house.

Tree felt so close to his brothers.

"We've got seventy-two hours," Curtis said. "What do we do first?"

"Give up," Larry suggested.

Curtis shook his head, held on tight.

"Scrub the basement walls and floor with Clorox," Grandpa ordered. "No joke."

Rubber gloves on, face masks tight, the Benton brothers formed a fighting unit to kill all bacteria left by the dirty floodwaters.

They lugged ruined boxes of photos and videos to the street.

Grandpa demonstrated how you pull down Sheetrock walls.

Slammed a sledgehammer into the wall, yanked as much out as he could with a crowbar.

Tree and his brothers stood by the wall, holding sledgehammers, too. No one wanted to go first.

Finally, Curtis said, "I keep thinking how it used to be, how Mom drove us crazy picking out the paint for the walls. It's stupid. I don't want to knock them down."

Larry dropped his hammer. "I don't, either."

Tree wanted a magical wind to dry everything up and put it back in place.

"You've got to take a thing apart before you can fix it," Grandpa explained.

Tree, Curtis, and Larry looked at one another.

"The best thing about a sledgehammer is how it lets you release your frustrations." Grandpa pounded his into the wall. "You fellas should try it."

Three sledges rammed the wall.

Grandpa shouted, *"And watch the plumbing in there!"*

Larry went at this with everything he had.

A clang and a crack.

Larry hit a pipe.

Grandpa limped over, marked the crack with tape. "You got many more frustrations left?"

Larry gulped. "Not too many."

"Good. Watch how your brother does it." Grandpa motioned to Tree. "He hits it just right. Swings easy, keeps up a steady rhythm."

Tree liked hearing that, but he wasn't sure Larry would. He hit the wall with the sledge to demonstrate, ripped off the wallboard. Hit it again.

Larry tried, but wasn't getting it.

"Here." Tree stood behind him, held his arm back, let it go. "Hit it like this."

Larry tried it himself.

"That's it," Tree said.

By night, they'd knocked the wallboard down in the hall and the living room.

They pulled out the insulation.

Those rooms stood stark like a tree without leaves.

Dad came in, beat—he had to work at the store *and* help at the house.

Stared at the sight. "You guys did all this?"

"I did most of it," Larry said.

Tree and Curtis pounced on him.

TWO A.M.

Tree was in his room at Mom's house. It felt good to be clean, felt good to be someplace that didn't smell like sewage.

He'd scrubbed Larry's home run medal and Curtis's athlete of the year trophy in hot, soapy water.

Dried them off.

Poured metal polish on a cloth and began to rub the medal. He went over and over it, let it dry. Did the same thing with Curtis's brass cup.

He rubbed the dried polish off. Still a few scratches, but the metal looked gold again.

Took another cloth, polished both pieces till they shone.

He sprayed Windex on the marble base of Curtis's trophy to make it gleam.

The trophy looked good, but Curtis's name in raised black letters wasn't clear. He filled in the C, the T, the BENTON with a laundry marker.

Turned to the medal. It was in an open leather box. The box had water stains all over. It looked awful. Tree had seen his dad restore a baseball glove left in the rain with saddle soap.

He poured saddle soap onto a damp cloth and cleaned the box.

That made it better, but not good enough.

He opened a can of mink oil—put some on a cloth, rubbed it deep into the grain.

You've got to be patient to fix a thing right.

He felt the leather get softer, rubbed more and more mink oil in. Gradually, the color deepened. The water stains disappeared.

Tree rubbed for an hour until he'd restored it to something you'd be proud to put on a shelf.

He fell into bed at 4:30.

CHAPTER THIRTY

"It's going to be better here now." Curtis surveyed the first floor of Dad's house. They'd gotten all the wallboard off, down to the frame and joints.

A contractor friend of Grandpa's was going to put up new walls next week.

Curtis and Larry were heading back to school.

"One game!" Larry ran outside, got the basketball that survived the flood.

Curtis ran outside as Larry dribbled the ball in the driveway. They'd hosed the driveway down. It was clean now.

"Come on," Larry shouted. Passed the ball to Tree.

Tree bounced, passed to Curtis, who made an easy basket. Larry got the ball under the net. Passed it to Tree again.

"Come on."

Larry got in front of Tree to guard him; all arms.

Tree tried to get around him.

Larry laughed.

Tree tried a basket from too far away.

Missed.

Curtis threw the ball back to him. Larry got out of the way.

"Nice and easy," Curtis said. "Set up the shot, then shoot."

Tree did that. Watched in triumph as the ball popped through the net.

"Awesome, Tree Man," Curtis said.

Larry slapped him on the back.

It was one of those moments you want to cover with plastic to keep safe.

Dad pulled up in the car with Grandpa, honked the horn.

"We've got to go," Curtis said.

"Wait. I have something for you guys." Tree ran to the porch, grabbed the presents wrapped in tissue paper. Handed one to Larry, one to Curtis.

"Open them."

Dad and Grandpa were heading up the walk.

Larry tore his open.

Couldn't believe what he saw.

Curtis unwrapped his carefully, held it solemnly to the light.

"I washed them off and gave them a polish. That's all it took," Tree said.

Larry touched the leather box, ran his finger across his name. "I thought it was gone." He looked up at Tree.

Tree shrugged.

Dad stepped forward to say something, but Grandpa motioned him back.

Larry slapped Tree on the shoulder. The slap turned into a hug.

Curtis put an arm around Tree, an arm around Larry.

"We'll be back on Memorial Day," Curtis promised.

"Try to get the house finished by then," Larry added. "And don't grow anymore, okay?"

Over the next weeks, Tree knew something had changed.

In school, he and Sophie walked down the hall and Amber and her friends moved aside fast when they saw them coming.

At Dad's, Grandpa started rewiring the downstairs. The new walls went up, and what had seemed like a construction site began to feel like a home again.

At Mom's, Tree looked at the picture of his parents laughing at the beach, and for the first time, he didn't get too torn up about it.

Mom sat him down. "How are you doing with the divorce stuff? How are you feeling about it?"

Tree said honestly, "I wish you hadn't done it. I wish you and Dad had tried harder to stay together. But I'm okay, Mom. I'm okay."

Phantom pain does get better.

CHAPTER THIRTY-ONE

Rat a tat tat tat.

Rat a tat tat.

Luger hit the snare drum two-handed.

Rrrrrrrrrrrrrrrrrrrrrrrrrrrrrrrrrrrrrrrrrrrrrrrrrrrrrrrrrrrrrrrrr.

Drumsticks rolled.

"Move it out!" the Trash King shouted.

The Vietnam vets marched in formation as the Ripley Memorial Day Parade began.

The vets were right behind the League of Women Voters float honoring the women's suffrage movement. Mayor Diner, as Susan B. Anthony, was chained to a post, screaming that women need the right to vote.

Rat a tat tat.

Grandpa was marching next to the Trash King, swinging his right leg out as sharp and smooth as he could manage.

People lined the streets four deep, applauding, whistling.

No town needed a parade as badly as Ripley.

And now, Scotty McInerny, decorated twice for courage in

battle, nodded to Luger, lifted his bagpipes to his mouth, and let the first mournful wail of "The Highlander's March" rise from that instrument.

A bagpipe and a snare drum make everybody stand a little taller.

Tree held the American flag and marched alongside Grandpa.

He was there in case Grandpa pushed too hard. If he did, he'd be riding in the Army Jeep driven by Wild Man Finzolli, who was honking the horn and waving to the crowd like he was running for governor. Bradley was sitting in the passenger seat.

Tree raised the flag high. It caught the wind, billowed full.

He felt so proud.

Raising a flag is the best thing going.

Rat a tat tat.

Rat a tat tat tat.

Rrrrrrrrrrrrrrrrrrrrrrrrrrrrrrrrrrrrrrrrrrrrrrrrrrrrrrrrrrrrrrrrrrr.

They marched.

Not for themselves.

They marched to remember the ones who didn't make it back.

They marched because seeing so much loss can teach you about life.

They marched because we're all fighting a war whether we know it or not—a war for our minds and souls and what we believe in.

Bagpipe sounds rising in the air, overcoming the Eleanor Roosevelt Middle School marching band a block ahead, struggling through the only known band rendition of "(I Can't Get No) Satisfaction."

Vets from World War II, Korea, the Gulf War.

Kids on Rollerblades.

Realtors in flag shirts.

Riding lawn mowers driven by Ace Hardware employees.

The high school jazz band blowing strong.

Grandpa feeling wobbly, but he didn't want to stop.

Luger was behind him, watching.

The drummer is always in charge.

Luger slowed the beat.

Grandpa marched slower; his limp was getting worse.

"Grandpa, are you okay?"

Pushing, frustrated. But he was too stubborn to stop.

Tree moved closer. "Grandpa, I'm worried you're going to hurt yourself."

Mona Arnold was standing by the halfway mark at the parade route with her husband and son.

She watched the Vietnam vets marching sharp, except for Leo.

He looked at her, looked away.

He tried to walk better, but his leg was hurting.

She was alongside him now.

"Enough of this, Leo. I want you to ride."

"A half mile more," he said. Keep pushing. Just like Vietnam.

"This isn't about making it until the end or you lose. You already went farther than I figured you could."

"You losing faith in me, Mona?"

"I'm losing patience."

The Trash King and the vets stopped marching.

Tree held the flag high.

Bradley barked.

"We're all just ordinary heroes here, Leo," the Trash King said. "No supermen allowed. Get in the Jeep."

"All right, all right." Grandpa climbed in good leg first, yanked up the other. Bradley crawled in the back.

Wild Man sounded the horn. "You did real good, Leo."

Grandpa took off his fake leg and raised it over his head.

Wild applause from the crowd.

Sophie, dressed like a soldier of yesteryear, was standing with Tree by the big white oak. They were waiting for Mayor Diner to change out of her Susan B. Anthony costume so the rest of the Memorial Day festivities could begin.

"I stand here in this park, Tree, and I see your story."

"What do you mean?"

"Look at these plants. There's a bush that isn't exciting. There's a vine that means nothing. There's a bunch of weeds. And there's this tree that you can't ignore." She hit the bark. "It sticks out like a sore thumb. That's who you are."

Tree liked that thought, except for the sore-thumb comparison.

Mayor Diner was onstage now.

"Aunt Peach wants me to march in place while I'm playing my solo and salute when I'm done."

Tree wasn't sure about that. "Be yourself, you know?"

Sophie cleared her throat and spat big into a tissue.

They walked to the stage.

She played her flute medley of great war hits with true feeling for the instrument, even though the wind blew her cap of yesteryear off during "Yankee Doodle." Tree could tell she was getting a mouthful of spit toward the end of "Over There," but he bet he was the only one to notice. She got a great round of applause from everyone except the popular eighth-grade girls, but the unpopular seventh-grade boys and Aunt Peach more than made up for it.

Mrs. Clitter and the Senior Women's Modern Dance Society formed the Memorial Day teardrop that symbolized the loss and courage of those who had died to make this country free.

Mayor Diner read, "In Flanders fields the poppies blow / Between the crosses, row on row..."

Then Inez, the ministry intern from Ripley Presbyterian Church, walked forward carrying a large candle, followed by the town's clergy.

She faced the crowd as a strong wind blew, and said the words she'd been practicing over and over.

"We light this candle of hope to help us remember that hope can always be with us. We light this candle to thank God for helping us through the flood. We light this candle of hope now..."

She struck a large match, but the wind blew it out.

Tried again.

"We light this candle of hope now..."

A flicker on the candle this time, but the wind was too strong.

A few ministers surrounded her.

"We light this candle of hope . . ."

"Lord," shouted Rabbi Toller. "We need a blowtorch."

"We light this candle of hope . . ."

Not today, they didn't.

Inez turned to the crowd, her big moment snuffed out. She was going to have to write this up for her weekly intern report.

"It's a metaphor, okay? We'll just be hopeful—no flame."

"Amen," said the people.

Sophie pushed Tree forward.

"What?"

"You're bigger than those people. Stand in front of the candle. Stop the wind. You can do it!"

No. Tree couldn't.

"Go on!" She shoved him forward.

Sully walked up, slapped him on the back. "That wind is history."

Inez gazed up as Tree, embarrassed, lumbered across the stage. "I can stop the wind, maybe."

He smiled. Not many kids could say that.

Tree stood over the candle, tucked in, felt the wind trying to crash past him.

Inez shouted, "We light this candle of hope to remember that hope can always be with us. . . ." She looked at Tree.

"Light it!" he said.

She lit it.

The flame caught, burned.

Tree guarded the flame until it got serious.

Inez raised the candle, triumphant.

The people applauded.

"I told you!" Sophie screamed from the crowd.

"Yes!" Sully stamped his feet. "Yes!"

Tree felt like he'd just made a winning free throw in the fourth quarter.

Cameras flashed, flags waved.

His mom smiled proudly from one end of the crowd.

His dad smiled proudly from the other.

Curtis and Larry were clapping and shouting.

Tree looked at his grandpa, and he could see the face of war and peace right there, backlit by the sun.

McInerny lifted his bagpipes and played "From the Halls of Montezuma," which was the Marines' song. McInerny himself was in the Army, but he thought the Marines had a better tune.

The purpose of a bagpipe is to reach deep into the heart.

Everything's got a purpose, really—you just have to look for it.

Cats are good at keeping old dogs alive.

Loss helps you reach for gain.

Death helps you celebrate life.

War helps you work for peace.

A flood makes you glad you're still standing.

And a tall boy can stop the wind so a candle of hope can burn bright.